The African Quest

THE
AFRICAN
QUEST

Lyn Hamilton

BERKLEY PRIME CRIME, NEW YORK

THE AFRICAN QUEST

A Berkley Prime Crime Book
Published by The Berkley Publishing Group,
a division of Penguin Putnam Inc.,
375 Hudson Street, New York, New York 10014.

The Penguin Putnam Inc. World Wide Web site address is
http://www.penguinputnam.com

Book design by Tiffany Kukec

First edition: February 2001

Library of Congress Cataloging-in-Publication Data
Hamilton, Lyn.
The African quest : an archaeological mystery / Lyn Hamilton.
p. cm.
ISBN 0-425-17806-4
1. Carthage (Extinct City)—Antiquities—Fiction. 2. Underwater
archaeology—Fiction. 3. Antique dealers—Fiction.
4. Shipwrecks—Fiction. 5. Tunisia—Fiction. I. Title.
PS3558.A44336 A69 2001
813'.54—dc21   00-039840

Printed in the United States of America

10 9 8 7 6 5 4 3 2 1

For Jane and Tim

Acknowledgments

I owe a debt of gratitude to so many people who have given generously of their time and expertise. I would like to thank marine archaeologist Peter Engelbert; curator Alison Easson of the Royal Ontario Museum; Claudine Bazin for sharing her memories of growing up in Tunisia; Jim Polk for his sage advice; my traveling companions Jane and Tim Marlatt and Sherrill Cheda; Mark Stanfield of Tam Dive; Susie Wilson; and as always, my parents and sister Cheryl for their steadfast support and encouragement. Last, but not least, I would like to thank the members of the 1999 Maltese Goddess tour, who, unlike the occasionally churlish individuals depicted here, were a delightful group of individuals, tolerant and even benevolent in their support of my own fledging efforts as a tour guide.

A word about setting: The places named in these pages all exist, and I hope I have portrayed them accurately, with one exception. The town of Taberda, while typical of many of the coastal villages of Tunisia, is, like all the characters depicted herein, a figment of my imagination.

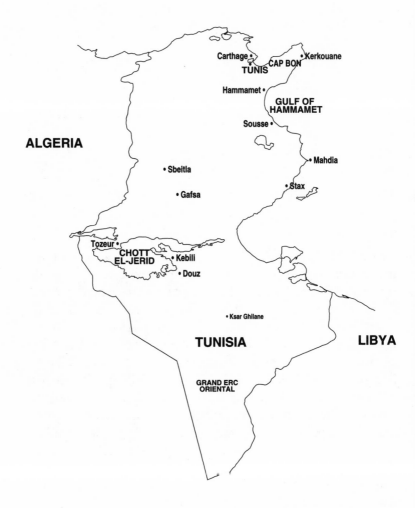

The following is a chronology of actual historical events referenced in the story:

B.C.E.

12th century Phoenicians establish their culture in Eastern Mediterranean

1100–1000 Beginnings of Phoenician expansion throughout Mediterranean

820–774 Reign of Pygmalion of Tyre

814 Elissa's flight from Tyre and the founding of Carthage (Qart Hadasht)

600–300 Continuing conflict between Carthage and Greece

333–331 Siege of Tyre; city falls to Alexander the Great

310–307 Agathocles of Syracuse invades North Africa, challenges Carthage

309–308 Attempted coup d'etat by Carthaginian general Bomilcar

263–241 First Punic War between Carthage and Rome

218 Hannibal crosses the Alps, beginning of second war with Rome

149–146 Third Punic War

146 Carthage falls to Rome, city destroyed, Roman rule until 439 C.E.

438 Vandals capture Carthage

533 Byzantine rule beings

647 Arab rule begins

797 on Succession of dynasties: Aghlabites, Fatimids, Al-mohads, Hafsids

1574 Tunisia becomes part of Ottoman Empire

1881 France invades Tunisia; French protectorate in 1883

1956 Tunisia granted independence, Habib Bourguiba is president

1964 Bourguiba nationalizes lands of remaining French settlers

1987 (November 7) Zine El-Abidine ben Ali seizes power

Prologue

I T IS CARTHALON, CITIZEN OF QART HADASHT, WHO stands before you, great Council of the Hundred and Four, to bear witness to a strange and terrifying event. It has taken me a very long time to gain the honor of this audience, and I pray I am not too late.

My story, a tale rife with perfidy and betrayal, but courage and loyalty, too, takes place at a time of the greatest peril to our city, when, despite the heroic efforts of our generals, our enemy was able to mobilize sixty ships and 14,000 men, and slipping through our blockade of Sicily, sailed for our shores. Until that moment, the Greeks were a nuisance, the cause of endless skirmishes in our territories in Sicily, destabilizing the sea trade that has proven to be the foundation of our power and prosperity. Now, though, they threaten the very walls of the city.

This much of my report is well known to you, how Agathocles, after landing on the shores of the Beautiful Promontory, burned his ships so we could not take them. Then he began his bloody and inexorable march *toward Qart Hadasht, ravaging our gardens and orchards, stealing our livestock and slaves, and enticing our allies and subjects, the Libyans, who perhaps smelled a change in the fortunes of our city and therefore an opportunity for themselves, to betray us. Not since the founding of our great city has defeat come so close to our gates.*

Many among us thought that our gods had forsaken us. Others, however, warned that it was we who had forsaken our gods. It is true that there were new gods in Qart Hadasht, the Sicilian goddesses Demeter and Kore among them. Had we brought our enemy's gods right to the heart of our city, built a temple to the divine powers who would destroy us?

The way to salvation was clear, a return to the molk sacrifice, long gone uncelebrated, to our own god, the great god of sun and fire. Hundreds of mothers and fathers, perhaps some of you among them, and certainly many of our generals, stood dry-eyed as their first-born sons and daughters were offered to the flames of Baal Hammon.

It was during these terrifying times that my story begins, when I put to sea for the first time on a small merchantman, ably captained by one Hasdrubal, he who has Baal's help, and a crew of about twenty men, some, like me, inexperienced and naive, others seasoned hands. Among them, I fear, were those who hid their real intentions behind a mask of patriotism and who would stop at nothing to advance their treacherous cause. I am aware that my youth speaks against me, that you, my elders and superiors, will greet what I say with skepticism and even perhaps, disbelief. But I swear by Baal Hammon, Tanit, and Melqart, the god who protects sailors, that the account of events I am about to give you is true.

PART I

Arma virumque cano

Of war and a man I sing

1

W<small>E WERE A STRANGE LITTLE GROUP, THINKING BACK</small> on it, some of us saints, some of us sinners, and at least one of us with murder on our minds.

The story of how we all came together, collided might be the better word, is, on the surface at least, an account of my short and something-less-than-successful career as a tour guide. On closer examination, however, it is a cautionary tale about the depths to which greed and obsession can plunge the human soul. If I have learned anything from the experience, it is that courage is found in the most unlikely of people, while evil lies hidden behind the blandest of faces.

My tale, the facts of which are true, but, as is always the case, subject to some sifting through the mind and memory of the teller, begins with two words I was coming to dread whenever they emanated from a certain source.

"I'<small>M THINKING,</small>" <small>CLIVE SWAIN, MY EX-HUSBAND,</small> and through a series of events much too long—and painful—to get into, my current business partner, said.

Don't hurt yourself, Clive, the little voice in my head retorted. I keep these uncharitable thoughts to myself because, in addition to his aforementioned status in my life, he is also my best friend Moira's lover.

"I'm thinking," he said again. Clive is a veritable fountain, no, a geyser, of ideas on how to promote our antiques business, McClintoch & Swain by name. These notions of his, I've not failed to notice, require the oozing of copious amounts of charm on his part, and a great deal of hard work on mine.

I could see Alex Stewart, a dear friend and retired gentleman who comes in four days a week to help out in the shop, give a wry smile. For some reason that eludes me, Alex and Clive, as completely different as they are, get along just fine. Even more astonishing is the fact that Diesel, an orange cat who holds the title of Official Guard Cat at the shop, and who, like most cats, treats the rest of the world with pure disdain, positively fawns on Clive. As this fateful conversation was unfolding, Diesel was looking up at Clive as if he were brilliance personified, purring his approval. Come to think of it, the only one of my friends who doesn't get along with Clive, is Rob Luczka, a member of the Royal Canadian Mounted Police. Rob and I are good friends, and occasionally toy with the idea of getting closer. Maybe his considerably less than favorable opinion of Clive is part of the attraction.

"We have to be top of mind in the antiques business, right? The first store that people think of when they're in the market for furniture and design," Clive said, stepping over the cat. It was a statement, not a question. Clive had recently taken a week-long marketing course, attendance at which apparently entitled him to liberally pepper his every utterance with terms like "top of mind," "extending our reach," and "market niche." Any moment now, he'd be calling our business a strategic alliance.

"So I have a great idea." He paused for effect. "Wait for it, Lara," he said, a devilish grin on his face. I waited.

"Antiques tour!" he exclaimed triumphantly. "Brilliant idea, isn't it? One of my best. We do a couple of promotional evenings—in the store, of course: a little cheese, a little wine to loosen things up, a little time to look around and perhaps to buy. We get some free publicity for the tour, and therefore the shop, in the travel rags. In no time flat, we get a group together. Price of the tour includes a couple of lectures before they go about what they'll see, in the shop again—another chance for them to make obscenely large purchases—then a week or ten days somewhere interesting with an expert along—that's you—to help them make their selections, and to ship the big stuff home. Nothing too ostentatious, of course, but unusual and quietly elegant. Loads of charm, just like us. Trip of a lifetime. What do you think?"

"I guess it's not the worst idea you ever had, Clive," I conceded.

"I knew you'd love it," he said. "You see the beauty of it, don't you? The price of the tour includes all your expenses. You do some buying while you're there, and the trip costs us nothing. If people buy a lot of stuff, we might even get a container paid for out of it. Great isn't it?"

"Where?" I asked. It was useless to protest. "How about London? Portobello, Camden Passage, the Silver Vaults? A visit to the furniture galleries at the Victoria and Albert so they start to develop an eye for what's really good. Maybe take in some theater while we're there? Tea with scones and cream and strawberry jam served from a trolley in some elegant courtyard." I was beginning to warm to this idea.

"Too dull," he replied, with a dismissive wave.

"Okay then, France. Paris first. A charming Left Bank hotel, a sweep of *les marchés aux puces,* the flea markets at Clignancourt and Montreuil. Great wine, good food, magnificent art. An afternoon sipping pastis in Place des Vosges. Then we could take a few days and go to Provence. Stay in town, Avignon perhaps, or maybe even a farmhouse . . ."

"Too French," he interrupted, unburdened as he is with even the remotest concept of political correctness.

I sighed. "How about Rome? That would work, wouldn't it? A cappuccino in the Piazza Navonna, then a leisurely stroll through the antiques shops right around there, with a little diversion to the market in the Campo dei Fiori, then a side trip to Florence, the Uffizi . . ."

"Too common," he sniffed.

Rome? Common? He took me by the arm and led me into the office where we keep a map of the world dotted with little colored pins that mark the where-abouts of our shipments. We don't need the pins, of course: We have a computer to do our tracking now, but we like the look of it a lot. At least I do.

"We need something more exotic," he said. "Some-where everybody else isn't going. The way to be suc-cessful in this business of ours is not to spot the latest trends; it's to start them. That's a good line, isn't it? I'll have to use it again." His hand waved over the surface of the map, index finger pausing for a second or two over Afghanistan, then sweeping on to Libya.

"Too dangerous," I said firmly.

"There!" he exclaimed, tapping his finger on the north coast of Africa. "Of course. The medina and souks of Tunis, the mosaics at the Bardo, a little time wandering the ruins of Carthage, a visit to the mosque at Kairouan, the ancient Roman cities in the desert— what are they called? Thuburbo Majus, Dougga, I think. You remember what that was like." I tried to look vague. "You do remember," he said leering at me. "Moonlight on the water, the garden of the hotel, you in my arms."

Of course I remembered. Tunisia was where Clive and I spent our honeymoon, nigh on twenty years ago. And I suppose the souks and mosques and ruins and moonlight were lovely. What I remember most about that trip, however, was the realization that I had made a mistake, although it took me something like twelve years to do anything about it. The question was, did I want to go back there, with Clive or without him?

"Think blue and white everywhere," Clive was saying, as I returned to the present, "tiles with that North African look, those charming wire birdcages, useless maybe, but they look wonderful and people love them, copper, maybe one or two of those splendid box beds with all the carving. We could do up the back show-room in a come-with-me-to-the-casbah look. People would lap it up. And carpets. We need lots more car-pets, and as you say, Pakistan and Afghanistan are a bit dicey these days. Beautiful," he said. "Don't you agree?"

I nodded. "Beautiful," I said, shrugging in Alex's general direction. I figured it would never happen. Clive's enthusiasm would wane as quickly as it usually did, and he'd be on to something else. Even if it did come about, there were things to be said for it. We were always on the lookout for new merchandise for the store, that was true, and, speaking personally, a week or two away from Clive and his brilliant ideas would be just fine with me. I had to admit that it really wasn't the worst idea in the world.

"I DON'T USUALLY TAKE TOURS," THE THIN, ELE-gant woman was saying to her companion, in a tone that implied this kind of travel was far beneath her. "When my husband was alive, he always took me on his business trips abroad, first class, of course. I've never traveled economy. But since he passed away . . ."

"Don't you worry, honey," her companion said, patting her hand, and completely misinterpreting the other woman's words. "I'll keep my eye on you. I take at least two trips every year now, since Arthur passed on. He hated to travel, so now I'm making up for lost time—with his money." She chuckled gleefully. "Now, what did your husband do, Catherine. It is Catherine, isn't it? Can I call you Cathy?" Catherine looked horrified.

Susie Windermere, group busybody, I thought, checking her off my list, and Catherine Anderson, group snob. The two women couldn't have been more unlike, the one with outlandishly dyed red hair, dressed in a long T-shirt that did its best to hide her pendulous breasts and little potbelly, her legs, clad in green and pink tights, surprisingly thin, making her look like a plump little bird on spindly legs; the other rather well turned out in a quietly expensive pantsuit, and just loaded with jewelry. She wore a gold watch laced with diamonds, an impressively heavy gold chain around her neck, and pear-shaped diamond earrings that were probably worth a fortune.

"Mrs. Anderson," I said joining them. We were not yet on a first name basis, most of us, and with Catherine Anderson, quite possibly never would be. And for certain it would never be "Cathy." "Perhaps you missed my advice not to bring expensive jewelry on the trip. It can be a magnet, I'm afraid, for thieves."

The woman looked faintly surprised. "But I did take

your advice," she said. "I left all of my best pieces at home."

"You just put that lovely necklace and earrings in your purse, honey," Susie said. "When we get to the hotel, that Bear place, what's it called?" she asked, turning to me.

"Taberda," I replied.

"Whatever," she said. "You can put your jewelry in a safety deposit box, honey, so you won't have to worry. Now, did I tell you about the cruise I took down the Nile? Have you been down the Nile?"

Inwardly I groaned. The two women, while traveling solo, had indicated that if possible they'd like to share a room, Susie to save money, and Catherine, presumably, for the company. We'd put the two of them together, but already I was wondering how bad an idea this was going to be.

"I thought Muslims didn't approve of homosexuals," another of our fellow travelers, Jimmy Johnstone from Buffalo, said, elbowing his wife, Betty, and pointing toward two men across the row from them.

"Don't worry," one of the men said cheerfully. "We won't hold hands in public." The "we" referred to were Benjamin Miller, a large teddy bear of a man, with a reddish beard and thinning hair to match, brown eyes that crinkled at the corners, and a handshake to be reckoned with, and the speaker, his traveling companion, Edmund Langdon, tall, thin, dark, and devastatingly good-looking, with long, curving eyelashes to die for, a man about ten or fifteen years Ben's junior.

"Stone them in public squares, I've heard," Jimmy went on without noticing.

Group bigot, I thought. It had taken me only minutes to realize that Jimmy would spend his entire vacation dissing everything and everybody even a little bit different from his comfortable world at home. With about twenty years in retail, I consider myself a pretty good judge of character, able to size up almost anyone at a glance. I shouldn't do this, of course, but, experience being a painful teacher, you do learn to spot the customer who can be cajoled into a purchase and the one that needs to be left alone to decide, or, more negatively, the visitor who is likely to shoplift, or the one whose check will bounce sky-high. As unfortunate as this tendency to categorize may be, I've found I'm right about ninety-five percent of the time. The other five percent, that is when I'm totally and utterly wrong, I attribute to a fluke of some sort. Having said that, while Jimmy might have leapt to some conclusions about the two men's relationship, the sleeping arrangements, to which I was privy as the group leader, were inconclusive. The men had requested single rooms, and Ben had told me, when he'd signed up for the tour, that Ed was his nephew.

"I'm tired, Mummy," Chastity Sherwood pouted. Why do parents do that to their children, I wonder, giving them names like Chastity? Chastity was about fifteen, I'd say, and, in addition to being whiny, was one of those people who haven't yet acquired a sense of their personal space. She had a very bad habit of swatting anyone in the vicinity with her backpack every time she turned around, and although people had known her for only eight or nine hours, they were already diving for cover when they saw her approach. "How much longer do we have to wait in this stupid place?" she said in a petulant tone.

"This stupid place" was the transit lounge at Frankfurt's airport, an admittedly dreary spot. The tour, which we were billing as an antiques and archaeology excursion, started in Toronto, where eight of our group had gathered: Chastity and her mother, who went by the sensible name of Marlene; Jimmy and Betty, Canadians who had moved across the lake to Buffalo twenty years earlier and never come back; Susie, Catherine, and the two men, Ben and Ed, who hailed from Boston, but who had opted to join the group in Toronto.

In Frankfurt, my task was to find the rest of our fellow travelers, someone by the name of Richard Reynolds, a businessman from Montreal, whom I'd only spoken to briefly on the telephone; Emile St. Laurent, a colleague from Paris, who'd been a late addition to the trip, having signed up only three days previously, and a couple who seemed certain to up the glamour quotient of the trip: Curtis Clark, a professional golfer from California, and his wife, whose name on her passport read Roslyn Clark, but who was far better known as Aziza, one of those models of one name only, who are regularly featured in the fashion pages of numerous magazines, and on the runways of the haute couture houses of Europe.

And indeed the couple was easy to spot, he with the even tan, beautiful teeth, and the shock of blond hair so familiar from the sports pages and CNN, and she, taller than he at about six feet, with gorgeous toffee-colored skin, elegant long neck and high cheekbones, a beautifully shaped head, accentuated by very, very short dark hair, and graced with a regal bearing that left the men she met drooling, and the women suicidal. There was no question about it, she was lovely. But then again, so was he.

Curtis, as far as I knew, had never won a major tournament of any kind, and might well have gone unnoticed forever, were it not for the fact he'd snared Aziza, thereby making himself the envy of half the world's population, but also because of his ability to be charming on television, a skill he was given the opportunity to demonstrate once he'd married Aziza. As a result, he snagged some very lucrative product endorsements, and his dazzling smile was much to be seen. He also functioned as her manager, if the stories in the tabloids were true, there having been some dustup with her former manager, which had been the subject of juicy speculation for a period of time. Why they were on this tour, when they could afford to travel first class, just the two of them, I could not imagine, but the fact they were had the potential to bring us some wonderful publicity. Clive had told me about a hundred times to make sure they enjoyed themselves.

Emile St. Laurent I had met on several occasions, and so I found him easily. He was seated near the gate, reading an antiques magazine. He was about sixty, with a nice head of gray hair, dressed in gray flannels and a polo shirt, with a houndstooth sports jacket over his arm, stylish in a lovely Parisian sort of way. He looked decidedly fresh and unrumpled, after what surely had been a decent meal and a good night's sleep, something the rest of us, having endured airline food and cramped seating on the transatlantic flight, were sorely missing. The truth of the matter was that, despite my annoyance with Chastity's complaining, I, too, was very tired, having just finished a stint at a design show that had kept me up till all hours and required a great deal of packing and unpacking of merchandise. Then there were all the last-minute arrangements for the tour, and hours of boning up on various subjects so I could be the expert Clive had envisioned. Even though I knew a fair amount about the part of the world we were going to see, I still felt I needed to do a lot of study before we left. Just looking at the neat and squeaky-clean St. Laurent made me feel even grubbier and more tired.

"Lara McClintoch!" he exclaimed, rising from his seat and extending his hand. "How nice to see you again."

"Nice to see you, too, Emile," I said, as he kissed my hand rather suavely. "Glad you'll be joining us."

"I'm delighted, too," he replied. "I found there was a space in my calendar after a business trip fell through, and I thought I'd just call up and see if you had room for one more at the last minute. This antiques and archaeology tour of yours is an inspired idea! Nice concept for a trip, and the publicity won't hurt business at all, will it? Gets the McClintoch and Swain name around internationally. Wish I'd thought of it first."

While Curtis and Aziza were the celebrities of our group, in some circles St. Laurent might have arguably been considered even more famous. Emile was a numismatist, a coin collector. This occupation might be a hobby for most, but for Emile it was a serious, and in his case, very lucrative, business. We'd first met about twenty years earlier, when I was just getting into antiques, and was beginning to go to antiquarian shows. Emile, too, was just starting up then; now, he was considered one of the most successful coin dealers on the planet, and his company, ESL Numismatics, had an international reputation. I doubted that in his business, at least, he needed the publicity he was referring to.

"Is this just a vacation for you, Emile, or is there something special you're looking for?"

"Just a holiday," he said. "Although, if I came across a silver tetradrachm or two from ancient Carthage, I wouldn't mind, now, would I? seeing as how they're selling at auction anywhere in the range of fifteen hundred to twenty thousand dollars these days. Rather more than enough to cover my expenses on this tour. But this is, as I say, a holiday, and something of a homecoming. I was born in Tunisia, actually. Haven't been back in forty years, so it will be interesting to see how it's changed, or at least how wrong my youthful memories of the place are." He winked at me through the little round wire-rimmed spectacles that gave him a rather scholarly appearance. "I hear you and Clive are back together," he said, changing the subject. "Professionally speaking, of course."

"Professionally only, I can assure you, Emile," I said, rather tartly. "Why don't you come along and meet the rest of the group? I'm sure they'll be interested in hearing stories of your youth in Tunisia." While I do know that it is a complete waste of time to contemplate such things, I could not help but idly wonder, as I led him over to the group, where I'd be if I'd chosen coins twenty years ago, instead of furniture. The kind of prices he was mentioning left me breathless. You wouldn't think there'd be that kind of money in coins, but Emile was the living proof there was. He'd had his ups and downs, though. At one time I'd heard he owned homes all over the world, including a spectacular apartment overlooking Central Park in New York, and an equally wonderful villa near Nice, and he'd gotten out of coins for a while. Then he'd lost all his money in some business scheme. His return to the coin business about three or four years earlier had created quite a stir at the time. I took his presence here as a good sign, that he was well on his way to a full economic recovery.

"I teach," Ben was saying at Susie's prompting, as Emile and I approached. "Harvard. Classics. Greeks, Romans, that sort of thing."

"And your friend?" Susie said, glancing Ed's way. The woman was going to know everything there was to know about everybody before we even hit Tunis.

"I'm a parasite," Ed replied. Susie looked taken aback.

"He means he's temporarily unemployed," Ben said, glaring at Ed.

"Oh, I see," Susie said. "Well, I'm sure it's not your fault, honey. It's those politicians."

"You can say that again," Jimmy exclaimed. "Should take the whole lot of them out back and shoot them."

"And what do you do, Jimmy?" Susie asked.

"Chicken parts," he replied.

"Chicken parts?" she replied dubiously. "You mean...?"

"Feet, necks, gizzards. I sell to the Chinese."

"The Chinese," Susie repeated. "Oh," she said, then brightened. "Chicken feet. Dim sum, right? You sell to Chinese restaurants in Buffalo!"

"China," he said. He looked at her. "I sell to the Chinese in China."

"From Buffalo?" she asked incredulously.

"Sure, why not?" he replied. "The rest of us don't want the stuff. Good business, actually. Helps to keep my bride here in style." The bride smiled and self-consciously patted her hair. She reminded me of nothing so much as a TV mom from the fifties.

"Oh," Susie said. "Isn't that sweet. How long have you and Betty been married?"

"Thirty years," Jimmy said.

Susie thought about this for a moment and then wisely decided to move on. "And you are?" she said to Emile.

"Emile St. Laurent, at your service," Emile said, bowing slightly.

"And what do you do, Emile?" she asked, rather coyly, I thought. He was an attractive man.

"I just dabble in a few things," he replied.

"Like what?" she prodded. There was no stopping this woman.

"Coins, that sort of thing," he said.

"Oh," she said. "Then you should meet Ed here. He doesn't do anything either." Emile had the good grace to look amused. I gave him the title of group diplomat on the spot.

"How much longer do we have to wait?" Chastity pouted, looking balefully in my direction. "I'm just miserable," she added.

I could kill Clive, I thought. Although I would never admit it to Clive, up until that moment I had been warming to this idea of his. Determined to make the tour a success in a more tangible way than Clive's rather sketchy notions of publicity value, I was aided, unwittingly on his part, by a film star who had recently purchased a huge house in Rosedale, a Toronto neighborhood that many aspire to but few attain. He called on McClintoch & Swain to furnish the place.

"I want to make a statement," the actor had said, pulling at his short and spiky bleached blond hair. "Something that expresses the real me."

I'd taken him sketches, swatches, and photos of Thai-style, Indonesian, and Greek decor, Tuscan farmhouse, Provençal villa, and just about everything else, but nothing appealed to him. Then, almost in desperation, I called him one last time. "North Africa," I said.

"Way cool," he'd replied. The house had ten bedrooms, six fireplaces, and a living room the size of a football field. Way cool, indeed. Clive and I made up a list of furnishings I was to locate during the tour. My plan was to get the group to Tunisia, hand them over to the local guide and the archaeologist we'd hired, then undertake the one activity that might actually keep us in business: scouring the country for the rather lengthy list of antiques and carpets needed for the Rosedale home. There are few activities I enjoy as much as hunting down the perfect antique for a client. From my perspective, the chase is as much fun as the purchase, and finding something really unusual for a good price is positively exhilarating.

"I'm hungry," Chastity said.

"Have a potato chip," Ben said, thrusting a bag in front of her. The girl eyed it, and him, suspiciously. "Okay, don't have a potato chip," Ben said, reaching into the bag to help himself to a handful. Ben, I could already tell, liked to eat. I hadn't seen him for even a moment without some food in his hand. Keeping him from getting hungry on this trip might be a challenge.

I turned my attention to finding the last member of the group to meet us in Frankfurt, one Richard Reynolds, another last-minute addition to the trip. The only thing I knew about Reynolds was that he was a stockbroker and had flown in from Montreal. I found him right away, though. He was the only person in the bar talking in English on a cell phone. I had no idea who he might be talking to, it being 2 A.M. back home, but they say the market never sleeps.

I had a minute or two to look him over while he talked away on his phone. His entire outfit was brand-new, right down to his belt and the carry-on bag at his side: new denim shirt, with the folds still showing, Reeboks so white they hurt my eyes, and a just-purchased khaki jacket. I knew that, because one of those nasty plastic price-tag clamps that require garden shears to remove was still protruding from the edge of one sleeve. I debated whether or not to point it out, but decided I wasn't his mother, just the tour guide, and anyway, given the self-important way he was leaning against the bar and talking loudly on his phone, I wasn't sure his ego could stand it. I hadn't seen his luggage yet, but I had no doubt it would be absolutely pristine, too, minus the usual wear and tear of the transatlantic flight. If I wasn't mistaken, this was the first trip of its kind Reynolds had ever taken. Whatever had possessed him, I wondered, to take an antiques and archaeology tour to Tunisia instead of, say, a sun, sand, and sex excursion to the Caribbean.

"Hold on a sec," he said into his cell phone as I hovered nearby. "You Lara, by any chance?" I nodded. "Hey, how ya doin'?" he asked, giving me one of those overly hearty handshakes that set your rings digging painfully into your fingers. "Call you back in a sec," he said to the phone.

"Glad you could join us, Mr. Reynolds," I said.

"Hey, call me Rick. I'm glad, too. Touch and go, let me tell you. Didn't know if I could make it right up until the last minute. Market's pretty hot, right now. But a guy's gotta take a break every now and then. You know what they say, all work and no play. Hope I don't get called back, though. I assume I'll be in cell phone range at all times? This thing is digital, of course. The satellite will find me just about anywhere, I should think."

"Maybe not always," I said, feeling sorry for the busy satellite whose job it was to keep an ear out for Rick. "But you know, I expect there'll be regular phones just about everywhere."

"Have to do," he said. "I promised I'd check in regularly. In fact, we'll have to talk some more later. Still got a couple of calls to make before we leave. Got to find out how the Nikkei did, get a few deals ready for tomorrow. Nice meeting you, Lara." he said, turning back to his phone.

If I was supposed to be impressed by this notion of Richard Reynolds' indispensability, I confess I wasn't. Indeed, when it came right down to it, if I had money to invest, which I don't—I have only one investment, and it's called a store—I already knew Rick was the last person I'd have look after it for me.

But at least, all were accounted for, except for one couple meeting us at Taberda.

"I think they're calling our flight, Rick," I said, gesturing toward the gate. I'd leave it to Susie to find out all there was to know about Rick Reynolds.

"I find a hatpin is very effective in warding off unwelcome advances," Susie was saying to Catherine as I caught up to them in the boarding line. "I always have one with me when I travel," she added, pointing to a rather lethal-looking pin in her felt chapeau. The pin was about four inches long, with a large fake ruby gemstone at one end and an unprotected point at the other. I wondered if they'd let her on the plane with it.

"I'd have said a Swiss Army knife would be better," Marlene said. "I have one."

"A gun works best of all," Jimmy said, turning to look back at the two women. "But Betty here made me leave mine at home." He gave his wife a baleful glance.

"Have a chocolate," Ben said from behind me. This is going to be quite the trip, I thought, helping myself to a large chunk of candy.

TABERDA IS A GLORIOUS LITTLE TOWN BUILT ON THE top and down the sides of a cliff high above Tunisia's Gulf of Hammamet. It is a sun-drenched cluster of brilliant white houses, domes, and minarets, accented with a distinctive blue, with terraces cascading down the sides of the hill to a tiny harbor and fishing port, and farther along, a small but very pretty beach. Originally a Berber village, it was now the haunt of wealthy Tunisians and travelers who eschewed the more crowded and popular tourist zones that lay to the south and north of it.

I had first crossed the threshold of the Auberge du Palmier twenty years earlier as a new bride. I fell in love instantly: the gentle rattle of the palm tree in the courtyard, the intense blue of the shutters and doors against the stark white of the walls, the smooth feel of the marble beneath one's feet, tumbling vines set against glowing tilework, and from somewhere, the scent of oranges and jasmine. I'd loved it then, and, despite everything that had transpired in the intervening years, I loved it now. Better still, I could see the magic working on my weary little band of travelers, who were as enchanted as I was.

"My, isn't this nice!" Susie sighed.

"Perfect," Aziza agreed.

"It's very good to see you again, Madame Swain," said Mohammed, the concierge, taking my carry-on bag. I winced. Mohammed had insisted on calling me Mme. Swain when I came here with Clive, despite my protestations that my name was still McClintoch, and I didn't think anything would change him now. He looked older, his face a little more weathered, and he stooped a little, too, but his friendly smile was the same. He was probably past it, as concierges go, but it said something about the nature of the place that the management had kept him on. I found, despite all my misgivings about revisiting the place, I was pleased to see him, the Swain name notwithstanding, and more than that, delighted to be there.

The auberge was built as a family home in the 1930's by the father of the current innkeepers, a Frenchman who'd come to North Africa to make his fortune, and stayed because he loved it. The house had been his passion, a folly of sorts, a magnificent home, a villa or a palace really, on which he'd lavished his attention, and much of his cash. He'd lost the place in the troubles in the late 1950's and early 1960's, when the country was agitating for independence from French rule. Like most of his compatriots, he'd fled with his wife and daughters, Sylvie and Chantal, to France. But Tunisia had been in their blood, and Sylvie and Chantal had returned to Taberda a few years later, now to run the hotel for the current owner, a charming man by the name of Khelifa Dridi.

Like most houses in Taberda, the inn showed a virtually blank wall to the street, dazzling white walls broken only by large solid wood gates in the traditional keyhole shape, decorated with metal studs, and painted a glorious blue that mirrored the sky and sea, and the cascading branches of bougainvillea in purple and pink. Once inside the gates, it was a different story. The house was on the outskirts of Taberda, about two-thirds of the way up the hill, and had a wonderful view back to the town's terraces to one side, and the Mediterranean on the other. The gardens were truly lovely, with palms and orange trees, and a profusion of flowers, hibiscus in yellow and scarlet; pink, lilac, and white oleander, and a small, but pretty swimming pool.

The large double entrance doors opened into a two-story space, the second floor supported by white marble columns which created a gallery on either side of the entrance. The upper portions of the columns and the arches between them were so delicately and intricately carved that it was almost impossible to believe they were marble. The walls in this area were sheathed in an incredible rose marble, and the floors were marble, too, covered at regular intervals with beautiful carpets. The most wonderful feature of all was the carved wood ceiling, painted dark red and gold.

To the right of the entranceway was a sitting room, which doubled as a tearoom and bar, with several couches, all covered with kilims, tapestry-woven rugs, or throws. There were niches in all the windows, filled with benches and pillows, and to one side a chessboard was set up. At the back, in a spacious alcove under the overhang of the floor above, was an eating area. Farther along was the so-called music room, with lovely light streaming through the windows, and a little library and reading area.

To the left, past the stairs to the second floor and through large doors, was a courtyard open to the sky. In it was the palm tree after which the auberge was named.

The hotel was to be our base during the stay in Tunisia, a pleasant refuge from which we'd head out every day to see the sights—Tunis and Carthage to the north, Sousse, farther south, and later, the Roman ruins on the edge of the desert, and then into the desert itself. Despite its size as a family home, as hotels go it was small, intimate. Our group had, in fact, pretty much taken over the whole inn, and in recognition of that fact, Sylvie, Chantal, and Sylvie's daughter Elyse were waiting for us when we arrived.

"Mesdames, messieurs, bienvenue à l'Auberge du Palmier," Sylvie said.

"Can't she speak English?" Jimmy said in a somewhat irritated tone.

"French is the country's second language after Arabic," Aziza said. "Tunisia was once part of France's empire. She is welcoming us to the hotel. *Merci, madame,"* she added in Sylvie's direction. *"Votre auberge est très gentille."* Aziza speaks French, I realized. That was good to know. She wouldn't need as much assistance getting around as some of the others.

"You are all most welcome," Sylvie said, switching to English. "We want you all to have a wonderful stay here in Taberda. And now, may I attend to some formalities?"

In short order, everyone had their room keys and been shown to their rooms. The guest rooms were located off the upstairs hallway, which overlooked the main space below. As tired as I was, there was no time for me to rest. I had only a moment or two to see my room, a small but almost perfect single, formerly an artist's studio, where according to Sylvie, she and her sister once had weekly art lessons. The room had a tiled entranceway, marble floors, and one of those boxed beds Clive was so keen to acquire for the store, and which I thought would be perfect for the film star, a bed essentially built into an alcove, and surrounded by a glorious carved wood frame. I sat on the bed for a moment or two. Perfect, and I was looking forward to falling into it. It had been a very long day: the overseas flight, the stopover in Frankfurt, another flight, and then the usual customs formalities, and an almost two-hour bus ride to our destination. Sleep was something I needed very badly.

In the meantime, however, I had work to do. First I checked that the remaining two members of our group had arrived, which indeed they had: Clifford Fielding, an American, and a woman by the name of Nora Winslow, who described herself as Fielding's companion, whatever that meant. They had requested adjoining rooms. "M. Fielding, he is resting," Sylvie said. "*Très charmant,* our M. Fielding. And the other one, she has gone jogging," she added, her distaste for such an activity, and the person engaged in it, plain in her tone. She had a point. Why would anyone travel all the way to North Africa to go jogging? "Ah, there she is. Madame Winslow, this is Madame McClintoch," she called out to a very fit-looking woman in jogging attire who was heading up the stairs.

Nora Winslow had a nice firm handshake, and the body to go with it. Rather androgynous in appearance, with long legs and a slim, wiry body with good muscle definition, she was about my age, early to mid-forties, and had short-cropped hair, bleached by the sun, and an even tan. Group athlete, I decided. "I'm very glad you'll be joining us," I said aloud. "You'll meet the others at dinner, cocktails are from seven-thirty to eight, here in the lounge. Will you tell Mr. Fielding for me?"

"Of course," Nora said rather abruptly. "See you," she added, before bounding up the stairs two at a time. Not a great conversationalist, our Ms. Winslow.

Next, with everyone accounted for, I met briefly with the guide who had greeted us at the airport and who would accompany us on all our excursions, a pleasant young woman named Jamila Melka, to make sure the arrangements for the next day's tours were in good shape. Then I telephoned our resident expert guide, an archaeologist and historian called Briars Hatley—an unusual name to be sure, but one I'd take over Chastity any day. I'd found Briars through some contacts I had in the field. He was a professor of archaeology at UCLA, a specialist on the Phoenician period in Tunisia, and was on sabbatical, working at a site on the Gulf of Hammamet. He confirmed he'd be at the hotel shortly to meet me, and was ready to start the next day.

"Can they spare you at the site?" I asked. I had been told he was the project director, and was pleased we'd been able to hire him.

"They can," he chuckled. "I have a very competent assistant. And I'm delighted to have a real paying job for a few days."

"Why don't you join us for dinner at the auberge this evening, then?" I suggested. "We'll throw in a good meal, too. We're having a Tunisian-style feast tonight to get things off to a fitting start. You can get acquainted with everyone."

"I never turn down a good meal, particularly given the grub I've been eating lately. Regrettably, our housekeeper quit and we've had to do our own cooking," he said. "I'll be there, with bells on."

"About seven-thirty or eight," I said, concluding the call.

Next I typed up a list of all our guests and their room numbers, had it copied, and arranged to have the list slid under everyone's door. I figured it would help people remember names that evening.

Then it was off to the kitchen to consult with Chantal, who was head chef for the evening. We went over all the details of the menu. Then, with Sylvie and Jamila, I went to see about setting up the tables. Clive had insisted we start with a big dinner, even though I protested that people would be too tired. "You start big, and end big," he insisted. "Then everyone will be happy. You'll see."

We had two large tables of eight, plus an extra setting at one of the tables for Briars. I decided to split up the couples, except for the group whiner and her mother. "Who do you figure will get lost first?" I said to Jamila, as she helped me put out place cards.

"Catherine," she replied. "She is the kind of woman who has been looked after all her life, and can't find her way anywhere by herself."

"You could just as easily say Betty by that criterion," I said, laughing. "I vote for Rick. He'll be too busy making deals over his cell phone to notice the rest of us have all moved on. Why do you figure he came on a trip like this?"

"I see that type all the time," Jamila said. "Men who work day and night for years and years. Never marry, or the wife leaves them because she's alone all the time. Then one day, right around forty or forty-five—I think that's his age, don't you?—they wake up and realize life is passing them by. They find they have few close friends, just casual acquaintances from the office, and no real stories to tell. But they do have money, so they try to buy some experiences: this trip, for example. Rick's got the look all over him. I agree he is a candidate for first person lost, but my money is still on Catherine. Want to bet a dinar or two?" she asked, referring to the local coinage.

"A dinar," I said. "You're on."

Cocktails were to be served at seven-thirty, and I had barely enough time to shower and change into something more partylike before it was time for the festivities to begin. I threw on a silk dress, some lipstick and eyeliner, looked longingly at the bed, and then headed down to the bar. We'd taken over the lounge, by and large, for the party. There were a couple of local businessmen there, but they soon left the place to us. It started quietly enough, but gradually our travelers began to drift in, and as the drinks flowed, the decibel level rose. On the bar were lovely pottery dishes decorated with elaborate Moorish patterns, heaped with glistening olives and sun-dried sweet peppers. Waiters passed plates of tiny *briks,* succulent warm and savory pastries filled with eggs or meat and perfumed with olives, capers, and cilantro. Other waiters passed platters of *doigts de Fatma,* Fatima's fingers, slender tubes of golden pastry filled with potato and onion. Still others brought artichokes stuffed with ricotta and tuna. And then there were slices of baguette—the French might have gone from Tunisia, but they'd left a number of culinary traditions behind—topped with goat cheese and roasted tomatoes.

Susie was the first to arrive. She'd exchanged her pink and green tights for white pants and a pink T-shirt. Catherine was one of the early birds, too, in a very elegant long skirt and starched white cotton blouse with a lace collar. She was wearing pearls this time, and while they make pretty authentic-looking fakes these days, I was reasonably sure these were the real thing. I sincerely hoped she had taken the advice to lock up the rest of her jewelry, and debated about mentioning it again, but it wasn't necessary. Susie was on it right away. "I'll do it after dinner," Catherine replied. "I was just too tired when we first got here."

"Don't you forget, honey," Susie said. "I'll remind you." That would have been enough to make me dash right back to the room to get the jewelry just to make her stop, but Catherine was made of sterner stuff than I.

Most of the others arrived in one big bunch. Aziza was absolutely spectacular in a royal blue silk sheath, and Curtis looked rather fetching, too, in a white suit that showed off his admirable tan to perfection. Marlene and Chastity arrived in similar little black dresses, with Emile in tow, casually elegant in a dark suit and white turtleneck. Betty wore an attractive yellow pantsuit, her husband rather flashy slacks and a blazer. Ben came in looking fairly casual, in slacks and sweater over a shirt and tie, Edmund, the fashion plate, wore a white T-shirt and black slacks, and a heavy silver bracelet. It was all rather festive.

Nora arrived with her arm linked through that of a rather debonair older man, about sixty, I judged, with a smashing red cravat, blue blazer, and gray trousers. While he looked very distinguished, she was dressed in white shorts and a sleeveless T-shirt with a very low scooped neck and large dangly earrings in the shape of a parrot. I made a mental note to tell her that when we were out visiting the sites, particularly the mosques, she would have to cover up.

"Hey, how ya doin'?" I heard, and realized that the last of our group had arrived: Rick, in a spanking new leisure outfit, who proceeded to bore everybody with how many calls he'd had to make to his office since we'd arrived. "Market's open back home, now," he said. "Gotta stay on top of it." Rick, I had already decided, was going to redefine the word *shallow* on this trip. Even Clive at his worst had more interesting things to say than he did, and was less self-centered. I left Rick to it, and moved on.

It was my first opportunity to meet Cliff Fielding, but I had barely introduced myself, when Susie was on the case. "Where are you two from?" she asked him and Nora.

"Dallas," Cliff said pleasantly. Up close, I decided Fielding was older than I'd originally thought, closer to seventy than sixty, but in remarkably good shape for his age.

"Dallas!" Susie exclaimed. "Didn't you say your name is Winslow, Nora? I have a cousin in Dallas by the name of Fred Winslow. Small world, eh? Do you know him? Maybe we're related."

Nora looked startled at the notion of being a relative of Susie's. "No," she said. "I don't." Making conversation with Nora was hard work, even for Susie.

"I should send him a postcard," Susie went on. "Maybe the two of you could get together when you get back." Nora looked less than thrilled with the idea.

"What do you do, Cliff?" Susie went on, oblivious to the fact that Cliff and Nora were trying to move away.

"I'm a dentist, but I'm retired now," he replied. "I have a little company, only five employees."

"My husband, Arthur, had a small business, too. He was an engineer. What does your company do?

"It manages my investments," he said. For once, Susie was speechless.

Group tycoon, was what I was thinking. "You'll have to meet Rick," was what I said aloud, however. "He's in a similar business, I believe." Cliff was about to allow himself to be led over to meet Rick, when Nora grasped his arm and steered him in another direction. It seemed that Nora was the one to decide who Cliff was to meet, and when, and although so far as I knew, she hadn't as yet had any opportunity to be bored to tears by Rick, she had other plans for Cliff.

Shortly after eight, Sylvie clapped her hands for attention and announced that dinner was served. We went into the candlelit courtyard, and sat at the tables around the palm tree. The setting was magnificent, with brass cutlery and gold-trimmed glassware gleaming against rich red napery. In the background, the music of the Malouf could be heard, exotic and soulful. At each place there was a small round or oval metal container, some engraved with flowers or swirls, others with brightly colored enamel work, against which the place cards were set. I'd dashed out in the afternoon to buy them. They were not expensive, but they were very attractive, and I thought they would make nice, and portable, mementos. As Clive had said a hundred times, if he'd said it once: Make sure everyone has a good time. It seemed to work. Everyone admired the workmanship, and wanted to know what they were. "Small powder cases," I explained, "as in gunpowder. Now you can use them for whatever you wish—tie tacks, rings, pills, whatever." Everyone seemed delighted with their keepsakes.

There was a fair amount of confusion at first about the seating arrangements, with Nora insisting that she had to sit with Cliff. "He's not as strong as he could be," she whispered to me. "I want to sit with him in case he needs my help." He didn't look as if he needed much help to me, but I decided not to argue, and we rearranged the seating to accommodate them. Cliff sat with Nora to his right, and Catherine Anderson to his left.

The meal started with a traditional Tunisian soup, *chorba el khodra,* a nice thick vegetable soup thickened with tiny pasta. Then, with a flourish, the waiters strode from the kitchen with platter after platter of various delectables. There was couscous, at least two or three kinds, one with lamb meatballs, one with vegetables, another with chicken; *mechouia,* a dish made of grilled tomatoes and peppers, spiced up with harissa, the Tunisian hot sauce, and the spice blend called tabil; heaping bowls of carrots, glistening with olive oil, redolent with caraway and sprinkled with parsley; and plates of grilled meat of various kinds. The air was filled with the scent of cumin and coriander, fennel and cinnamon. A collective sigh of contentment went up as the group tucked into their meal. "This is just divine," Betty said, and several others murmured their agreement. It occurred to me that what Betty really liked best was sitting at a different table from her husband. She immediately engaged Ed Langdon in conversation and was soon giggling away happily.

Everyone seemed to be having a good time, except for one or two people. "What's this?" Chastity said, poking at the food on her plate.

"I don't know, dear," her mother said. "And we do have to be very careful what we eat in these primitive countries."

"Chicken," Jimmy said. "I should know. But they've put something strange on it." I assume he meant the cumin. Chastity looked at her plate rather dubiously.

"I'm sure there must be a McDonald's or something around here somewhere, dear," Marlene went on. "We'll find it tomorrow."

"Actually, there isn't," I said, with some satisfaction. "I don't believe there are any burger joints in this country."

Marlene looked horrified. Her daughter looked as if she was about to cry. "Tragic," Chastity said.

Ben just smiled. He was a man who enjoyed his food. He'd sampled all the appetizers and gone back for his favorites more than once, and had heaped his plate at dinner. He took a large bite of the suspect food, poured himself a generous glass of wine from the decanter on the table, and raised his glass. "Delicious," he proclaimed. "Whatever it is."

Nora ate silently, sharing only a word or two with Cliff and hardly anything with Marlene, who sat on her other side. Cliff, though, seemed to be enjoying himself, engaging in animated conversation with Catherine, on his left. From time to time, both of them would erupt in laughter. When that happened, Nora would insinuate herself into the conversation for a moment or two before drawing back into her shell.

Curtis did not appear to be having as good a time as the rest of us, but for a different reason. He kept looking over at the other table where his wife, the beautiful Aziza, was talking animatedly in French to the handsome and flirtatious, although in a relatively harmless way, Emile St. Laurent. He's jealous, I thought, not surprisingly. She was lovely, but more than that, she was his meal ticket. Golf wasn't going to make Curtis's fortune, his relationship with Aziza was, and he wasn't about to give her up any time soon. Betty tried manfully to engage him in conversation, but soon gave up, and turned her attention back to Ed.

We were already on the main course and well into the wine when Briars arrived. "Sorry," he said. "Problem at the site. Shall I go round and say hello to everyone, or can I eat first?"

"Sit down and eat," I said, remembering he'd been cooking for himself. "Make your own introductions here, and I'll introduce you to the other table later."

"Thanks," he said, reaching for some couscous. "I'm starving."

"Man after my own heart," Ben said. "Eat first. Deal with problems later. Try some of this excellent local wine. Magon, I think the waiter says it's called. I'm Ben Miller, by the way. Harvard. I understand you're from UCLA."

And so the conversation went, and by and large, the evening seemed to go quite well. Everyone made an effort to get along with everyone else, even with Chastity. When she began to whine that there was nothing she wanted for dessert, Ben picked up a branch of dates, and offered her one.

"Try it," he commanded in a voice I expect he put to good use in the lecture hall.

Chastity took the proffered piece of fruit, and carefully placed it in her mouth. "Oh," was all she said, a look of surprise crossing her face as she reached for another. Ben grinned across the table at me.

"Excellent evening," he said.

And it was. People stayed at the tables long after they needed to, and lingered over coffee and fruit. Briars, a good meal in him at last, was charming and funny, and had everyone eating out of his hand within minutes. People came and went. From time to time, someone would get up to get another drink from the bar, or go to the bathroom, but no one seemed inclined to cut the evening short, not even Ben when Chastity, pushing back her chair suddenly without looking behind her, and nearly flattening Susie in the process, also knocked over a glass of red wine, splattering it all over Ben's sweater. He just got up, disappeared for a few minutes, and returned wearing a clean sweater, his good humor intact. Aziza left for a few minutes to fetch a wrap as the evening air turned cooler, and Curtis followed her. People switched places from time to time to talk to someone new: Ed got up and came over to chat with Ben for a few minutes. Susie bobbed around the courtyard continuing her interrogation of anyone she'd missed at the airport or the cocktail party. Emile and Cliff, two businessmen who'd presumably found much in common, got into a discussion about fine cognac, then went into the bar to see what they could come up with, leaving Nora, who went to exchange a few words with Rick before going after Cliff. Even Marlene felt secure enough to leave her daughter alone for a moment and went over to talk to Betty Johnstone. I kept up my end of the conversation as best I could and tried not to fall asleep right then and there. In my sleep-deprived state, I was even beginning to credit Clive with being the genius he always said he was.

All that changed in an instant. "It's gone," Catherine gasped, almost falling into the courtyard in her distress. "My gold necklace. It's been stolen!"

2

*T*HE MAN SNIFFED THE AIR AND CURSED UNDER *his breath. Storm coming, he thought, looking longingly back as the hills and battlements of Qart Hadasht receded behind the thin white wake of the boat. Bad storm, he added a few moments later, when the first large drops of rain smacked the deck and the rectangular sail began to luff briefly as the wind abruptly shifted. Superstitiously, he touched the silver pendant around his neck that held the magic words—painstakingly copied on a tiny piece of papyrus—that would keep him safe.*

He stamped his feet on the wooden deck to keep warm. Why had he ever agreed to this? He didn't even know the ship's destination, let alone how long he would be away. A sudden vision of his tiny baby daughter made him smile. She was the reason why, of course, and the other one on the way. He wanted a good life for them all, and there would be extra profit in this voyage. The captain, Hasdrubal—he'd sailed with him many times before—was a stern but honorable man and had promised him that much.

But what was it about this journey that made it neces-sary to leave on such a night, to steal from his warm bed and the loving arms of his young wife, to slip across the courtyard, then through the silent city streets past the metal workshops and the artisans' quarters to the har-bor? What need was there for the ship to slip its moor-ings when the night was darkest, maneuvering the squat little freighter quietly out of the harbor, where the sail was raised and the wind and the current took her? Did they think they could outrun the storm? And why now, with winter coming? He'd be sitting out the storm season at the voyage's destination, wherever it might be—that much was certain. His new child would be months' old when he got back.

Even in good weather, why sail at night, and alone? What were they worried about? Pirates? His eyes quickly scanned the coastline, peering into the dark coves where danger might lurk. But if pirates—and here he smiled— thinking that his own people had made piracy an art, and a rather lucrative one at that, then why sail unac-companied? There were warships aplenty in the harbor when they left. They could have escorted the ship.

Pirates should not be a hazard at night, surely. Few except his fellow citizens ventured to sea at night. Even fewer knew the secrets of the polestar, and the aid to navigation that star could be. And fewer still had the courage it took, preferring to huddle in little bays until the light, then scooting to the next landing place before darkness fell once more.

A foreign power, perhaps? Possibly. There were other nations that challenged their supremacy at sea from time to time, but they did not enjoy the protection of the city gods, Baal Hammon and Tanit, nor the god of the old city and sailors, Melqart, to whom he, Abdelmelqart, sailor of Qart Hadasht, had been pledged at birth. It was unbelievable that Agathocles the Greek tyrant should have outrun Hamilcar's blockade, but it was said he'd burned his ships once he'd reached the shore, so he should be no worry at sea, no matter how much a threat on land.

And where were they going? It was a puzzle, to be sure. East, that much was clear. Egypt perhaps. He had done that route often enough, hugging the Libyan coast all the way. The great pharaoh always had need of their goods, the riches they brought from the lands at the ends of the sea. Or Tyre, the mother city, from whom Qart Hadasht's founder, the great Elissa Dido had once sailed? Now, that he wouldn't mind. Even if Qart Hadasht had outstripped Tyre in grandeur and importance for some time now, since Alexander had captured the city, Abdelmelqart would still like to see it. He could picture the amazement in his wife's eyes as he recounted where he had been, the things he had seen and done. A vision of her long, long dark hair caused him to look back again. He could no longer see the city. Soon enough they would round the headland, and if there was an offshore breeze—and he hoped there wasn't, because it was the worst stench in the world, no matter what wealth it brought—he'd catch a whiff from the vats where the purple dye fermented. Then he'd need to keep a lookout for Iranim, a shadow on the sea off to the port side of the ship, and if the ship turned south toward the Libyan coast, for Hadramaut—what was left of it after Agathocles had captured it—then the island called Meninx.

But if not pirates, and not enemies, what then? The cargo? He had seen the last of it loaded into the hold, the hundreds of amphorae filled with wine and oil, the pithoi filled with glass and ivory, the piles of silver and copper ingots. A rich cargo to be sure, but still, nothing unusual there. A few slaves for sale, also nothing out of the ordinary. They remained chained below.

Only one thing had caught his attention, a plain cedar box tarred black to keep it watertight, now lashed to the deck, and the stranger who had seen it stowed. Nothing all that special about either the box or the man, really, but if the rumors in the port were true, and Abdelmelqart was reasonably sure they were, both the stranger and his cargo had come in on a ship from the colonies to the west. Not that this was in itself unusual: All ships from the west stopped at Qart Hadasht.

Too bad we aren't headed west, he thought. Those lands, he would give much to visit. Just once he'd like to brave the tricky currents of the pillars of Herakles and see for himself the lands that marked the ends of the earth. He'd heard that the ground burned there, and rivers of pure silver flowed from its depths, fabulous riches that could be purchased for a few amphorae of oil and a trinket or two. What treasures must come from there! Tartessus. Even the name seemed exotic.

He looked at the wood crate, then scanned carefully about him. Most of the crew had found shelter from the rain. The men below dozed at their places, and no one looked his way. Well, shouldn't he as watchman know what he was guarding? He advanced silently on bare feet toward the box, which was about six feet long, and not quite three feet wide and high. It was, he found, securely fastened with rope. Still it might be possible to pry the lid up just enough to catch a glimpse of what was inside once there was a little more light. Carefully he took the short-sword from his belt and slid the blade between the lid and the box. He looked around again. He could see no one.

Holding his breath with the effort to be quiet, he levered the blade so that the lid began to pull up and away from the box.

Too late, he turned to the sound of a board creaking behind him.

"Arriving tomorrow American Airlines flight 124. Meet me at airport. KE," the fax said. A little peremptory in tone, one might say, but I suppose Kristi Ellingham, travel writer for the upscale—dare I say snotty?—*First Class* magazine, had come to expect such attention. The fax was not entirely a surprise, Clive having put prodigious effort into getting a travel writer of Kristi's stature to come along with us, in an attempt to "extend the reach"—to use his expression—of this particular public relations endeavor called an antiques and archaeology tour. Once we'd gotten underway, however, I'd assumed, with some relief, that she wouldn't show. An enthusiastic call from Clive, however, disabused me of that assumption.

"I have fabulous news," he said, without even saying hello, as I groped in the dark for the light. "Kristi Ellingham is joining the group. Kristi Ellingham!" he enthused.

"Clive," I said, finding the light and peering at the clock. "It's four in the morning here."

"Oh," he said. "Right. Sorry. But make sure she has a great time, won't you? We'll be famous the world over."

Fortunately, there was still room at the inn, the best suite in the place, in fact, which I was certain Kristi would consider her due. Chantal and Sylvie had offered to give us the room for free in return for the hoped-for publicity; McClintoch & Swain was paying her airfare and all her incidental expenses, *First Class* magazine not being among those publishers with any scruples about their writers accepting freebies. Kristi's appearance meant that we wouldn't make a dime on the trip, but the publicity, as Clive kept telling me, would more than make up for the few dollars it was going to cost us to have her along. The problem was that the first thing she might hear about this tour was that we had a thief in our midst.

Which we surely did. In the uproar that followed Catherine's announcement, I'd forced myself into some semblance of alertness and looked about me. Every one of our guests was in the courtyard at that moment, and all had something to say. "I told you," Susie said to Catherine. "You should listen to someone like me. I'm an experienced traveler." True, but maybe Catherine didn't need to hear it at this very moment. Aziza took Catherine by the arm, led her over to a sofa in the lounge and sat with her.

"You should have let me bring my gun," Jimmy said to Betty. "You can't be too careful in these Muslim countries."

"You're going to shoot yourself or some innocent person, one day," Betty said, a hint of steel in her voice. Perhaps she wasn't the submissive little wife I'd taken her for. "You almost shot our future son-in-law, remember? Just because he was sneaking in to see our daughter during the night." The couple glared at each other. I wasn't sure the marriage would survive this tour.

"Are you insured?" Rick asked, going over to Catherine. Catherine just sat there numbly, but that question gave Betty another thought.

"Do you think she hid it herself to collect on the insurance?" she whispered to her husband. If she had, I thought, she was a rather good actress. The poor woman was white as a sheet, and her hands shook as she sat there.

"She has a roommate, doesn't she?" Jimmy replied, not all that quietly. "That nosy little woman. Maybe she took it."

"Why don't we go up and have a look at Catherine's

room?" Ed suggested. "Perhaps she just misplaced it. Jet lag can do that to you."

That struck several of us as a very sensible course of action, and so Ben, Ed, Marlene, Chastity, Betty, and Susie went to look. They came back empty-handed.

Speculation then began as to who was responsible, and regrettably, although perhaps predictably, everyone decided it was the staff. "I saw the concierge—what's his name?—skulking around over there when I went to get some aspirin in my room," Rick said.

"We did, too," Curtis said. "When Aziza and I went up to get her wrap."

"His name is Mohammed," I said, "and it's his job to be checking around the place. He's been here for years." I did not like the way the conversation was going.

"I didn't see any signs that the room was broken into," Ed said.

"Someone with a key, then," Jimmy said, forgetting his earlier comment about Susie, "Pretty clear, if you ask me. The staff. Has to be."

Sylvie and Chantal protested that their employees were absolutely honest, had all been with them for years without any such incident, but I could see that the tour group much preferred to think it was one of the staff rather than one of their fellow travelers—which I suppose was understandable, as unfounded as that conclusion might be.

I took Catherine back to her room, Susie jogging along behind, and then got her into bed. Sylvie said that a guard would be posted in the upstairs hallway that night, and that seemed to soothe Catherine a little.

As we left her to get some rest, I ran my finger along the edge of the door near the lock, and pulled it back quickly as a splinter pierced my hand. Hardly conclusive, but the possibility was there that the door had been forced. If the door was opened with a key, it pretty well had to be staff or Susie. If it was forced, then the pool of possible thieves widened considerably. I went to my own room and had a closer look at the lock, which was just a button in the door knob, standard in all the guest rooms. There was a security chain, but it only worked when someone was in the room. I decided the door could be forced, and rather easily at that.

I went downstairs to see Sylvie, who was still upset about what had happened, and about the implication that her staff was involved.

"It could easily have been someone from outside," I said soothingly.

"No, it couldn't," she said. "There are three gates into the hotel grounds. Only one is ever left unlocked, the main one, and when it's open, there is a guard on duty every minute. Even that one is locked at night. That's why the guests are given keys to the gate when they check in, so they can let themselves in anytime. There are also regular patrols of the grounds from dusk until dawn, in case an intruder tries to scale the wall. I've asked the guards. The gates are all locked, and there has been no sign of anyone coming in from the street. So it has to be someone in the hotel. I have to tell you I believe in the honesty of my staff absolutely. That leaves her roommate, Mme. Windermere, I'm afraid."

"I'm not so sure," I said.

"We've never had any trouble before. This is a law-abiding country. Who else could it be?"

The question really was, was it one of us, and to my way of thinking, the answer was yes. Catherine had put the chain and earrings in her purse when we were leaving Frankfurt, so the staff wouldn't have seen it. Several of the rest of us did. I tried to think who had heard that conversation about Catherine's jewelry in the airport: Betty and Jimmy for sure, Ben and Ed, Marlene and Chastity. Emile hadn't joined us at that point, nor had Curtis, Aziza, and Rick.

However, Catherine had continued to wear the necklace right on to the plane, so the others might have seen it when we were all lining up to board. It was very obviously a good necklace. That was my problem with it in the first place. It just screamed "steal me." And Susie made a big thing about it at the cocktail party, so I couldn't even leave out the people who joined us there.

Given the possibility that all of them not only knew she had the chain, and also that she hadn't got around to putting it in the hotel safe, I had to look for motive and opportunity to narrow the field a little.

These people were all strangers to me. I'd met a couple of them at the shop before we left—Susie and Catherine and Marlene, to be specific—but none of the others. But if money was the issue, then surely at least a few members of the group could be eliminated. Susie seemed a little anxious about finances, but she was hardly alone in the world in that. Clifford Fielding, the group tycoon, didn't need the money. I could leave him and Nora off the list of suspects, I thought, unless, of course, they had tendencies to kleptomania I didn't know about.

By the same token, I'd have to eliminate Emile, too. For all his charm, Emile, the group diplomat, was a tycoon, too, or at least well on his way to being one again. Rick was a tycoon wannabe, and Curtis and Aziza were not exactly hurting, either. I was a little surprised by the people who signed up, in fact. I'd expected antiques and archaeology lovers, certainly, and this wasn't a budget tour, but neither was it a luxury junket, just—how had Clive described it?—upscale and charming. But somehow we'd attracted some real financial powerhouses.

So if motive wasn't immediately apparent to me, who had the opportunity to do this? I walked about the lower floor and looked up at the upstairs hallway. Because of the atrium-style design of the building, most of the guest-room doors were visible from downstairs. But not all of them, my own room and Catherine and Susie's being two that weren't. Our rooms were off small corridors at opposite ends of the building. Yes, you could see someone walking along the hall outside the rooms, but the thief could have ducked quickly into the corridor, and then into Catherine and Susie's room.

As I stood there, Susie hailed me from upstairs, then came bounding down to talk to me. "Catherine's asleep now," she whispered to me, as if her roommate could hear us from the floor above. "I've been sitting there thinking about which one of us could have done this," she went on, gesturing me to a seat in the lounge. "I know it wasn't me, and I don't think it was you, either, because you were here when Catherine and I came down to dinner, and you never left the whole time. So who was it, do you think?"

"I have no idea," I confessed.

"What might help would be figuring out who left the courtyard," she went on. "Aziza did, I know, and Curtis with her. Ben left, too, after Chastity doused him with wine. At my table, the only person who didn't actually leave the room was Chastity, and maybe her mother, although even she went to get a liqueur at some point, I think. Cliff and Emile headed off somewhere, although they came back at different times, so they weren't together the whole time," she said, barely stopping for breath. "Aziza left a second time with Betty: they went out to the garden to see the lights of the town. Rick went off for a while. I shouldn't say this, but I was happy to see him leave for a few minutes. My, that man is a bore. I don't know where he went, and I didn't ask. I was sure if I did, he'd tell me he'd phoned Japan to see how his stocks were doing, and I couldn't bear to hear it. The Lord strike me dead for saying it, but that's the truth. Didn't Rick say he went to get aspirin, or something, and that's when he saw Mohammed?"

"He said at first he'd gone up to call Montreal to see how his stock portfolio was doing, and he also said he went to get some aspirin. Did he go twice?" It felt a little strange having this conversation with the number one suspect, Susie having both some motive and all kinds of opportunity, given her room key—but if anyone had noticed what was going on, she had, and furthermore she was prepared to talk about it.

"Maybe," she said. "I'm not sure. But do you really think you can eliminate Chastity? She caused quite a stir with that wine, and nearly knocked me over with her chair. Maybe it was a diversionary tactic so her mother could dash upstairs and do the deed. I'm trying to recall whether Marlene was in the room at the time. Do you remember?"

"I don't," I said. If it had been a diversionary tactic, it had been very effective with me. I was so mesmerized by the pattern of the wine splatters on Ben's sweater, I didn't see anything else. Chastity had certainly done a job on the poor man. He'd been awfully good-humored about it. It was possible, of course, that the thief was Ben, taking advantage of the opportunity, but he'd have had to move rather fast to change his clothes and then rob another room.

"Somehow I don't think Chastity's move was deliberate," I said.

"I guess not. Did you notice how Nora managed to

get out of Chastity's way, unlike slow old me? Nice reflexes that woman has."

"She jogs, apparently," I said. It was the most compelling argument I'd heard in some time for getting back to jogging: to avoid being knocked senseless by Chastity Sherwood's backpack. For a moment I even toyed with the idea of getting up early the next morning and going for a run. "I've got to get some sleep," I said dismissing the idea. "We are not going to solve anything tonight."

"When I think about it, I don't think we've eliminated anybody, have we, except maybe Chastity? What should we do?" she said.

"I think we should just carry on with the tour, but keep our eyes and ears open," I said.

So that is what we did.

"THIS IS WHERE IT ALL BEGAN," BRIARS SAID. We were standing on the summit of Byrsa Hill, with the city of Tunis around us, the water of the Gulf of Tunis behind, and the hills of Cap Bon across the gulf. "These are the very foundations of one of the most important cities of the ancient world, the great city of Carthage. Its history begins with a love story. A tragic one, perhaps, but a love story, nevertheless. It is the story of a woman called Elissa.

"At the time I am speaking of, the ninth century B.C.E., the whole of the Mediterranean," he said, waving his arms toward the sea behind him, "all of it, right to the Pillars of Hercules and beyond, was dominated by a merchant nation we have come to call the Phoenicians. They didn't call themselves that. In fact, we really don't know what name they went by: Canaanites, perhaps.

"Be that as it may, we do know these people controlled much of the trade in the Mediterranean from a city-state called Tyre, located in what is now Lebanon. They were fabulous sailors, having mastered the art of celestial navigation, and knowing intimately the currents and winds of the Mediterranean Sea. No other nation at that time could touch them on the seas.

"At this time, there was a king in Tyre called Mattan. He had a daughter and a son, and he made his wishes quite clear. On his death, Tyre was to be ruled jointly by both of them. You could say he was a man ahead of his time. When he died, though, the people wanted just one ruler."

"Could you possibly guess which one they picked?" Marlene said.

"The people chose the son," Briars went on.

"No kidding," Marlene sneered. "I would never have guessed that, would you?" Her face was framed against the backdrop of the ancient city, the bright sun behind her casting part of her face in shadow. Marlene, I realized, was in the grip of what might be permanent cynicism, which was etching itself into bitter lines about her mouth and eyes. Chastity cringed at her mother's tone.

"The son's name was Pygmalion," Briars said. The wind ruffled his hair, what was left of it, that is. He was an attractive man, in a burly, outdoorsy kind of way, his face and forearms freckled from so much time spent outdoors—a kind of maleness that draws a woman. Nora noticed it, too. For a moment she gave him her undivided attention. Then Cliff and Catherine shared a chuckle, and hearing them, Nora turned away from Briars and returned to Cliff's side, as if reminded of her duty.

"Pygmalion!" Chastity exclaimed. "I've heard of him." I noticed with relief that she looked interested for the first time since we left home.

"His sister's name was Elissa," Briars continued. "Elissa was married to the high priest of Tyre, a man by the name of Zakarbaal. The high priest would have been the second most powerful person in Tyre, after the king. Perhaps Pygmalion thought Zakarbaal a threat, or maybe he was just plain greedy. In any event Pygmalion had Zakarbaal killed. Elissa fled the city with some of her followers, and headed to sea. She stopped first in what we now call Cyprus, added a number of temple priestesses to her retinue; then after sailing from port to port, eventually found this spot on the north coast of Africa.

"When she and her followers arrived here, they were welcomed by the inhabitants, led by a Libyan chieftain named Hiarbas. In this case, the term Libyan refers to one of the groups of people living here when the Phoenicians arrived. Elissa asked to buy some land, and Hiarbas agreed to sell her as much territory as could be covered by the hide of an ox. Elissa, a clever woman and never one to back down from a challenge, cut the hide into the narrowest of strips and encircled this hill, which is called Byrsa now, after the Greek word for ox hide. It was here, on this hill that, in the year 814 B.C.E., she founded what was called Qart Hadasht, or new city, the place we now call Carthage. Qart Hadasht was not the first city the Phoenicians founded on the shores of North Africa, nor would it be the last. But it was unquestionably the most important, eventually outstripping its parent, Tyre, in both grandeur and power. Its people, now called Carthaginians, dominated the Mediterranean for many hundreds of years. It was to become a cultured, cosmopolitan city of temples and marketplaces, ateliers and beautiful homes. And it was strong enough to hold off even the Roman juggernaut for a very long time."

"I thought you said this was tragic," Chastity pouted.

The others laughed. She flushed with anger or embar-
rassment.

"Wait," Briars said, smiling at her. "For a while the
two peoples, the Phoenicians and the native Libyans,
lived in harmony. The woman who had been Elissa in
Tyre, became known as Dido, or the wandering one,
in North Africa, and it is by this second name that she
has come down to us through history. Then Hiarbas
decided he wanted to marry Elissa. She, still loyal to
her dead husband, refused him. When his entreaties
failed, he resorted to threats, saying if she didn't agree,
he would kill all her followers. Elissa built a huge bon-
fire for what looked to be a great ceremony. And a
great ceremony it was. Try to picture it: all the people
gathered to see the lighting of the great fire, Dido in
the magnificent robes of city founder. Perhaps off in
the distance, Hiarbas and his followers stood watching
and waiting, Hiarbas, in eager anticipation of the prize
that was about to be his. And then, as the flames licked
at the wood, crackling and spitting and soaring higher
and higher, Elissa Dido threw herself into the flames,
which became her funeral pyre. Rather than submit to
Hiarbas, rather than betray her dead husband, Dido
sacrificed herself."

"Tragic enough for you, Chastity?" Ed joked. But
Chastity stood transfixed by the story. As I watched
her, a single tear left the corner of one eye and began
its journey down her cheek. She was a lonely and impressionable young girl.

"The astounding thing about this story," Briars went
on, "is that parts of it may actually be true. While the
archaeological evidence to date goes back only as far
as the eighth century, it is close enough to give some
credence to the stories of Carthage's founding. We do
know that there was political upheaval in Tyre during
Pygmalion's reign, and we know that he ruled at the

time traditionally given as the founding of Carthage. We also know that sacrifice by fire was an important ritual for the Carthaginians, that in times of great danger they may even have sacrificed their own children, and that the wife of the last leader of Carthage threw herself into the flames, along with her children, rather than be taken by Rome at the fall of the city in 146 B.C.E. Be that as it may, Dido's story—her journey, her steadfast love for her husband, her courage, and her tragic death—has resonated through the ages.

"The Romans liked the story, of that we are certain, because they adopted it as their own, with some variations that suited their particular egotistical view of history. To the average Roman citizen, Rome was, let's face it, the center of the universe," Briars said, smiling.

"Writing in the first century B.C.E., Virgil, one of the great storytellers and poets of ancient Rome, began his tale of the foundation of Rome with the words, *Arma virumque cano,* of war and a man I sing, and tells the story of Aeneas, a Trojan, who flees the defeat of Troy at the hands of the Greeks, and sets sail, later to found Rome. *Fato profugus,* exiled by fate, *multum ille et terris iactatus,* much tossed about, buffeted, on land and sea, as Virgil describes it, Aeneas arrives on these shores to be welcomed by Dido herself. In this version of the story, Juno, consort of the Greek god Zeus, casts a spell on Dido, under the influence of which the Queen of Carthage falls madly in love with the dashing Aeneas, only to be left behind when duty calls and he sets sail again to meet his destiny. Overcome with grief at his betrayal, Dido casts herself into the flames." Briars paused for a moment. "Now let's go and have a look around the site, before you proceed from ancient Carthaginian rituals to modern-day Tunisian commerce with Lara and Jamila, who will be taking you on a tour of the medina or marketplace." Everyone laughed.

"THE FORMAL PART OF OUR TOUR OF THE MEDINA of Tunis ends here," I told the group sometime later. "You now have some time to explore on your own, shop a little if you want to, or just sit in a coffee house and watch the world go by.

"I have maps of the area for each of you," I said, handing them around. "You are here," I explained, holding up a map and pointing, "in the Souk des Chéchias, so if any of you want to buy one of the red skull caps, the chéchia, this is the place to do it. Also, right over there," I said, pointing once again, "is the Café Chaouechin, the oldest coffee house in Tunis. There's also Café Mrabat in Souk el Trouk, the souk of the Turks, which is over that way. The café is actually built right over the tomb of a saint. For the more adventurous among you, there are some public baths in the medina; they're called hammams. Most are for men, but there is one that has women's hours about now," I said, checking my watch. "You would be sampling a very important part of Tunisian life, if you opt for the baths. You'll recognize them from the very distinctive red doorways." From the shaking of heads, I gathered that public baths were not a popular option.

"If you get lost, just remember that the medina was built around the mosque, so look for the Zitouna Mosque. I've marked it, and Jamila," I said, referring to the efficient woman who shared guide duties with me, and who was looking after all the arrangements as we went, "has put the name in Arabic on the map, so you can ask directions in any shop. We'll meet at the main door of the mosque in about an hour, say one hour and ten minutes.

"For those of you who would like to shop, Jamila is going to an area where you can sometimes find antiques, old lamps and such, and I'll be going over to the Souk el Trouk and the Souk de Leffa to look at carpets. Anyone who wants to come along with either of us, is quite welcome to do so. Now, one hour and ten minutes, main door of Zitouna Mosque. See you there."

"Something smells good around here," Ben said. "I vote we go and get something to eat."

"I could use a coffee and a sit-down," Susie said. "I'll come with you. You coming, too, Catherine?"

"I guess so," Catherine said.

"Why don't you go and buy yourself something nice, Nora?" Cliff said reaching for his wallet.

"No, I'll stay with you, Cliff," she said.

"You don't need to do that," he said, a trifle irritably. "I'm not an invalid."

"I'm going to explore a little bit more," Ed said. "Anyone want to come and have a look at the hammam with me?"

"I knew he'd head for the baths," Jimmy muttered to his wife.

"Shush," she said.

"I'll go with you," Chastity said to Ed.

"You will not!" her mother exclaimed. "You just come and have some tea!"

"I'll go," Cliff said. Nora started to protest. "You can come, too, if you want to, Nora. I don't want to miss a thing."

"Excellent!" Ed declared. "Let's go, Cliff. I'll take good care of him, Nora. Don't worry." Nora stood there looking like a little lost child.

"He'll be fine, Nora," I assured her.

"You never know what can happen," she replied.

"There has to be a coin dealer around here some-

where," Emile said. "I think I'll see what I can find."
Gradually the others dispersed.

So far, our plan to carry on in as close to a
normal manner as possible seemed to be working.
While the majority still thought that someone on the
staff had to be responsible for the theft of Catherine's
necklace, many of them were coming around to the
view that she had been very careless. Catherine still
seemed a little delicate, but she was rallying, and we
stuck to our original schedule.

And so, while the others had been exclaiming over
the exquisite Roman mosaics in the Bardo museum, I'd
been dashing out to the airport, as directed, to meet
Kristi Ellingham.

I don't know what I expected Kristi Ellingham to
look like, with her chichi name and her job as travel
editor for *First Class* magazine, a journal that catered to
the upscale tastes and acquisitiveness of newly wealthy
boomers as well as old money types. Tall, thin, elegant,
perhaps, with an imperious attitude, Vuitton luggage,
and a Burberry raincoat. Kristi was, in fact, rather ordi-
nary-looking, of average height and weight, with short
brown hair. Her only distinguishing feature was a scar
that ran from the corner of her lip down to the line of
her jaw. The expensive luggage was in evidence; the
attitude, however, was not. "Hi," she said, handing me
her business card. "Thanks for meeting me. I'm really
looking forward to covering this tour." She reached
into her large shoulder bag, and pulled out a silver
lighter and pack of cigarettes. "Those transatlantic non-
smoking flights are killers," she said, inhaling deeply.
"Filthy habit, I know," she added. "Can't seem to kick
it. No willpower. Now, where do we go?"

It should be said that I don't much like *First Class*

magazine. Let's just say that if you are looking for thoughtful commentary on social and political issues, inspiring stories of people overcoming adversity, or indeed for articles of any redeeming social value whatsoever, then *First Class* may not be the magazine for you. I knew only too well how influential it was, though. A few months earlier, *First Class* had run a photo of a condo we'd furnished for an up-and-coming young Canadian starlet—an assignment Clive still referred to as The Job from Hell, but which *First Class* called "New Life in Old Houses"—as one small part of a feature they were running on young swingers who liked old places, and it had led to a surprising number of inquiries.

I took Kristi back to the hotel, and with Sylvie, showed her to her room. The suite was gorgeous, spacious, with beautiful tilework on the walls in the entranceway, a large canopy bed, and a huge tiled bathroom. A carved wooden archway led to a small sitting room. There were flowers everywhere, and I'd sprung for a bottle of real champagne, the only foreign wine, I believe, the Tunisian government allowed into the country. It was set out, with two crystal flutes, on an elegant brass tray. There was also a lovely bowl filled with apples, pears, and dates. "Isn't this delightful?" Kristi said. "I hope you don't mind, but I'm going to rest for the remainder of the day. I'll join the group tomorrow when I'm feeling a little less jet lagged. I'm looking forward to meeting them all, and seeing the sights." Pleasantly surprised by her generally agreeable demeanor, I left her and headed back to the group, just in time to take them to the medina.

FOR THE BETTER PART OF AN HOUR, I TOOK AZIZA, Betty, and Jimmy, to look at carpets, explaining the different grades, the methods by which they were produced, and in general what to look for in buying one. With my help in the bargaining, Betty and Jimmy purchased two rather large and handsome carpets in a traditional Persian design. Or rather Betty did, Jimmy being essentially uninterested in both the carpets and all the bargaining that went along with their acquisition. Nonetheless, Betty was delighted, and I arranged to have her choices shipped.

Aziza was more interested in the more informal Berber *allouches,* but couldn't decide on one. Instead she purchased a lovely silk and linen *sifsari,* the traditional shawl and headcovering, in which I knew she'd look spectacular. She and I then went hunting for a chicha, a water pipe, something she said Curtis wanted, and I helped her distinguish the good ones from the junk made for the tourist trade. She was rather pleased with her purchase.

Taking a few minutes for my own search, I found six rather large, old but not antique, carpets for my film-star client. In addition to the six, I ordered two custom carpets, huge ones, for the living room—silk, in lovely shades of red and green. I was off and running on the Rosedale house.

I got my little group back to the Zitouna Mosque right on time. Jamila was already there with several of the others, and a few stragglers turned up within five minutes of the appointed time, laden down with their purchases. Susie, spectacular in blue and yellow tights and an emerald-green sweatshirt, was buzzing around asking to see what everyone had bought and exactly how much they'd paid for it. There were more little stuffed camels than anything else, which just goes to prove that people who come on an antiques tour aren't necessarily interested in antiques, nor are they terribly discriminating. I noted that Marlene and Chastity had succumbed to the lure of the large wire birdcages, as Clive said people would. I would have to figure out how to get these rather unwieldy objects home for them.

When Ed and Cliff arrived, everyone crowded around to hear about the baths. "They were really interesting," I heard Cliff say. "A real social place."

Emile, among the last to return, told me he hadn't found any interesting coins, but had picked up a small terra-cotta lamp. "What do you think?" he asked me. "This isn't my field. Is it worth anything?"

I examined it closely. "Roman, I should think, and probably authentic." He beamed. "However," I said, "see here, it's been broken and repaired." He pushed his glasses up onto his forehead and studied the place I'd pointed to. "So a nice piece, but the repairs bring the value down."

"Ah, I see what you mean. I'll have to take you shopping with me next time." He smiled ruefully. "I confess to being a little embarrassed."

"You shouldn't be," I consoled. "It's not your field, and the repairs are really expert. I can't imagine how badly I'd do if I went looking for coins. It's very attractive and you should just enjoy it as a lovely memento of your trip."

"I will," he said, but, as I began to turn my attention to the group, I saw him hand the lamp to Catherine, who'd admired it. "Keep it," he said to her, "with my compliments." Catherine flushed with pleasure. It seemed Emile St. Laurent was only interested in the finest specimens, and he was not prepared to live with his mistakes. Come to think of it, though, I might have felt the same way if he'd told me a coin I'd found was worthless. An occupational hazard, I suppose.

"Time to go," I called to the group. "Let me do a head count."

"Guess I owe you a dinar," Jamila said after we'd

counted everybody three times. We were one short, and it was Rick Reynolds who was missing.

"You do, and I'll expect to collect the debt this evening," I told her. I was not worried in the least about Rick. "Anyone seen Rick since the Souk des Chéchias?" I asked the group. No one had.

After another ten minutes or so, I did begin to feel a little anxious. Certainly it was easy enough to get lost in the medina, but the area is really not that large, and with the map I'd given him, getting directions should not have been a problem. A few minutes later, with still no sign of Rick, and the group becoming restive, I suggested to Jamila that she accompany the others back to the bus to wait, then circle back to help me try to find Rick.

Jamila and I got out a map, and decided who would go where, agreeing to meet back at the mosque in twenty-five minutes to check on each other's progress. The medina, the historical center of the city of Tunis, indeed the original city, was built in the seventh century by the Arabs. It is a semicircular walled town which has at its heart the grand mosque. It is a vibrant mix of monuments and tombs, former palaces and tiny homes, hammams, and the Koranic schools called medersas, white domes and minarets. Everywhere there are shops: one tunnel-like souk, or covered market, leads into another in a confusing maze. The streets are, for the most part, narrow, winding, and inevitably crowded during the day, so looking for Rick was a daunting task. Jamila was to retrace the most direct route back to the Souk des Chéchias, where Rick had last been seen. I was to circle a little farther afield.

For several minutes I looked carefully about, traversing pillared arcades and peering into various souks, the air filled with smoke, and sharp streaks of sunlight penetrating the haze from skylights above. Little children tugged at my sleeves, and salesmen, ever on the lookout for tourists, followed me for a while, extolling the virtues of their particular establishment. Several invited me in for a look. I made my way past workmen at their benches making red felt skullcaps and leather goods, cafés where the men sat drinking strong, black Turkish coffee and smoking the chicha, then past the gargotes, where the aroma of kebabs and kefta wafted into the street. It was hot, and crowded, and I was beginning to think it was hopeless. I wondered if Rick would know how to get back to Taberda on his own, or indeed if he had enough money with him for the hour-long trip, when he realized he was late and the group had left him behind.

I had just come up on the heavy wooden gates of the Souk des Orfèvres, the souk of the goldsmiths, when I thought I caught sight of him. I entered the souk, with its narrow little shops, the sun casting patterns on the street through the awnings overhead, but couldn't see him. Perhaps I'd been mistaken, but it seemed worth a closer look. I went up and down the souk, and was just about to give up and look elsewhere when I caught sight of him again. This time he was standing in the doorway of one of the shops, stuffing what looked to be a wad of cash into the money belt at his waist. He appeared to have just made a purchase and was putting his change away.

I was about to go over to him and, as with a wayward child, either hug him in my relief at finding him, or berate him for being so late. Something stopped me, though, something in the way he was looking about him carefully before stepping fully into the street, or the fact that he wasn't carrying any parcel. Instead, I pulled back into one of the shops, and watched as he went by. He didn't look worried, or lost, for that matter.

I waited until he had left the souk, and was about to follow him, when, struck by an unpleasant thought, I went into the shop he had just left.

"Can I help you, miss?" the man behind the counter asked.

"Perhaps," I said. "I'm looking for a gold necklace."

"We have many," the man said enthusiastically. "Here," he said, pointing to rows of rather elaborate filigree work, a trifle ornate for my taste.

I looked at several, feigning some interest, but not too much. Shopping in the medina requires nerve, skill, and not just a little acting ability.

"Where are you from?" he asked. "England? Germany?"

"Canada," I replied.

"Excellent," he replied. "I give a good price for Canada. You like which one?"

"I don't know," I said. "Maybe something simpler. Plain, but good, you know. Heavy," I added.

"I might have something like that," he said, turning to the counter behind him, where the object I was really interested in, lay. "Something like this?" he asked, holding the necklace up for me to see.

"That's a little closer to what I was thinking of," I said, carefully emphasizing the words *a little*. "Can I have a look?"

"Of course," he said, handing it to me. "Lovely, isn't it? Eighteen karat, too. It's very fortunate you came in here. I just got it in today, and I'm sure it will sell very quickly. How much do you want to pay?"

"I'm not sure this is the one," I said. "It's a bit like what I had in mind, but not exactly right. Are there others?" I looked at a few more necklaces, then turned back to the one I was determined to get, and at the lowest price possible.

"I'll give you a good price, I told you," he said. He made a big show of thinking, did some figuring on a pocket calculator, named a breathtaking sum, and the haggling began.

"Oh, I don't know," I said again. "Maybe . . ." I looked about me, then took a couple of steps toward the door. He lowered his price slightly. I paused and countered with a much lower offer. He looked hurt, but came back with something less than his previous price. I named a sum slightly higher than my original offer. He offered me a cup of pine nut tea. Back and forth it went between sips of the lovely minty beverage. Finally he threw up his hands. "I must be feeling very good today"—he sighed theatrically—"to agree to such a low price. But, it's for such a lovely lady. And Canada, too." I thanked him for the compliment, we shook hands, I forked over the cash, and he wrapped it up for me. It was a lot of money, but probably considerably less than Catherine Anderson's late husband had paid for it back home. Rick Reynolds had rather a lot of explaining to do.

But Rick did not so much as bat an eyelash when I produced the necklace with a flourish at dinner that night.

Catherine almost cried with delight, and the rest of the group burst into spontaneous applause. Cliff reached over and patted Catherine's hand. "Where did you find it?" they exclaimed.

"In a shop in the Souk des Orfèvres," I said. "While I was out trying to find Rick." I looked at him pointedly. He shrugged and looked a little sheepish.

It was either a magnificent performance or the man was entirely innocent. While I was sorely tempted to take him aside and demand that he pay up for the necklace, every last penny I'd shelled out for it, I had to admit that just being in the same shop didn't make him a thief, and the fact I'd seen him putting money away didn't incriminate him either. As for the lack of a parcel, it could be as simple as his having purchased something small enough to carry in his money belt. A pair of earrings for a girlfriend, for example, or even a ring.

"Hey!" he exclaimed. "Maybe that will make up for the fact that I kept everybody waiting. Sorry about that, really I am. My watch stopped, and I didn't notice. But I won't be late again. I managed to buy a battery for it, right in the medina."

Or a watch battery, I conceded.

Still, I felt a small twinge of triumph, however tempered by a certain ambiguity about the identity of the thief. Kristi Ellingham, whose opinion could make or break the reputation of McClintoch & Swain, had not yet emerged from her room, and at least one major stumbling block to a positive report on her part had been removed, in a fashion at least. Yes, it had cost a pretty penny to get the necklace back, but it was worth it, wasn't it?

3

HASDRUBAL STRAIGHTENED FROM EXAMINING THE *body, and sighed. What had happened here? An accident surely, but how could that be? To such an experienced sailor as Abdelmelqart! The sea was choppy perhaps, but not dangerously so, the deck a little wet from the brief squall that had passed through, but not, he thought, sliding his foot tentatively across the surface, so slippery that someone as surefooted as this sailor would stumble. It was not possible!*

But there to prove him wrong, Abdelmelqart lay, the life gone from him, eyes staring upward, as if fixed on some distant place, the dark plait of hair on the right side of his head now matted with blood. It was easy to see how he had died: a severe blow to the back of his skull. There was something wrong about it, though, the way the man lay, and Hasdrubal had a sense of a body disturbed, somehow, something missing, perhaps, from the way he usually saw the man. He would have to think about this when he was more able, when the shock of seeing him dead had passed a little.

"Did anyone see how this happened?" he asked the group of men crowded around the body. They all shook their heads.

"Hit his head, I expect," one of them, a man by the name of Mago, said.

"Obviously," Hasdrubal replied dryly. "But how?"

Mago shrugged. Hasdrubal didn't like Mago. He thought him untrustworthy. There was nothing in Mago's words with which to find fault, ever, but something about his attitude, the mild defiance that crossed his face whenever Hasdrubal gave him an order, the treachery in his eyes, bothered the captain. Mago might be telling the truth; then again, he might not. And was that not Abdelmelqart's silver pendant already hanging around Mago's neck? Ah, there it was, the missing object. He recognized the design, a solar disk set into a downward crescent. Abdelmelqart would not be without his talisman, just as he, Hasdrubal, would not set sail without his. Swift, that Mago. Swift and nasty.

Hasdrubal looked over at the others. "Anyone?" he demanded.

"We thought we heard a cry over the sound of the wind," replied Safat, a friend of Mago's and equally untrustworthy, although not as clever. On a mission such as this, one took on whatever crew one could. Even then, Hasdrubal would not have hired Mago and Safat, had the man who had commissioned the ship not insisted upon leaving immediately, making it impossible for the captain to round up his usual crew.

"But we didn't think anything of it. We thought it was a bird," a man named Malchus said, picking up the story from Safat. "But later, when dawn came, we found him lying there. We didn't see it happen."

Now there's another one, Hasdrubal thought. The man could hardly contain his glee at the sight of Abdelmelqart's body. Hadn't the two of them been rivals for the hand of the lovely Bodastart, and Abdelmelqart the lucky one? Now perhaps Malchus was thinking of expressing his condolences to the widow in person. Abdelmelqart had not been pleased to see Malchus aboard, but Hasdrubal had persuaded him that it was better to have him here than hanging about Qart Hadasht while Abdelmelqart was at sea.

The others were nodding now, in agreement. All but the young man, a boy really, who was going to sea for the first time. Hasdrubal had selected him for the voyage because he looked intelligent and observant. Now, though, the young man looked wary, and perhaps even frightened.

Hasdrubal dismissed the crew with a wave. "Back to your duties," he said. The men turned to go. "And Mago," he said, extending his open hand toward the man. "The pendant, please. For Abdelmelqart's widow." Mago gave him a look of pure hatred as he unclasped the pendant and hurled it at Hasdrubal.

The captain turned back to the body. He would be sorry to lose Abdelmelqart. He was a good man, cunning certainly, and useful when it came to negotiations with the locals in the various ports of call, but an honorable man when it came to dealing with his fellow citizens and sailors. And in such a silly, unnecessary accident, a moment's carelessness, perhaps, in an occupation that allowed few mistakes.

But what had he hit his head on? Surely there would be some blood that would show the point of impact. The ship's captain tentatively reached out and touched the gunwales near where the man had fallen. Nothing that he could see there. He turned to the cedar box. There was no sign of blood there either, but he ran his fingers along its edge. A splinter jabbed his hand, and he pulled it back abruptly.

He looked at the spot where the splinter had caught

him. Could it be, he wondered, that someone had tried to pry open the box? He bent to study the wood. The marks were faint, but they were there. Some very slim instrument had been inserted between the lid and the box, and pressure exerted to force the lid up.

He turned back and bent over Abdelmelqart's body. His short-sword was not there. Perhaps he had forgotten to bring it with him, having had to leave his bed in the middle of the night. Unlikely, though, the captain thought. Abdelmelqart was very proud of that sword. He had purchased it from a mercenary soldier years earlier. It had cost him a silver drachm, he once told Hasdrubal. The mercenary could hardly refuse to sell it at that price. But Abdelmelqart had paid the man with a coin that he had stolen from him the night before. Abdelmelqart always laughed when he told that story, how he'd paid the man with his own money. Yes, Abdelmelqart was a crafty one, that much was certain. Had Mago stolen that, too? Probably not, the captain concluded. There had not been enough time before the others arrived to have hidden it. Unless . . .

He looked ahead to the sky, now red with dawn. Two men stood watching him, the stranger and Mago. Now he had two problems, Hasdrubal thought. The sky meant a storm, and a bad one at that. And there was something seriously amiss on his ship.

"Come," he said to the boy, who hovered nervously nearby. "Come and talk to me."

THE NEXT ITEM TO GO MISSING WAS MAR-lene's Swiss Army knife, followed closely by a rather large sum of money, large by my standards anyway— about seven hundred dollars, that Jimmy was carrying around with him.

"At home we leave the back door unlocked all the

time," he said. "This country is full of thieves. A man can't leave his belongings in a hotel like this, even for a minute."

I wanted to tell him that Tunisia, while it had its share of the problems every country has, was a relatively safe place, but there didn't seem to be any point. His mind was made up. And certainly, on the face of it, it appeared he was right: two serious thefts in the first few days. The truth of the matter was that he had been very careless. He'd taken the money with him when he'd gone to the pool, and had left it with his towel while he went for a swim. Then, still in his bathing suit, he'd left the pool to watch a croquet match his wife was playing in. Hardly just a minute—more like fifteen or twenty, during which time just about everybody had passed through the pool area. Inattentive though he might have been, however, the thefts simply had to stop for any number of reasons, not the least of which was that we had a reporter on the scene. Kristi Ellingham said she wanted to interview me for the article she was writing on the tour. I was dreading a question or comment about the theft, but she never mentioned the subject, and her questions surprised me.

"It's rather unusual to be in business with your ex-husband, isn't it?" she began, pen poised over her notebook, and a cigarette in her left hand.

I was taken aback, but rallied. "It works for us," I said. In a fashion, I thought.

"Clive was telling me that the two of you were in business together before, then sold the store when you divorced."

"Yes," I said. The less said about that, the better, as far as I was concerned. Clive should learn to keep his mouth shut. I'd had to sell the store to give him half the proceeds, even though I'd started the business alone, long before he and I even met.

"But now you're back in business again," Kristi said.

"That's right," I replied. "How about you? How long have you been writing for *First Class*?"

"I'm interviewing you, remember?" she said, but she smiled to take the edge off the remark. "About ten years," she added.

Then, sensing I wasn't about to be more forthcoming on the subject of Clive and me, she switched gears. "You have quite a diverse group of people on this tour, don't you? They come from all over the place, and have such varied interests and occupations."

"I think most people are interested in seeing different cultures, and of course, the focus of this tour on antiques and archaeology makes it unusual." I hoped Clive would be pleased with my response here, although I couldn't believe these words were coming out of my mouth. It certainly sounded like PR talk to me.

"Emile, for example," she went on. "He sounds French. Is he from France?"

"Yes," I replied.

"Very charming, isn't he?" she said in a tone that implied she was confiding in me. "What does he do?"

"He's a numismatist. A coin dealer. He has a company called ESL Numismatics, very influential in the field of ancient coinage."

"How interesting," she said, taking a sip of her gin and tonic. If there was fault to be found with Kristi, it was her fondness for gin. She was on her third drink since we'd sat down together, charging each of them to her room. Tunisia being a predominantly Muslim country, alcoholic beverages are generally served only in tourist establishments, and even there, are prohibitively expensive. A rather unexceptional gin and tonic can run as high as $8 or $10, and Kristi managed to consume several every day. As Ms. Ellingham's host, the bills came to me every morning from either Sylvie or

Chantal, who clucked sympathetically as they handed them over, while I swore Clive's marketing initiative was going to bankrupt us. Still she was pleasant enough, and if we got some positive press, presumably Clive would think it was worth it. Praise be for my film star's ten-bedroom house. It was going to save the day, financially speaking.

"And that fellow Rick. He must be involved in the stock market some way." She laughed, and I did, too. It was impossible not to know that about Rick. "Where's he from?"

"Montreal," I replied.

"What company is he with?" I told her. We went through the list of everyone on the tour, where they were from, and what I knew about them, which frankly wasn't much.

"Aziza and Curtis I know, of course," she concluded. "I'm surprised they're here, but you're lucky to have them along. They have lots of influential friends."

"They're lovely people," I said, tactfully. When, I wondered, were we going to get around to the trip itself?

She asked some questions about the next few days' itinerary. I waxed poetic about the Roman ruins in the desert, the mosque at Kairouan, and so on, and that was it. It was a strange interview, I thought, but then *First Class* was a peculiar magazine. I hoped this wouldn't end up being a gossipy piece, but with *First Class* that was always a risk.

But it was done, and I didn't have time to worry about it. After the first flurry of buying, I was not making as much progress as I'd hoped to on furnishing the Rosedale house. I'd found lots of carpets, some lovely ones, and furniture, too, but I really wanted to find unusual decorative elements that would pull it all together, and so far I hadn't seen anything that seemed just right. Furthermore, I didn't have as much time to do it as I'd thought I would. My idea of just turning the group over to someone else once we got there, and from time to time dispensing sage advice on antiques, had essentially been wishful thinking.

In the first place, whether I liked it or not, there was a tour to be run, people's needs and desires to be met: Ben's insatiable appetite had to be assuaged, Marlene's and Catherine's nervousness about foreign lands needed soothing. And Curtis, with his jealous nature, had to be kept away from Emile, who had the bad habit of flirting without realizing he was doing it. And Jimmy with his prejudices had to be kept away from Ed, who had taken to countering Jimmy's remarks with some inflammatory ones of his own. My ally in this last challenge, although we'd never discussed the subject, was Jimmy's wife, Betty.

And then there was teenaged Chastity, in a category all her own. Everything was "tragic" to Chastity. "I'm bored," she was always saying. "I'm tired. I want to go back to the hotel. I'm hot." It was like dealing with a squalling baby, and I didn't know how her mother could stand it, or why she let her get away with it.

To be fair, there were some easy people on the trip. Cliff was a pleasant fellow, although a bit forgetful, and Nora, despite her overly protective manner toward him, was no trouble whatsoever. Susie, too, seemed happy with just about anything. I sometimes wondered why she bothered to travel at all, when she was more interested in the people on the trip than the sights themselves, but I suppose it was meeting new people that made it all worthwhile for her. Aziza seemed to enjoy herself, and despite what I'd heard of her prima donna tendencies on the fashion runway, there was no evidence of them here.

But the person who was most cutting into my buying

time was Rick. Leaving aside his insatiable need for a telephone, and my herculean efforts to find him one in the most obscure places, his cell phone not working as well as he expected it to out in the Sahel, there was what I, on admittedly scant evidence, presumed to be a nasty tendency to theft. I decided I would dog his every footstep, and if I caught him at it, he'd be on the first plane out. I stayed as close to him as possible, trying not to be obvious about it, but never leaving him completely alone for long. If he went to the bathroom during dinner, I made some excuse, and more or less followed him, watching until he went into his room, and then again until he returned to the table.

It was always a relief when everyone turned in for the night. That was when I got to stroll the grounds alone in the darkness, looking back to the lights of the town, and breathing in the heady scent of the night flowers. Sometimes I'd leave the security of the hotel, and just walk the cobblestone streets of the town for a while, enjoying the solitude. Taberda, I decided, was at its best at night, when the tourists departed, leaving the streets to the cats, who flitted like tiny ghosts through the jasmine-scented air.

My enjoyment was spoiled the evening of my interview with Kristi, though, by the sight of Rick slipping through one of the hotel gates—not the one with the guard on it—and heading down the hill. I couldn't help but wonder what he was up to this late at night. Worried, I followed him at a distance, staying away from the streetlights, which was a good idea, because about halfway down the hill he met Curtis Clark. I was surprised to see the two men together, as they'd had virtually nothing to do with each other until this moment. The pair continued down the main street to the lower town, past the shops, now boarded up until the morning, and the little white houses, some with slivers of light still showing through the shutters. At the traffic circle at the bottom, where only a few stragglers were still sitting in the cafés, they turned left along another residential street, then right, onto a steep and rough path that led down to the harbor. I stayed back in the shadows, far enough behind them that they couldn't see me, but not so far that I lost them.

The path was really treacherous for someone unfamiliar with it—steep, and the stones that made up the surface were rough and uneven. It was also apparent, from the billing and cooing, and the occasional louder and more passionate yelp, that we were in the local version of a lovers' lane.

The moon was full that night, which was the only thing that kept me from breaking my ankle, I am certain, but it also meant that if either man turned around, they would probably see me. It was hard going, trying to negotiate the path in the moonlight, and at the same time keep a watchful eye on the two men ahead of me. At one point the path curved around, and I lost sight of them. I quickened my pace, and then unintentionally almost caught up to them where they stopped in the middle of the path.

I edged forward as quietly as I could to try to hear what they were saying, sticking to the shadows at the side of the road. At first, I could catch only the murmur of their low voices, not actual words. Curtis sounded angry, Rick almost frightened, gibbering something to the effect that it wasn't his fault. I moved closer.

"I told you to take care of it, you incompetent little twit," Curtis said.

Rick muttered something that sounded like "I promise you we'll get it," although I couldn't swear to it. His back was to me, and his words got swallowed in the breeze from the sea.

"Go back to the hotel," Curtis said quite clearly. "If

you're not capable of it, then I am." Rick, after a word or two of protest, turned abruptly away from his companion and started back up the hill. I flung myself hurriedly into the brush at the side of the road, stumbling, as I did so, upon a couple in, shall we say, the throes of ecstasy. The man in question, though startled no doubt, managed to hurl a string of epithets in my general direction—I do not know Arabic, but I am reasonably sure the word pervert must have been among them—as I moved past the couple to hide behind a tree. Rick, silhouetted against the moonlight, stopped for a moment and peered into the darkness, but, apparently satisfied it was only lovers, and presumably not knowing Arabic either, he moved on. I heard his footsteps, dragging a little as if he were a defeated man, recede into the distance up the hill. I stayed behind the tree, and the couple, now nervous at my presence, pulled themselves together and slunk away. I counted on the fact that they wouldn't want anyone to know they were there, and therefore wouldn't sound the alarm.

I waited for several minutes, expecting to see Curtis also move past my position, but he didn't. I certainly didn't want to be seen there by either man. My appearance in this part of town at this time of night would require an explanation that even my vivid imagination would have trouble inventing. I wondered whether there might be another route back to the hotel by going downhill, and decided there was, but not on foot, since it involved climbing up the very long and steep cliff below the hotel and the town. I would have to chance finding a yellow taxi on the harbor road, and I couldn't imagine there'd be too many of them down by the waterfront at this time of night.

Finally, after deciding that I couldn't wait all night, I stepped out onto the path, listening for footsteps below me as I did so, and was startled instead by the clatter of tiny pebbles coming down the hill toward me. Afraid that it was Rick coming back, I tried to plunge back into the shadows quickly, but twisted my ankle in the attempt. Despite my efforts to be quiet, I gasped out loud. There was a sliding sound, as if someone higher up on the path had lost their footing for a second on the slippery slope. I held my breath and listened carefully. I had a sense that whoever was up there was doing the same. In a moment or two, to my relief, I heard footsteps retreating back up the hill.

I sat on the side of the path for a few moments, until the throbbing in my ankle subsided to manageable proportions, and then hobbled as quickly as I could uphill. Several yards above my original position, about where I would have assumed the mystery walker had stopped, the moonlight caught a shiny strip of something on the path. I leaned over and picked up Kristi Ellingham's notebook. I recognized it immediately, one of those leatherbound, six-ring diaries, this one with protective metal corners that had caught the moonlight and my attention. It seemed obvious to me that it must have been Kristi on the hill above me. She would have dropped the notebook when she slipped. I stuck the book in my handbag and made my way slowly and carefully back to the hotel, hoping the bar was still open so I could get some ice for my ankle.

The bartender was beginning to close up and the lounge was almost empty when I came in, trying not to limp. There was no sign of Curtis, nor of Kristi, but Rick was there, the remains of a large drink in front of him, and another one coming his way. He was having a nightcap with Briars Hatley and another man I didn't know. The three men were engaged in a rather heated discussion and did not hear me approach until the last moment, when the conversation abruptly stopped. "Just stay away," I heard Briars say. "I'm warning you."

"Don't you threaten me. I've had enough," Rick replied. "You . . ." They all stopped at my approach. The stranger, a young man with dark hair and eyes, looked at me briefly, and then turned away.

I put on my most innocent face and smiled sweetly. "Good evening, gentlemen," I said. "I've just come for some ice. We'll see you tomorrow morning, breakfast at seven-thirty sharp. We have a big day out on Cap Bon tomorrow." They looked at me suspiciously, no doubt wondering what I'd heard, but I gave no indication I had heard anything at all. I was not introduced to the young man.

What was going on here? I huffed to myself. What could all these men possibly be going on about? *Taking care of something,* and *staying away,* and heaven knows what else. What was Briars doing threatening one of our guests? This was an antiques and archaeology tour, for God's sake, and he was the archaeologist! Was I going to have to say something to him about this? I gingerly mounted the stairs, leaning heavily on the railing to spare my ankle, as Briars and the stranger both left the bar and disappeared into the night. Rick remained, and drained his drink. I expected he'd be prevailing on the barman to get him another before closing. Back in my room, I threw Kristi's notebook on the night table—a quick peek at the first page confirmed that it was hers, although there had been little doubt in my mind—iced my ankle, and got ready for bed, fuming.

For about an hour I tossed and turned, my ankle paining me, rehearsing over and over what I'd say to Briars, cursing him and Curtis and Rick. What was it Rick had promised they would get? Kristi's book? It was lying right there on the path. Still, if the moon hadn't been just right, I wouldn't have seen it, either. Maybe they weren't talking about that at all. The whole episode made me cross. Worse still, the book on the night table kept calling out to me. What was she going to say about us? Don't stoop so low, I told myself. But what was she doing out on the path? Spying, like me?

Finally I succumbed to my more primitive self, and turned on the light. What I found in her notebook made me so angry, I could barely see. Kristi Ellingham was keeping a list of what she considered to be deficiencies in the McClintoch & Swain antiques and archaeology tour, shortcomings that no doubt would appear in good time in the pages of *First Class* magazine. Things like: *No Elevator!!* Or, *No Diet Cola!!! Boring Ruins!! No Room Service after 10 P.M.!!!!* Or even, since she apparently did not restrict herself to the location itself, *Peculiar Bunch of Tourists!* All her comments were punctuated with capitals and exclamation marks, the number of the latter presumably indicating the depth of her displeasure. It was a long list, and presumably getting longer, and the trip was shaping up to be a public relations disaster rather than the triumph Clive had envisioned.

All smiles and compliments, she hadn't voiced any of these criticisms, just scribbled them down in her notebook. Her comments were by and large unfair. True, there was no elevator in the Auberge du Palmier, but it was only two floors, and with abundant helpful staff at her every beck and call, the only weight Kristi had to heft up the one flight of stairs was her own. And surely, it should be possible to go without diet cola for a day or two. As for me, it was a source of considerable relief that there was no room service after ten at night, thus bringing Kristi's drink orders to a close for the day.

Rarely have I felt as angry as I did at that very

moment, and helpless, too. Thinking rationally, I doubted that she could actually ruin McClintoch & Swain. We were not really in the travel business, after all. But she could seriously harm us, and furthermore could adversely influence business, at the Auberge. The staff, including Sylvie and Chantal, had worked so hard to please her. And she hadn't paid one thin dime for the trip. We and the Auberge had covered everything, even her taxis. I wanted to scream at her, tell her how unreasonable she was being.

Calm down, Lara, I told myself. Everything will be fine. The other people are enjoying the trip. Perhaps they'll write letters to the editor; you never know. Aziza and Curtis speaking up for us certainly wouldn't hurt. And Emile must have some influence in this business.

Should I say something to her? Probably not. I couldn't do it without losing my temper. Should I tell Clive? He was going to be awfully disappointed. He'd get over it. He always did. And we'd survive this, no matter what she said. But the idea of poisoning her gin did cross my mind.

But even these unjust observations were nothing compared to what I found toward the back of the book, something she called her To Do list. I wasn't entirely sure what it was all about, but what I saw I didn't like. Ms. Ellingham had written down the initials of every person on the trip, and in several instances, had made some rather nasty insinuations. *CC—freeloader or blackmail?* it said. *Aziza—too thin. Drugs? St. Laurent—rings a bell—fraud? CS—Lolita complex. Abusive father? Check RR—something fishy. NW—trailer-park trash/ master manipulator. Get the poop on her and CF. BM/ EL—uncle/nephew: Not!* The list went on and on, and the fact that there was nothing noted next to LM, while something of a relief, didn't make me feel any better.

Maybe it was just idle curiosity on her part, but it had the look and feel of what she seemed to be accusing Curtis of—assuming CC stood for Curtis Clark—blackmail, in other words. Some of the comments were just uncharitable, like referring to Nora, NW that is, as trailer-park trash. Yes, it was true the woman didn't know how to dress, and her perfume made her smell more like a salad than a flower, but this was just plain unkind. And yes, she did seem to have Cliff under her thumb a little, and the relationship was a little ambiguous. As for Ben and Ed, did it really matter about their relationship? Maybe they were trying to be discreet, which was more than you could say about Kristi. But accusing a young girl of being a Lolita, and hinting that she'd been abused made me more than a little uncomfortable. What bothered me most of all was that I'd helped her compile that list, unknowingly, of course, during our talk. She hadn't been interviewing me, she'd been pumping me for information. Clearly she had to be stopped.

Maybe what it would take would be a list of my own: Just how much gin was that dreadful woman drinking? Was it enough that she might lose her job if her employer found out about it? I certainly had the receipts. What would her employer think of this little list of hers? Would they think she was no longer an asset to their fancy publication, or would they commend her for her brilliant investigative journalism?

Stop this, I told myself. Don't sink to her level. So what if she thought Curtis was a freeloader; I did, too. As for RR, I had heard enough that very evening to think something was fishy myself, to say nothing of the fact that he was probably a thief.

It occurred to me that I had another problem: what to do with the notebook. It was bad enough that I'd found it somewhere I wouldn't normally be, but now that I'd read it, the situation got a whole lot worse. Should I just hide it in my luggage? I didn't think so: It would drive me crazy knowing it was there. Should I take it into town and toss it in a dumpster far from the hotel? Or should I be very bold and hand it right back to her at breakfast, saying I'd found it outside? If I opted for the latter course, should I hint that I'd read it, or just hand it over with an "I think this is yours, Kristi"?

I carefully copied out the two lists—heaven knows, I might need them sometime, and most certainly I wasn't asking the front desk to make a copy for me—then extinguished the light and surprisingly, considering the huge weight of guilt and anger I was carrying, went to sleep. I awoke very early in the morning with an idea. Kristi would soon figure out, if she hadn't already, that she'd lost the book. I hadn't run into her in town as I returned to the hotel, so if she'd gone back for it, it would have been later. I wasn't sure I'd want to be out there on that path in the middle of the night again, and I suspected she wouldn't either. Presumably she wouldn't know exactly where she'd dropped it. If I got up right away, I could toss it in the bushes near the main gate. While there were three entrances to the hotel property, there was only one way into the grounds at night, a gate which required the use of a key, which all guests had in case they were late returning. She would have had to come in that way, unless she'd climbed straight up the hill from the beach way down below, a feat I'd already decided was too much for me. I didn't think she'd be up for it either, given her whining about one flight of stairs. She was always the last to arrive at breakfast, and by then the gardener proba- bly would have found her book and turned it in at the desk. Failing that, I could go out a little later myself, preferably with one of the others along as a witness, and "discover" it, with some appropriate dialogue along the lines of "Is that something in the bushes over there? Oh, look. A notebook." That kind of thing.

I pulled on a pair of shorts, a sweater, and my sneakers, carefully sliding my still swollen foot into the shoe, and crept down the stairs, my handbag with its unpleasant contents over my shoulder. If I'd thought I could slink out undetected, I was mistaken. The staff was setting up for breakfast, and Sylvie waved cheerily to me. Several members of the group were already up, Catherine reading a romance novel in the lounge, a cup of tea at her side, and Cliff at the front desk asking if the previous day's *International Herald Tribune* had come in. Emile stood at one of the bay windows, just looking outside. From the upstairs hallway I could hear Jimmy railing away at some issue that concerned him, his wife quietly murmuring by his side. "We're still setting up, but we can get you a coffee," Sylvie called to me.

Despite the tempting aromas of warm croissants, pain au chocolat fresh from the oven, and hot coffee, I had my insalubrious task to accomplish before I could indulge. "Thanks, but I'm going for a morning constitutional," I told her. "I'll be back soon."

"Don't tell me you are getting into this jogging," Sylvie said disapprovingly.

"Ah, Lara," Briars said from behind me. I started at the sound of his voice, the notebook in my shoulder bag making me nervous. "Sorry to startle you," he said, as I turned to speak to him. He was accompanied by the young man I had seen the previous evening. "I was just about to leave you this note. Can we talk privately for a minute?"

"Good idea," I said. There were things I wanted to say to him, too.

"I'm sorry to do this, but I have to leave for a few hours. Hedi here—sorry, have I introduced you two?

This is Hedi Masoud, Lara. He's the supervisor at the project I've been working on, and has been filling in as director in my absence. Hedi, this is Ms. McClintoch." We shook hands briefly. "Hedi has just told me about a problem at the site which requires my attention," Briars continued. "I've talked to Jamila: She's perfectly capable of doing the guiding we need this morning. It's just the scenic tour of Cap Bon. I'll rejoin you at the Punic city site, Kerkouane, this afternoon to explain that to everyone. I'm sorry about this. I really am, but it can't be helped."

"That's fine, Briars," I said. "As long as you meet us at Kerkouane by about two, it won't be a problem. There is one thing, however, I'd like to talk to you about," I added, drawing him aside a little so that Hedi couldn't overhear us. I realized I was still very angry with Briars. "About that rather unpleasant conversation you were having with Rick Reynolds last night . . ."

"I was afraid you'd overheard that. It won't happen again, I can assure you," Briars said.

"But—" I wanted an explanation.

"It won't happen again," he said firmly, and turned away. It appeared our conversation was at an end. Annoyed, I would have liked a fuller explanation of his behavior, but with the task at hand preying on my mind, I just watched him leave with Hedi, and then continued out the door to do the evil deed.

It was just about dawn, a sliver of pink on the horizon, and the haunting chant of the muezzin for the first call to prayer drifting across the town from the mosque's tower. I shivered a little in the cool of the morning, then stepped out briskly, looking the part of a morning exercise enthusiast. I'd gone only a few steps when I met Aziza, returning to the hotel. It surprised me that everyone was up, but of course, I was the one who had told them we would be on our way early that day. "Lovely morning, isn't it?" Aziza said. "And this is such a delightful spot. I must go and wake Curtis. He's missing the best part of the day."

Didn't she think that Curtis might need a little more beauty sleep after all that wandering about late at night? She must know he'd been out. They were in the same room. An unbidden thought surfaced: Perhaps she was drugged up to her lovely eyeballs, and wouldn't have a clue as to whether her husband was in their room or not. I dismissed the idea with some annoyance. That was the trouble with people like Kristi Ellingham, wasn't it? They dropped these ugly little hints, allegations that would never have occurred to you, and then suddenly you found yourself looking for evidence that would support them. Aziza wasn't on drugs. Anyone on the tour could tell you why she was so slim. She didn't eat. She was always just picking at her food, saying it was delicious, but that she wasn't terribly hungry. Anorexic, maybe, but no drug addict. Kristi was wrong. Not that anybody had seen the accusations but me, of course, and I shouldn't have. *Get rid of that horrible diary,* I told myself, *just as soon as you possibly can. And forget everything that's in it,* I added.

As I neared the gate, I looked about me very carefully. I did not, after all, need one of my charges to come running after me, telling me I'd dropped something. Nor did I want to see Briars. My righteous anger at his deportment of the previous evening wouldn't stand up very well if he knew what I was up to. Seeing no one, I tossed the notebook into a bush beside the path; then, without looking around, headed right out to the road toward town, testing my ankle, which I found, to my relief, much improved. As I reached the main street, I saw Nora streak by. She waved briefly as she churned past me and up the hill, barely breaking a sweat. Lagging far behind her was little Susie, her flaming-red hair now plastered to her head, her T-shirt clinging wetly and unflatteringly to her body, puffing slowly up the hill. I moved in beside her. "If Nora can do it, I can, too," she gasped. "Do you know," she said stopping abruptly, "Nora lost forty-five pounds in one year. Forty-five!" Susie exclaimed, wiping sweat out of her eyes. "Just by taking up jogging. She runs marathons now. That's twenty-six miles or kilometers or something, isn't it? Don't you think that's amazing?"

"Amazing," I agreed.

"She lifts weights, too. Have you seen her arms? And when she has so little time for it," Susie went on, gasping for breath. "Looking after Cliff all the time. She's devoted the last year of her life to him, you know, since his wife died. Cancer, the poor thing. She lingered for months. I'm glad that Arthur went so fast. It was a terrible shock at the time, what with him being so much alive one minute, and stone-dead the next. But better that than what happened to Cliff's wife. He was lucky to have Nora as a neighbor. They both were. She saw them through the last few weeks of the wife's life, moved right in with them to stay at her bedside day and night, and then took care of him, too, when he developed heart trouble. The strain of seeing his wife go, I expect. That's why she's always telling him to rest. She had to give up her job, you know, to care for them both. And her apartment. It can't be much of a life for her, I wouldn't think. She's at least twenty-five years younger than him. But she doesn't complain, I'll give you that. And he's promised to look after her. They have a legal agreement of some kind. She's moved in with him permanently. He has a really large apartment. She told me," Susie whispered, "it's strictly platonic, you know. The relationship. I asked her."

"You didn't!" I exclaimed, in spite of myself. This woman was incorrigible.

"I certainly did," she replied. "I had to, didn't I? I think my roomie is sweet on Cliff, and so I had to get the lay of the land. Oops," she giggled, putting her hand to her mouth. "Bad pun. Well, I better shove off. I'll never get thin talking to you. If she can do it, I can, too," she repeated. "Gotta get myself a new man, you know. Can't stay a widow forever. You don't think Arthur would mind, do you?"

"No," I replied. "I don't." Still, there was no question in my mind that Susie would do better to find a man who would appreciate her as she was, rather than one who would go for the more streamlined version that I suspected Susie might never become.

"This is a really excellent trip in that way," she added, turning back to me again. "All those single men! Most of the tours I go on are filled with older widows like me. Cathy wants Cliff, so he's out for me. That Emile is single, you know, and about the right age, and very distinguished and foreign. But maybe not my type. What do you think?"

I chose not to answer that one.

"Marlene has her eye on him, too—Emile, I mean," Susie went on, barely stopping for breath. "I wish she'd exercise a little more control over her daughter, by the way, but I guess she's still recovering from the divorce: It sounded particularly nasty. Her husband walked out and took up with someone not much older than Chastity. Not that that's so unusual. Still, not very nice. Maybe she's too depressed to notice her daughter's behavior. There's something wrong with that girl, though. Now Briars . . ."

She paused for barely a second. "He's cute as a bug's ear. Too young for me, but how about you? You don't have anybody, do you? I'm pretty sure he's divorced, or soon to be, anyway. You could do a lot worse. Don't you think it's time you got over your divorce and moved on? There's Rick, of course, but he's too young for all of us, no matter what his real age. What about Ben? Good job. Harvard. You don't think he's you-know-what, do you, the way Jimmy does? Not that I care, but it does affect his eligibility."

"I have no idea," I said, managing to break into this torrent of words. "You'd better get going, though, if you want to catch up to Nora, and not miss breakfast!" My, that woman could talk, and such a meddler! Had I actually told her I was divorced? I supposed I had, that first evening. Perhaps it was the jet lag. I had to admire her determination, though, as I watched her lumber off after Nora, who, if we could have seen her at all, would be a tiny speck in the distance. And her gall. I had been wondering myself about the relationship between Nora and Cliff, but would never have dared ask. In fact, once I'd seen Kristi's insinuations, I'd have died rather than ask any one in the group a personal question.

"I think either Briars or Emile is for you," Susie called back to me. "Save me one of those buns with the melted chocolate inside, will you? Or maybe two. They're kind of small."

I was sorry in a way that I hadn't managed to steer Susie toward the hotel so that she could find the notebook. If anybody would spot it, it was Susie; nothing escaped her eagle eye. It was clear, however, that she was going to soldier on behind Nora. Alone, I circled back to the hotel, and, hoping to avoid another set-to with Briars as he left, cute as a bug's ear though he might be, entered the grounds through another gate, at the far end of the garden. I then walked slowly along a path that took me through the orange grove toward the pool, savoring the day.

Mist rose from the warm water, and as the sun climbed higher, the brightly colored chairs and umbrellas beside the pool were reflected in the still water, a perfect little world in reverse. I stopped for a moment to look. A pair of slacks and a golf shirt were neatly folded on one of the chairs, a pair of sandals nearby, and a towel lay beside the pool.

I realized then what deficiency would undoubtedly appear next on The List, the one right after *Boring Ruins!!* It was *Dead Body in Swimming Pool!!!!!*

Rick Reynolds, clad in emerald-green swimming trunks, brand new, no doubt, lay on the bottom at the shallow end, a slight haze of red slowly dispersing in the water above his head. I knew he was dead even before I got to him.

4

"WHAT DID YOU SEE?" HASDRUBAL ASKED THE boy. Outside, the sea was getting rougher, the sky darker, and the boy, unaccustomed to a life at sea, had to steady himself.

"Nothing," he said.

The captain looked at him intently.

"Nothing!" the boy exclaimed defiantly.

"But something frightened you," Hasdrubal said.

The boy shifted his weight slightly to adjust to the roll of the ship. "A shadow," he said. "It was only a shadow."

"Tell me about this shadow," the captain said quietly. He noticed the boy eyeing the food on his table. "First, eat," he said, ladling the cereal into a bowl.

"I heard a cry," the boy said finally. "I took shelter, it was raining a little, and I was cold, so I pulled my robe up to cover my head and face and took shelter as best I could. The cry—" He paused for a moment. "It sounded bad. I knew something terrible had happened. Then there was the sound of something falling. But I *was afraid to go out and look in the dark. Just when it got to be light, I crawled out and stood up, and Abdelmelqart was there."*

"Did he look exactly as he did when I first saw him?"

"Not exactly," the boy said reluctantly. The captain waited. "He was closer to the cedar box. Mago—" The boy stopped.

Too frightened to say anything bad about Mago, Hasdrubal thought with a sigh. "Mago moved the body when he took the silver pendant. How did he move him? How was Abdelmelqart lying when you first saw him?"

"Face down," the boy said. "Mago rolled him over to take the pendant."

Face down, was it? Hasdrubal thought. And with a blow to the back of the head. Rather difficult to do, wouldn't it be? To fall back and hit one's head, but to end up face down.

"And the shadow?"

"It was still dark," the boy said. "And raining. I thought I saw something, a shadow, a man, moving away. But I'm sure I was mistaken," he added miserably. "I called out, and the others came. It was too late, though. He was dead."

"Think carefully," Hasdrubal said. "Where did the others come from?"

"From all over," the boy said in a surprised tone. "Some from the bow, some from the quarterdeck at the stern . . ."

"And Mago?"

"The stern, I think," the boy said. "Although I can't be sure. The dead man . . . the rain, I don't know."

"And the one the crew calls the stranger? The custodian of the special cargo?"

"I don't recall seeing him at all," the boy said.

The captain took two silver coins from a little sack

he carried around his neck. "I have a task for you," he said to the boy, "for which I will pay you handsomely."

The boy's eyes widened as he realized the coins were for him.

"You have the run of the ship. I want you to search it, everywhere you can."

"For what?" the boy asked.

"For two things. Two coins," Hasdrubal said, "two objects I require. When you find them, I want you to leave them where they are, but to come immediately and tell me exactly where you found them. The first is a short-sword. Do you know what they look like? The swords used by the mercenaries from the western lands who fight in the armies of Qart Hadasht?" The boy nodded, and the captain continued. "This one has a fine carving of a horse's head on the hilt."

The boy nodded. "And the other?"

"I'm not sure. A strong piece of wood, perhaps, something heavy." He paused for a moment. "Something with blood on it. I want you to find the weapon that was used to kill Abdelmelqart."

The boy's eyes widened again, but he said nothing.

"You understand you must tell no one of this?"

"Yes," the boy whispered.

"Good," the captain said. "Here is one coin in advance. The other will be yours when you report back to me. You may go now."

The boy took the coin and stared at it for a moment in the palm of his hand. Then he turned to leave.

"And Carthalon," the captain said very quietly to his retreating back. "Be very, very careful. Shadows can be dangerous."

"LARA," CLIVE WAS SAYING IN A LOUD AND RATHER accusing tone, "I've just had a call from a reporter with the *National Post* about an article he's writing for tomorrow's newspaper. Something about an accident on our tour!"

"Rick Reynolds is dead," I said, holding the phone away from my ear.

"Dead! What do you mean dead?" he said even more loudly.

"Dead. You know, deceased, passed away, gone to a better place. Dead."

"Dead!" Clive repeated. "This is not the kind of publicity I had in mind, Lara."

"That may well be, Clive, but I don't think I can be held responsible for someone who is dumb enough to go out swimming all by himself before anybody else is up and then takes a very deep dive into a very shallow pool," I said. "Right in front of signs in four, count 'em, four languages, warning him not to do so."

"Oh," he said. "I see. Well, I'll just have to put the best spin on this I can."

There he was, using one of those odious marketing expressions again. "You do that, Clive," I said.

"You're rather touchy, aren't you?" he said. "How is everybody else taking it?"

"Surprisingly well," I replied. As indeed they were. It was a testament to just how unpopular Rick was, with his "hey" this and that and his incessant babbling about how important and busy he was, together with his inability to establish any kind of rapport with his fellow travelers, that, after expressions of shock—genuine, I'm sure—everyone on the tour seemed to be carrying on very much as before. Shortly after noon, we'd packed them onto the bus and sent them to catch up with the afternoon part of the day's itinerary, a visit to the ruins of the Punic city of Kerkouane.

"In fact," I added, "I think the only thing that's really worrying them at this point is how we'll make up the four-hour scenic tour of Cap Bon, which we had to miss this morning due to the police investigation."

"Idiot," Jimmy had said, echoing, I'm sure, much of the sentiment in the group. "Couldn't have made the No Diving signs much bigger, could they? Can't he read?"

"Not anymore," Ed said.

"Hush, Jimmy," Betty said. "You must have more respect for the dead."

"Too bad," Ben said, looking down at the body. "Do you think they're serving breakfast yet?"

"How can you eat right now?" Chastity demanded. "That's gross." For once I agreed with her.

"*Mors certa, hora incerta*," he replied. "Death is certain, the hour uncertain."

Nora didn't show up at all. I gathered she went into the hotel from her run without seeing what had happened. Susie turned up some time later, but she was remarkably subdued, perhaps having worn herself out trying to catch up to Nora.

Come to think of it, the only person showing much emotion was Marlene, who, acting in a fashion I would have expected more from her daughter, set about shrieking and screaming to such an extent that I almost had to hold my ears before she collapsed against Emile, who stood, a peculiar expression on his face, patting Marlene's head.

The good news, however, was that the auberge had nothing to fear from Rick's death. The depth of the pool was marked very clearly in both meters and feet and there were very prominent signs, as Jimmy had pointed out, saying NO DIVING in Arabic, French, English, and German. Khelifa Dridi, the hotel owner, was hastily called after efforts to revive Rick proved singularly unsuccessful. He did all the talking to the police, bless his heart, and there seemed no doubt about what had happened. Rick had gone out early for a swim and had taken a dive into only three feet of water. His head was thoroughly bashed in as a result, although the cause of death would later be officially listed as drowning. The blow had rendered him unconscious, and he'd died in the water. The police officer in charge of the investigation, perfunctory in the extreme, summed it all up rather succinctly. "Stupid tourist," he said, snapping his notebook closed with some finality.

Others were somewhat more charitable. "I think perhaps it's fortunate that he's dead," Khelifa said, holding Chantal's hand as he spoke. "He'd be almost certainly paralyzed if he wasn't." Khelifa and Chantal were, to put it politely, close. There was a wife around somewhere, I was reasonably certain, but both he and Chantal seemed perfectly happy with the arrangement. I wasn't sure whether Khelifa was basing his comments on any knowledge of what happened to people who did what Rick had done, or if he was just trying to make us feel better. If it was the latter, I wasn't sure it helped.

The Canadian embassy in Tunis was called, and staff there took over dealing with the arrangements to ship Rick's body back home. The local tour company handling our itinerary in Tunisia also assigned someone to deal with this problem, much to my relief, and it was all very straightforward after the initial shock of it all.

"None of them have asked for their money back, or anything, have they?" Clive asked rather nervously.

"Nope," I told him.

"Well, that's something," Clive said. "What about Kristi Ellingham? Where is she on this subject?"

"I think she's rather enjoying the whole spectacle, Clive," I said, a vision of Kristi as I'd seen her right after the accident flashing across my brain. She was standing, as she always did, off to one side, silver lighter in one hand, freshly lit cigarette in the other. I was certain she'd have been scribbling away in her nasty little notebook, too, were it not for the fact that the notebook was resting in a bush near the main gate at that moment, as I knew only too well. She was obviously trying to look concerned, but knowing what I did, I interpreted her expression rather differently.

She turned to me, and perhaps seeing something in my face, dropped the mask for a moment. "This is a rather fascinating tour you're putting on, Ms. McClintoch," she said. "I can't wait to see what will happen next."

"Is that good or bad?" Clive said.

"Who's to say?" I replied. Personally, I could almost see the headlines in *First Class* magazine: "Death Takes a Holiday with McClintoch & Swain." Or worse: "See Carthage and Die—the McClintoch & Swain Tour." In my opinion this idea of Clive's was well on its way to becoming an unmitigated disaster. "It's the only thing about the trip so far she's liked, though."

"What hasn't she liked?" Clive said.

"Just about everything," I said. "I don't think this trip is quite Kristi's cup of tea."

"For instance?"

"No diet cola. No elevators. Boring ruins."

"Surely you can do something about the diet cola," Clive said peevishly.

"I'm trying," I replied. "I've put out an all points bulletin. We may see a case or two come in on a ship in the next few days."

"Isn't there anything else she likes to drink?"

"Yes," I said. "Gin. Lots of it. At about ten dollars a shot, I might add."

"Whew!" he exclaimed. "I wonder if I could buy a case of diet cola and have it air-freighted to you."

"Not a bad idea, Clive," I said. "At the rate she's

going through the gin, you could just strap the case into a seat. Business class.''

"Oh. Well, keep on it," Clive said.

"How's the shop, Clive?" I asked, changing the subject before I got really riled.

"Great!" he said with enthusiasm. "We're reorganizing the place, giving it a whole new look."

"What's wrong with the old look?" I said, gritting my teeth.

"Nothing, really. But Moira has some neat ideas about making it look sleeker."

Sleeker! Why would anyone want an antiques shop to look sleek? And what was my friend Moira doing messing around with my store while I was out of the country? Now I was really steamed.

"I'd appreciate it if you and Moira wouldn't make that kind of decision when I'm not there," I snapped. "This is my shop, too."

"Lara, you really are in a mood. If you don't like it, we'll put it back the way it was."

"Goodbye, Clive," I said. He was right. I was feeling touchy, maybe even downright testy. I reminded myself that Clive and Moira had been thrown together because of me. I'd been in trouble, and worried about me, they'd taken to talking on the telephone, then in person, wondering if I was all right. And suddenly, I think, they realized there was something more. I was left to come to terms with their relationship. Eventually I'd agreed to get back in business with Clive, influenced by the fact that it was really important for Moira that Clive and I get along. What I hadn't expected was that she'd start having a say in what I still considered to be my, not our, store.

All in all it was not a happy conversation, but it was all sweetness and light compared to the one I'd have later in the evening with Briars Hatley minutes after he had returned to the auberge.

"Sabotage," he said. "In a word. Since you asked. And when I get my hands on the proof that sniveling little creep did it, his life won't be worth much." His face was flushed and he had one fist upraised. Tall as he was, it was not a pleasant sight, but I was too angry to be intimidated.

"I don't care about your problems," I snarled. "You were supposed to be at Kerkouane at two. You weren't, we were. And incidentally, we would have had a much better excuse than you do, if we hadn't shown up."

"And what big excuse might that be?" he asked.

"Oh, you think having a member of your tour party die wouldn't have been a good enough reason?"

"What are you talking about?" he exclaimed.

"Rick Reynolds is dead, that's what," I said. "In case you haven't heard."

"What do you mean, dead?" he said.

"I mean dead dead," I said. What part of the word *dead* did the men I was having to deal with that day not understand? "He dove into the shallow end of the pool."

"My God," Briars said, lowering his arm and taking a step back. "When?"

"Early this morning," I said. "Right about dawn, probably."

Briars slumped in a chair. He looked genuinely shocked. "My God," he said again.

"What do you say we start this conversation all over again?" I said, sitting opposite him. We were having this little altercation in one of the reading rooms upstairs, with the double doors closed so that we could say what we really thought. "I was asking you what you were arguing with Rick about last night, and why you hadn't shown up at Kerkouane to be our guide this afternoon as you promised you would. I may have sounded rather annoyed. I am sorry for that. My excuse, if I'm permitted one, is that last night I sprained my ankle, found out Kristi Ellingham was going to write awful things about the trip in her magazine; then, this morning, I found Rick face down in the swimming pool. After that I had a phone conversation with my business partner, Clive, who is also my ex-husband—don't ask!—who seemed to feel I should have made sure this drowning kind of thing didn't happen, and that furthermore, I should overhaul the entire Tunisian economy to get Kristi Ellingham a diet cola. It has been a rather stressful twenty-four hours, and it has made me, as Clive pointed out, rather touchy."

"I'm sorry, too," Briars said. "I really am. Your tour is very important to me, and I don't want to mess up here. God knows, we need the money, but it's more than that. I enjoy telling people about the archaeology of the area, and I want to do a good job. If I am to be permitted an excuse, it is that last night Hedi reported that two of our crew had quit to join a competitor, gone over to the dark side, as it were, and that the bank was getting nasty about the payroll. Then early this morning he came to tell me that he had discovered someone had gotten into the office and trashed the place, including some critical equipment. When I saw what had happened, I just lost it, I'm afraid. I went off to find the individual I think—I am quite certain—is responsible, a guy by the name of Peter Groves. He and I have been rivals for the last year or two, and he's the one who hired two of my people away from me. I found him down in Sousse, and I'm afraid I made something of an ass of myself, yelling at him, even worse than I've been shouting at you now. I have a bit of a temper. You may have noticed. He denied it, of course, and then some of his people threatened to call the cops, and I finally took off."

"I accept your apology," I said, "and hope you do mine. I have something of a temper, myself. Maybe I'm tired, but none of this is making any sense to me, Briars. You work on an archaeological project. Who is Peter Groves? An academic from another university? Is that what you're saying? You're going to hurl learned dissertations at one another? Why on earth would anyone be interested in trashing the office of an archaeology project?"

He looked puzzled for a moment. "Ah," he said at last. "I see what you thought. Obviously I have a lot to tell you," he went on, looking at his watch. "And it's time for dinner. We have to go and be charming for a few hours. Isn't tomorrow a rest day for the tour, a day to spend on the beach or whatever? The group doesn't need our help and wise counsel to do that, do they? How about we get together tomorrow at some point? I'll take you to the site, and we'll talk. I promise I'll explain everything. Agreed?"

"Agreed," I said. "I've had enough for one day."

But my day wasn't over yet.

I WAS STANDING HIGH ON A CLIFF ABOVE THE sea, in an emerald-green bathing suit. Behind me the earth was in flames. I knew I must choose between the fire and the water, but I didn't know what to do. Around me there were voices: Briars saying, "It won't happen again, I promise you," and Curtis, "I told you to take care of it, you incompetent little twit." I turned and looked back to a burning city, then at the sea as it crashed against the shore below. Decision made, my arms stretched up above my head, palms facing out; my elbows, straight as can be, hugged my ears. My legs pushed off and out and I left the burning soil. \The water rushed up to meet me. As I streaked toward it, I saw Rick Reynolds in the foam of the waves. A single strand of blood streamed from his head, and swirled with the motion of the water. Then I saw the rocks, huge ones, just below the surface. I knew I would be dashed to pieces. I pictured bone splintering, my skull smashed like a ripe melon thrown against a brick wall. I awoke gasping, my heart pounding. It took a second or two to get my bearings.

Then I realized I did smell fire, not in my dream, but there and then. I got out of bed and went out into the hall to find smoke seeping from under the door that led to Kristi Ellingham's suite. I tried the door but it was locked. I yelled as loudly as I could, and almost immediately heard footsteps behind me. Ben shouted, "Get out of the way," and then hurled himself against the door. Nothing happened.

"Together!" Cliff said, coming up behind us, and the two men, in unison, hit the door with their full weight. Mercifully the lock snapped, the door flew open, and Ben ran into a wall of smoke. Cliff tried to follow him, but Nora held him back.

"No, Cliff," she cried. "Your heart!"

I started into the room, but Cliff grabbed me. "Ben won't know where the bed is in that huge room," I said to Cliff. "I do." I wrenched myself free and dashed into the haze.

Nothing could have prepared me for how dreadful it was in that place, dense smoke assailing my lungs and eyes. "The bed is to the right in an alcove," I tried to shout to Ben, who had to be somewhere inside, but the words came out a croak.

"I can't find her," he gasped, a few feet away from me. "She's not in bed. We've got to get out of here. There's nothing we can do. Go for the door."

I knew he was right. I turned and, disoriented, tried to figure out the way back. My foot hit something and I went down. "She's here," I choked out. "On the floor."

I felt Ben pulling me to my feet, and then, with each of us grabbing one arm, we dragged her along the floor. I wasn't sure we'd make it, but then there was Cliff, anxious, framed in the light, and several hands—Mohammed and Ed and even Catherine—pulling us to safety, as several staff with fire extinguishers rushed past us into the room. We burst into the hallway, and then stood, stunned by what we saw.

"What the hell!" Ben exclaimed, because it wasn't Kristi. Aziza coughed and opened her eyes.

PART II

Multum ille et terris iactatus

Much buffeted by sea and land

5

Ship's manifest
Glass beads, one pithos
Ivory pieces, one pithos
Gold jewelry, one pithos
Wine, 200 amphorae
Oil, 200 amphorae
Olives, 100 amphorae
Copper, 250 ingots
Tin, 100 ingots
Silver, 100 ingots
Coins, 5 amphorae
1 Cedar box, contents unknown

*B*E CAREFUL. SHADOWS ARE DANGEROUS. NOT *if you keep to them perhaps. Where to look for the weapon? Mago. I don't like Mago. Cuffed me yesterday for no reason. But worse than that, he is an evil man. Safat, too. But Safat is stupid, and therefore not so dangerous. I found the short-sword, didn't I? Found it right away, in Mago's kit. Mago had Abdelmelqart's pendant, too, didn't he? Does this make Mago a murderer, or just a thief? The captain will know.*

Check the cargo, now. Pithoi, yes. Contents as specified. Amphorae, 505 amphorae, all accounted for. Tin, 100 ingots. Silver, 99 ingots. One missing. Theft again?

No, too difficult. All will be counted before the crew leaves the ship. Thrown overboard? Too valuable. It will have to be returned. I will hide in the shadows and wait.

Kristi LINGERED UNTIL MORNING, BUT SHE WAS gone by the time they released Ben and me from hospital. She'd obviously made an attempt to get out, but like me, had become disoriented. They found her huddled between the bed and an armoire next to it. I figured she was dead drunk, a condition that would have considerably reduced her chances of escaping.

Ben and I stopped by to see Aziza before we left. She lay propped up on pillows, pale and a little weepy. Her husband sat beside her, holding her hand. He got up when we came in.

"What kind of tour are you running here?" Curtis demanded. "People are dropping like flies!"

"Curtis!" Aziza coughed.

"That hotel is a deathtrap. You should never have brought us there."

"Now wait a minute, here!" Ben huffed. "It is hardly Lara's or the hotel's fault. I wouldn't put it past that Ellingham woman to have disconnected the smoke detector so she could smoke in bed."

"She brought that bitch on the trip, didn't she? For the publicity."

"Curtis, please!" Aziza implored.

"Aren't you forgetting something?" Ben demanded. It was a side of Ben I hadn't seen before. The two men were almost nose to nose, barking at each other. "If it weren't for the fact that Lara raised the alarm and went in there—risking her own life, I might add—your wife most assuredly would be . . ."

"Stop it, both of you!" I interrupted. "Can't you see you're upsetting her?"

They ignored that. "What exactly was your wife doing in that room, anyway?" Ben asked. It was a very good question.

"Silence!" a nurse ordered, coming into the room. "Mme. Clark needs rest. You gentlemen will leave the room, please. *Maintenant.* Now."

"I'll meet you outside, Ben," I said. "Do you need anything, Aziza?" I asked her. "A nightgown? Something to read?"

She shook her head. She looked just miserable. "The doctor said I could probably leave tomorrow. Thank you for getting me out," she added. "And don't mind Curtis. He's upset, that's all."

"Why were you in Kristi's room, Aziza?" I asked her. I might have objected to Ben asking the question, but I was just as determined to find out what had happened.

"I was out for a little walk around the hotel," she said. "I saw that Kristi's door was open very slightly. Just a crack. Anyone could just walk in, and after Catherine's necklace having been stolen, and Jimmy's money and everything, I just thought I shouldn't leave it like that."

"You were out walking at that time of night?" I said.

She didn't answer for a moment. "I couldn't sleep and didn't want to bother Curtis," she said finally.

"So you noticed the door was ajar, and then . . ." I prodded as gently as I could.

"I wasn't sure whether she had left it that way deliberately, you know, cross ventilation or something, so I tapped on the door and then went in. All of a sudden there was this whooshing sound, and the room filled with smoke. I tried to find the door, but I couldn't."

"The door was locked when I got there," I said.

"I suppose I must have closed it behind me when I went in, and it locked automatically," she said. She was picking at some lint on the hospital blanket, and didn't look at me once while she spoke.

"It's horrible what happened," she said. She started to cry a little.

"You rest, Aziza," I said. "And if you think of anything you need, anything at all, please give me a call at the hotel."

As I turned to leave, I looked back. She lay there, eyes closed, one small tear running down her face.

I was absolutely certain she was lying, but I didn't know what to do about it. It could have something to do with Curtis, given to nocturnal ramblings of his own. Not that I could blame him for being upset right now. His wife really was within minutes of being the third corpse on this tour. Which brought me back to the subject of the rest of the group: I had to believe that they were all considering asking for their money back and heading home any time now.

As we arrived back at the Auberge, two men were loading a very sodden mattress, or what was left of it, into a police van. It was an upsetting sight, and it all seemed so unnecessary. If anything, this was an even more idiotic death, to use Jimmy's expression, than Rick's had been.

But two people on the tour were dead, no matter how supremely careless both may have been, and it was a very subdued group that greeted us as we returned.

"Jamila," I said, taking her aside. "Ben and I are considering taking the rest of the day off." That was an understatement. "You've got to take these people somewhere special today. Do you know a really splendid restaurant around here that serves lunch outside? A patio overlooking the water or some such thing?"

"I can arrange something like that," Jamila replied. "I know just the place."

"Good. Just take them there and let them order whatever they want. We'll cover it. But you'll have to manage on your own today."

"I can do that. You rest," she said. "Hello, everyone," she called, crossing over to the group in the breakfast area. "If I may have your attention for just a minute, I have an announcement. We're going to do something special today, a little surprise."

"A few too many surprises already, if you ask me," I heard Jimmy say.

"A lovely lunch at one of the finest restaurants in the country," she went on, undeterred. "Something special we're including as part of the tour."

"Fresh seafood, I hope," Ben said. "Is wine included, too?" Ben apparently was recovering quite nicely, and contrary to what I expected, was carrying right on.

"Of course," Jamila said, after looking at me for a sign. I nodded. "Drinks, too."

"I'm going to bed," I said to no one in particular.

Tired as I was, I couldn't sleep, just a few minutes here and there, broken by horrible dreams. By noon, I gave up trying and went downstairs.

"Your husband called three times, Madame Swain," Mohammed said as he handed me little pink slips of paper with Clive's name on every one. "Mme. Sylvie said we were not to put the calls through to your room while you were resting."

"Thank you, Mohammed," I said, tearing up the messages. Word of Kristi's demise had apparently already made its way back home, and Clive would be beside himself. There'd be time to listen to him rant, later on.

A few minutes later, I found myself in town in what

is rather whimsically called a taxiphone, one of the few places, other than some of the large American hotel chains, where it is possible to dial direct overseas. I looked at my watch. It was 6:20 A.M., Toronto time, and it was Sunday. I put in a dinar coin or two and dialed, anyway.

"Rob," I said. "It's me."

"Oh," the sleepy voice said. "It's good to hear from you." He paused. "Is everything okay?"

"Not really," I said. "I needed to hear a friendly voice. I know it's early."

"That's okay. What's happened?" he asked anxiously. I told him.

"That's terrible," he said. "But it's not your fault, remember that."

"I know," I said miserably. "But it was really unpleasant, and Clive already thinks I'm making a mess of things—even before he heard about Kristi."

"I don't understand why you went into business with that fellow again," Rob said. He did not like Clive much, it was fair to say. "Moira would have understood if you'd said no when he suggested it."

"I know," I said again. That one phrase seemed to be the height of my conversational abilities at that moment. "You have no idea how bad an idea it was. Please don't ask me why. He may be right about my making a mess of this trip, though."

"That sounds unlikely to me," he replied. He was being so nice.

"I suppose you see this kind of thing all the time, being a policeman. Have you ever pulled someone out of the pool when they've bashed their head in?"

"Unfortunately, yes. Twice. Well, once in a lake. Same idea, though."

"What happens when they hit the bottom?" I asked.

"What?" he said. "Oh, I see. Your fellow died.

Drowned, I suppose. If you get them out in time, they're usually paralyzed. Quadriplegics in some cases."

"Actually, I meant what happens to their head?"

"Isn't this a little grisly, Lara? Why would you want to know?"

"I guess I need to understand this in some way, Rob," I said. "Maybe I'll feel better about the fact that I didn't get him out in time." There didn't seem to be much point in mentioning I was being haunted by a dream that was making me question the conclusions the local police had drawn.

"I'm not sure telling you this is a good idea, but essentially they break their necks. I'm not a doctor, but I think the top of the head and the neck take the whole weight of the body, and one of the vertebra is forced out of position, slicing the spinal cord. The extent of their injuries, or the paralysis, depends on where it gets severed."

"I think what I'm really asking is, did I kill him taking him out of the pool? I mean should I have known his neck was broken, or anything?"

"I don't think there'd be any way of telling that his neck was broken just by looking at him, and leaving him on the bottom of the pool for a while until someone who understood neck injuries arrived wouldn't have helped him much, now would it? Don't do this to yourself, Lara! You did what you could. If he hadn't gone swimming by himself, then maybe someone could have got him out in time. From what you've told me, he was the instrument of his own death."

"I know, but I keep thinking of him lying there conscious for a moment or two, unable to help himself. He wasn't a very nice person, maybe, but he didn't deserve that. And Kristi . . ."

"Lara, if you're going to ask me now what happens to the lungs of people who die smoking in bed, forget it. I'm not going to tell you. I think you should just try and get some rest. You'll feel better tomorrow," he said gently.

"Who's with you?" I said suddenly. I could have sworn I heard a sleepy female voice asking him who it was he was talking to.

"Nobody," he said. That, I realized with a pang, was a lie.

"I think I'll take your advice," I said. "And get some rest. Thanks for being there," I added.

"Lara," he said. "We'll talk about this, okay? I mean you, we, aren't really . . . are we?"

"Whatever," I said. "Goodbye, Rob."

It was true, we weren't, if by that he meant lovers. We'd never got past the necking stage. Something always seemed to intervene: his daughter, my shop, his job, and then one or the other of us would think better of it. But when I was feeling really wretched, Rob was the person I wanted to talk to, to hear his nice calm voice, and knowing there was someone else with him early on a Sunday morning, did nothing to improve my day. Looking on the bright side, I suppose, I'd found out what I needed to know, whether I liked it or not, about both Rob and Rick Reynolds.

"I thought you were supposed to be resting," a voice said as I passed through the lobby on the way back to my room. I turned to see Briars in the lounge. "Can't sleep?"

"It seems not," I agreed.

"Would you like a little fresh air?" he inquired.

"Sure, I guess so."

He hailed a little yellow taxi outside the hotel gate, and soon we were descending to the harbor, then picking up the coast road headed north. Just on the outskirts of Taberda we stopped at a pier, where several colorful fishing boats bobbed at anchor. Briars climbed down to a little outboard, and beckoned me to follow. Soon we were bouncing across the water toward a boat about a quarter mile offshore.

"Here we are," he said, as we pulled alongside. A smiling Hedi offered me a hand up the ladder.

"Welcome aboard the *Elissa Dido*," he said.

"And," Briars added, "our project site. Meet two of our divers: Ron Todd, one of my students at UCLA, and Khmais ben Khalid, a local archaeologist and diver. Hedi, you know, of course. He's our dive supervisor, and he's been filling in as project director while I've been with your group. We have two other divers—both, I gather, Hedi?—down below." Hedi nodded. "Gentlemen, meet Lara McClintoch. I shook a couple of wet hands. Briars reached into a cooler. "Something cold to drink, Lara? Cola? Mineral water? No alcohol allowed onboard, I'm afraid." I gratefully took the proffered mineral water. "Ron, see if you can find Lara a hat."

Ron emerged from the cabin a minute or two later with a black neoprene cap emblazoned with the words *The Elissa Dido Project* in white, and what looked to be some kind of ship, with a large square sail, the prow in the shape of a horse's head. Briars presented it to me with a flourish. "Since you're helping pay for this expedition," he said, "whether you knew it or not," he added, "you get to be an honorary crew member. Lara's had a bad day," he said to the men, "so we won't put her to work right away."

"Explain this to me, Briars," I said.

"About paying for the expedition, you mean, or getting down to work? I just meant that we're a little underfunded, and so your offer of a salary for a couple of weeks helped us out here with our expenses quite a bit. I knew Hedi would fill in for me admirably. Your tour may keep us going for another month."

"You know that's not what I meant. I thought you were digging away on some ancient city site around here somewhere," I said. "You did say you had a project on the Gulf of Hammamet, didn't you? You meant *on* the gulf literally, I suppose."

He smiled. "Perhaps I should have said *in,* rather than *on,* the gulf. I didn't mean to mislead you. I guess I'm so deep into this project that it never occurred to me there was more than one possible interpretation of that phrase. We're looking for a shipwreck," he said.

"What kind of shipwreck?" I asked. "A Spanish galleon or something?"

"We're not entirely sure, but I hope much older than that," he replied. "We're looking for a ship that dates back at least two thousand years."

"Is that possible?" I exclaimed. "Wouldn't the ship have rotted away?"

"The ship itself might have, yes. But not necessarily the cargo. Not only is it possible to find it, we *are* going to find it. First, I might add." The others clapped and whistled.

"You're nuts," I said.

He laughed. "You're not the first woman to tell me that. My soon to be ex-wife, for example, was quite convinced of it. When are Sandy and Gus due up?" he asked Hedi.

Hedi looked at his watch. "About nine minutes," he said. I looked over the side to see two trails of bubbles from below. Khmais and Ron started pulling on their gear, checking and rechecking their tanks.

"You asked me the other day—was it only yesterday?—what I meant by sabotage," Briars said quietly to me as the others moved out of range. "Come over here for a minute."

I looked into the wheelhouse: There were maps and

papers all over the place. "I think maybe you could use a little help with the housekeeping," I said.

"You should have seen it yesterday. We keep all our charts and records here. Someone got in: We lock up, but someone broke the padlock. The place was a shambles. Chart drawers open, and everything dumped on the floor, the scanning equipment wrecked. The fish—that's the piece of equipment that trails behind the boat when we're scanning and gives us the pictures—was severely damaged, maybe even permanently."

"Anything taken?"

"Hard to tell. The place was, and still is, a mess. But I don't think this was theft. As I keep saying, it was sabotage, designed to scare us off, or slow us down. After all, we leave the ship out at anchor so we don't have to pay marina fees, and whoever it was would have to get out to it. It wouldn't be a casual, spur-of-the-moment kind of smash and grab. I'll bet I'm not making any sense, am I? Why don't I start at the beginning."

"Please do," I said.

"Good. Back to the beginning. I first got interested in this part of the world in my university days. I came over under the auspices of UNESCO to work at Carthage in the early seventies, along with a boyhood friend of mine named Peter Groves. Peter and I had been chums since we were about seven. I think it's because we were both wimpy guys, lousy at sports, and good at school, the kind of lads the other kids despise. I had no idea what I wanted to be when I grew up. I was taking a general arts course at the university and had taken a course in archaeology, but nothing much had piqued my interest. I'd say Peter was about the same. I can't even remember how we got the job. I think Peter's father knew somebody who knew somebody; that kind of thing. So while our friends at school were spending their summer cleaning pools or flipping burgers, Peter and I headed for Carthage. Revenge of the nerds, they'd call it now.

"In any event, a whole new world opened up for Peter and me. I loved the job. I was a dig assistant, and worked for some very good people, and I found I had a real feel for it. Peter didn't like it nearly as much as I did: He thought it was boring, actually, while I found it endlessly fascinating. What we did agree on were the weekends. It was paradise. We sailed, swam, learned to scuba dive, met European and Arab girls.

"There was an old Arab who was working on the project as a laborer, and he kind of adopted Peter and me. He was awfully good to us—took us to meet his daughter and her family, made sure we ate properly, which considering our student status, was something. As with most kids, I'm not sure we appreciated him at the time. But oh, what stories that man had to tell! He claimed that in his younger days he'd been a sponge diver, and that he'd once seen the most marvelous sight: He said he'd found a graveyard of amphorae guarded by the god of the sea, who, as it turns out, was made of gold. We thought he was just kidding us, but the old man insisted that the story he was telling us was true, that the amphorae and the god himself were still down there in the depths.

"We asked around, and found that the old man— his name was Zoubeeir—had indeed been a sponge diver in his youth. At first we put the tale about the golden god and the graveyard of amphorae down to the Martini Law. Do you know what that is?"

"No, but I could probably guess the general idea," I replied.

"The Martini Law says that every ten meters you go down—that's about thirty-two, thirty-three feet—has the same effect as a double martini. You'll understand that when you're working at, say, a hundred and twenty feet, the Martini Law has significant impact. The more technical term is nitrogen narcosis, what they call the rapture of the deep, staying down too deep for too long. Bit of a nutter was how Peter put it at first.

"But the story seemed to worm its way into Peter's soul. 'What if there really is a golden statue down there?' he kept saying to me. 'It's possible, isn't it? Gold is essentially inert. It would stand up under water virtually forever. And the graveyard of amphorae? Doesn't that sound like a shipwreck to you? The wooden ship might be gone, but the amphorae that held the cargo would last for a very, very long time. Maybe we should go and look for it.' Or 'I've looked into this, and more shipwrecks have been found based on this kind of anecdotal information than on all the fancy technology in the world,' he would say. And there is a certain amount of truth in that. The Mahdia wreck, which was found toward the south end of the gulf here, was originally discovered by sponge divers. So was the Uluburun wreck off Turkey. Ready for another mineral water?

"That summer was a defining experience for both of us. I went home, changed courses to get into archaeology and eventually got my doctorate—my thesis was on Carthaginian shipping and trade—found myself a teaching job at UCLA, got married, and had a couple of kids. Peter dropped out of the university, got married, too, had a daughter, and went into business for himself, manufacturing plastic bottles, I think. Made lots of money at it, much more than I did as a professor of archaeology, that's for sure. We kind of lost touch. Just Christmas cards and things like that as contact. Then one day, he packed it all in, the company, the marriage, the works. He became—and he and I might quibble about the terminology—a treasure hunter. He'd say a marine salvage expert. He started looking for sunken treasure. He had some success right away, found a Spanish ship in the Caribbean, loaded with gold. Trouble was, he ended up in endless litigation over ownership of it. So he hired himself a fancy lawyer, and went on looking for shipwrecks. His initial success, regardless of all the legal problems, ensured that he was always able to get investors. His passion was sunken treasure, any sunken treasure, but I think there was a special place in his heart for Zoubeeir's amphorae graveyard and the statue of gold. He tracked down Zoubeeir, who was now blind, and essentially senile, and his daughter and son-in-law, and found out that Zoubeeir used to dive in the Gulf of Hammamet.

"There's a lot of water in the gulf, to that I can attest, and under water you could be almost on top of something and still miss it. Peter tried to get Zoubeeir to narrow it down a little, and in a manner of speaking, he did. The god of the sea, Zoubeeir maintained, lined up with a piece of rock that looked like a camel on the shore. Trouble was, there's been a lot of development along the gulf since Zoubeeir was sponge diving, so if that particular rock formation ever existed anywhere but in the old man's imagination, I expect it's long gone.

"Peter was undaunted, though. One day near the end of the term, not having had any contact with him for a few years, I get a phone call out of the blue. 'You've been mired in theory long enough,' Peter said. 'It's time to find Zoubeeir's graveyard of amphorae and the golden god of the sea.' I took the bait. Marine archaeology is a relatively new discipline—it simply wasn't possible to do much of it until underwater technology was developed, particularly the Aqua-Lung, which wasn't invented until the 1940's. It was true I'd been immersed in theory about Mediterranean shipping routes, currents, and trade routes and all the rest. It was an exciting idea to go out and see what all that study would get me, and I confess I got bitten by the bug a little, too."

He paused and looked out to sea for a moment.

"You and Peter aren't still partners?" I asked.

"Nope," he replied. "The second summer I came over to help him, we had a serious difference of opinion. There were a couple of incidents that summer, one that caused me to question Peter's commitment to the protection of the heritage resource, another to question his sanity.

"While we both wanted to find Zoubeeir's ship, I wanted to find it for the knowledge it could bring, although if I was being completely honest, I could also see it making my reputation in the field. He wanted the treasure. At the end of the day, these were essentially incompatible philosophies, no matter how much the salvage industry claims the two visions can co-exist. I've come to look upon salvage companies as the marine equivalents of tomb robbers—not all, maybe, but many of them. We actually found a wreck, south of here, not very old, maybe three hundred years, but I was very excited about it, concerned about dating the wreck, seeing it was properly mapped and photographed. I went into town to get some equipment, and when I came back, the divers had already raised a lot of the stuff and were dividing it up. I was furious. I told Peter he was just paying lip service to marine archaeology, that I was along for window dressing. He was suitably contrite, said it wouldn't happen again, and for a while I tried to make myself believe him.

"But then there was the other incident." Briars took a deep breath before continuing. "I don't want to get into it, but we lost a diver, a young man, a kid really, one of my students. The sea was pretty choppy that day. I thought we should call it quits and head for shore. But Peter had seen something on the side scan sonar that he thought was worth checking out. There was only one diver that had any time left that day. You have to keep very close track of how much time you can be down in any given day: It depends on the depth you're working at, essentially. And you never go down without a buddy. The kid was over the side before anyone knew what was happening. I am certain Peter told him to go, although he denied it. We lost the trail of bubbles almost immediately in the choppy water. You have no idea what that's like, standing helplessly on the deck counting the seconds, knowing you're too late. Two of us went in, even though we'd had enough for one day. He was gone. We never found him. That was it for me. I left Peter's expedition. I went home and gave up the search for shipwrecks for a year or two. I remember I phoned the kid's parents when I got home. Talked to his dad. It was one of the worst things I've ever had to do in my life. The man was just shattered. Told me he'd entrusted his son to me, and I'd let him die. Which maybe I did. Maybe I didn't protest enough, you know, turned a blind eye to Peter's shenanigans. Anyway, why am I telling you this? You've had a rather rough few days yourself. Are you feeling okay?"

"Not too bad, all things considered," I replied. "But you're back looking for Zoubeeir's ship."

"Yes. Peter and I eventually became competitors, maybe even enemies, two former friends, two boats, both looking for the same thing. I said that there's a lot of water around here, but apparently, judging from the mess they've made of my boat, there wasn't enough for the two of us."

"Why did you come back?" I'd heard about people like this, obsessed with hidden treasure, sunken or otherwise. People who saw clues everywhere, and who refused to acknowledge information that would say they were wrong. People who were prepared to risk everything for some elusive and probably imaginary windfall. Peter Groves sounded like one of those people. The question was, I suppose, was I talking to another one now?

"I'm not entirely sure. I do know that if we could find this shipwreck, if it does exist, it would be a tremendous find. Ships that old are not exactly a dime a dozen. What it would tell us about life at that time would be spectacular. That's the thing about shipwrecks, you know. Archaeologists often dig up graveyards, tombs, that kind of thing, but the people in them have been specially prepared, laid out for the afterlife. Shipwrecks are different. They are little microcosms of life at the time. If they're merchant ships, you get an idea of what was valued in those times. You might get to see the difference between the officers and the common sailors, in terms of the utensils they used for eating, and so on. You are getting a chance to see the here and now of a particular time period, not the great hereafter, if you see what I mean. That's what I say, anyway, and I believe it. But maybe another reason is that my wife and I are getting divorced, my kids are essentially grown up, and I decided there were worse things to do with my sabbatical. I made a proposal to a foundation and got some funding.

"I've often wondered," Briars mused, "whether the kid, Mark Henderson, his name was, found something at the end. That's a real danger, you know. You see something really important—you might be the first person to see a ship in centuries, if not millennia. In your excitement, you ignore the timer that says it's time to head for the surface. But if he did see something, I couldn't find that, either."

"Here they are," Hedi called. "Any news?" he said to the first diver up the ladder.

"No joy," a young woman said, pulling off her mask

and shaking her tank free. She pulled her blond hair back into a twist, and grabbed a towel.

"Ah, well. Come over and meet Lara," Briars said. "Lara, these are a couple more members of the team: Sandy Groves," he said, gesturing toward the young woman, "and Gus Patterson."

"Hi," they said in unison.

"Nothing?" Briars asked.

"'Fraid not," Gus said. "We found the formation that showed up on the scanner before it got trashed, but it turned out to be nothing. A wooden boat, yes, but one that went down about a week and a half ago, by the look of it. Nice to meet you, Lara."

"What did I tell you? Another day of great hopes dashed," Briars said, with a shrug.

The engines throttled up and the ship moved on several hundred yards, the outboard bouncing along behind. "We've got time for one more dive," Hedi said, slowing down and anchoring in a new position. "In you go, you two. You know the drill. I want you back up here on deck in no more than twenty-five minutes." Ron and Khmais sat on the gunwales, and then rolled backward into the water. "Watch for them," Hedi said to the others.

"I have an idea for tomorrow, boss. To try to keep us going while we get the scanner fixed," Hedi said to Briars, as the other two kept watch.

"Let's hear it," Briars said.

"Why don't we use a tow rope? I think I could rig something up that would work. We can send three divers down instead of two, to about sixty feet, put them about twenty feet apart, and just tow them slowly through the zone we want covered. It's shallow enough in here that they could see the bottom, at least well enough to see if there's something we might want to take a closer look at. We could cover a lot more ground that way."

"Not bad," Briars said. "Let's see what you can come up with. Hedi's terrific," he added, after the young man had moved out of range. "Very careful, doesn't let the divers take any chances. Meticulous about the equipment. I was lucky to find him. He's Berber, you know, not Arab. His family still lives out in the desert, way south of here. In tents, if you can imagine. Can't think why you'd take up scuba diving when you've grown up in the desert, but what do I know? I didn't think I'd ever take it up either, and I grew up in California."

"Did you say Groves?" I asked. "Sandy Groves?"

"You noticed," he said. "Sandy is Peter's daughter. She turned up here a few months ago, and has been with us every since. A little family feud, I expect. I don't ask questions about it. She's a solid, experienced diver. Khmais is Zoubeeir's grandson, by the way. We've got the whole original gang represented in some form or another."

"You mentioned that you got some funding from a foundation. I'm surprised a foundation would put money into something so . . . speculative," I said. "Couldn't this be an elaborate hoax? A little joke on the part of Zoubeeir, to tease the students in his charge?"

"Sure it could. But Zoubeeir never struck me as that kind of person. He took a fair amount of razzing about it from everybody, but he stuck with his story. I'm not convinced myself about the statue, by the way. It would be covered with centuries of silt, if it existed at all. But I'd be very happy to find the ship even without it. But I see you remain unconvinced. You really should meet my ex-wife. I'm sure the two of you would get along," he said with a smile. "Come, I'll see what I can dig up in the mess. You sit," he said, positioning a chair outside the entrance to the wheelhouse. "And I'll look.

"Okay, it must be here somewhere. One reason to believe Zoubeeir is that the old man was very specific about what he saw. He described it in some detail: how he'd found the amphorae—which are unquestionably one of the things that indicate the presence of a wreck. He said there was a mound in the middle of the amphorae, and he'd cleared the silt off it over the course of several dives, until he realized that what he had was a golden god. He was frightened by this, and stopped working on the wreck, for fear of angering the god. But he, too, was obsessed by it. He sketched it over and over, from memory, and his daughter had kept drawings: We've got the sketches, which I'd show you if I could find them in here, of both the amphorae and the statue. Here they are!" he exclaimed triumphantly. "A copy of the old man's drawings. What do you think?"

I looked at rather crude but surprisingly powerful sketches. They showed the outline of what I suppose were the tops and sides of several large jars. The dominant feature, though, was a man's, or, I suppose, a god's, head, in an elongated cone-shaped headdress. He was buried from about mid-chest, so that all you could see was the head, and part of one arm. He did, in a way, look as if he were guarding the amphorae, the right arm raised as if to ward off any attacker.

"I agree with you that these are interesting drawings, and I'll take your word for it that Zoubeeir was sincere, but how do we get to a two-thousand-year-old ship from this?"

"Good question. Do you know what I mean by transport amphorae? They are clay vessels, and can be very large, maybe four or five feet high, cylindrical in shape. They were used much the way we would use shipping containers now. They were used to carry olives, olive oil, wine, that kind of thing, and even glass beads and small objects like that. The merchant seamen stacked them on their sides with the handle of one at right angles to the handle of the one above or below it. That locked them in place so they wouldn't roll about and destabilize the ship. A large merchant ship would have hundreds and hundreds of these onboard. Now, does the term Dressel amphora form mean anything to you?"

I shook my head. "I'm afraid not," I said.

"Well, there's no particular reason it should. Heinrich Dressel was a nineteenth-century German scholar who developed a way for us to date amphorae based on their design—whether they were long and thin or round and more squat, what the tops looked like, the shape of the handles, and so on. He published a chart with Mediterranean amphorae listed in chronological order. All of them are numbered. So Dressel 1 forms, for example, were manufactured in Italy and used from the middle of the second century B.C.E. to the beginning of the first, often to hold Italian wine. A lot of them show up in wrecks in the French part of the Mediterranean. The Dressel forms are a wonderful tool for dating wrecks, because amphorae were used all through antiquity in shipping; they tend to hold up well over time on the bottom, unlike wood, for example; and they are relatively easy to spot."

"You're going to tell me these amphorae in Zoubeeir's drawings date the wreck to that time period, aren't you?"

"I am," he replied. "They do. If we believe the legends, Carthage was founded in 814 B.C.E. The archaeological evidence doesn't go back quite that far, but it's close enough to lend some credence to the myth. The city fell to the Romans in the spring of 146 B.C.E. The wife of the city's leader threw herself into the flames rather than be taken by the Romans."

"I hope you're not going to tell Chastity that story

again," I said. "She seems to be rather impressionable, especially on the subject of romantic notions about death by fire, or maybe it's dying for love. But anyway, you're saying the amphorae date to within that time period."

"Yes, they do. We can date them a little more closely than that. Something like the fourth century B.C.E., in fact. There are a couple of other clues as well. See here," he said placing a photograph in front of me. "It's a wine jug, terra cotta. Zoubeeir brought it up from the site. He brought up a few objects, I think, before he found the god and stopped looting the wreck. It's a beauty, isn't it? Not perfect. You can see there's a piece out of the rim. But this jar—you see it's shaped a little like a horse laden with amphorae—would probably date to the third and fourth centuries B.C.E. Given that it is associated with the ship, and not just something dropped at another time, it would help to date the ship."

"It looks very interesting," I said. "Where is it now?"

"Gone. Vanished. Zoubeeir's daughter had it, but it went missing shortly after Peter and I saw it. I figure Peter stole it, but that may be because I can't think of a positive thing to say about the man. Luckily I photographed it when I was there."

"Okay, but there were a lot of nations shipping cargo all over the Mediterranean at that time. Why couldn't this ship you're looking for be Greek or Roman, for example? Have I got the time period about right?"

"Yes. The amphorae, again, would say that this is more likely to be Carthaginian."

"And the statue?"

"Ah, the statue. Well, here it gets a little more complicated, and it's one of the reasons I try to view this all with some healthy skepticism. Assuming Zoubeeir really saw it, and as I've already mentioned, I personally am not sure about that part; I mean I know he believed it, but working at those depths does affect you sometimes. But, if we allow for a moment that he did see the statue, I think this would most likely be a much earlier artifact, older than the amphorae by maybe five or six hundred years. It looks to me to be a version of what we call a smiting god—the upraised right arm attests to that. Striking gods come out of an earlier Phoenician tradition, pre-Carthage. It could be Melqart, the city god of Tyre, or even a Baal, who much later, in a slightly different form, together with his consort Tanit, became the city god of Carthage."

"And this means what?"

"Who knows?" He shrugged. "A shipwreck can't be older than the latest thing in it. It could mean we have a shipwreck that dates to the fourth century B.C.E. which carried a cargo with a statue that was already old when the ship sailed, and I have no idea why that would be so; or, more likely, there are two or more wrecks here—they do tend to go down in the same general area—winds, currents, and so on. The debris scatters over a wide field, which also complicates the matter. Perhaps there's one from the fourth century B.C.E., another much earlier."

"I hear what you're saying, but I guess I just find it hard to believe that it would be possible to find ships that old."

"Older ships than that have been found. The Uluburun wreck that George Bass excavated off the coast of Turkey dated to the fourteenth century B.C.E., and recently Robert Ballard—you know, the fellow who found the *Titanic*—located a pair of Phoenician ships in very deep waters in the eastern Mediterranean. They were dated, using the amphorae again, at about 750 to 700 B.C.E. They were down really deep, fourteen to fifteen hundred feet or so, with no sunlight, and little sediment, so under those circumstances they might be in remarkably good condition. At the depths we're talking about around here, most of the wood would be gone, but ceramic lasts a very long time, virtually forever, and some of the metal, depending on its composition, too. Sometimes, though, even at these depths, parts of the hull have been protected by the cargo on top of it, and so you can find some wood."

"So is Peter still looking for it, too?"

"He is. He calls his outfit Star Salvage and Diving, out of California. They've got a ship in the area, the *Piranha.* Sorry," he smiled ruefully, "a little slip of the tongue there. The ship's called the *Susannah.* They showed up here this spring after not having been here at all last season. I heard Peter was on the verge of bankruptcy, but he seems to have recovered quite nicely. Got all the latest equipment, satellite stuff, underwater robots, deep-water tracking equipment, you name it. He must have spent last year raising a lot of money. Makes us look like the Clampetts. Am I ranting, do you think?"

"Maybe just a little," I said.

"Thank you." He laughed. "I hate to think what will happen if they find it first. I know Peter, remember. They'll strip the ship of everything they think is valuable, and destroy the rest. This would be such an important find. You need to understand that. But not if they find it first. There won't be a scrap left when they're done with it."

"But surely they can't do that with a ship that old! There must be a law of some kind that deals with shipwrecks like this."

"Yes, they can, and there is. It's called the Law of Finds. You find it, you get to keep it. It's that simple. Admiralty law would tend to support you, and anyway, when it comes right down to it, who is going to stop you? It's happening all over the world. These companies are only interested in profit, not scholarship. Sometimes, after they've stripped everything they consider of value from a vessel, they raise it, just to prove they can do it, or maybe because they think there's profit in it. Not with one this old, maybe. There wouldn't be much left. But with relatively recent ships—you know, War of 1812 in the Great Lakes, Spanish Armada, that kind of thing. Turn them into tourist attractions for a while, put them outside a seafood restaurant or something. Then, they're gone. These old ships just disintegrate when they're brought up, unless they are stabilized and cared for, and it costs a fortune to look after them, which these people are not often interested in spending. They've moved on somewhere else by then. Maybe ten years after the ships have been raised, they cart them away to the dump. They could almost vacuum them up, really. They're virtually dust. It's a crime. There are lots of organizations and countries that have tried to stop companies like Star Salvage, but it's really hard to do. So I intend to find this ship before they do," he said grimly. "Sorry," he added after a moment. "This is a sore point with me, as you may have guessed."

I looked out over the water. "As you say, there's a lot of water around here," I said. "Kind of a long shot, isn't it? And what's to stop somebody else coming along and looking for it, too, someone else who heard Zoubeeir talking about it? Another of these sponge divers, or whatever."

"It is a long shot," he agreed. "And as for someone else, a third party looking for it, you've touched a nerve there. While no one has announced a big find, there have been a few items coming on the market in the past year that make me wonder whether someone else has found something. Local divers are always on the lookout. As I said, that's how a lot of the wrecks are found. There were a couple of pieces of gold jewelry for sale in Brussels last year that date to that time period: authenticated and all. And a month or two ago, some terra-cotta pieces showed up in Tunis. It's not an avalanche yet, just a trickle, but yes, I do get a little agitated about it from time to time. On the other hand"—he smiled—"it's a helluva good way to spend an afternoon, don't you think?"

"It is," I agreed. "Incidentally, if you're thinking that hearing all about the ship, fascinating though the subject might be, will make me forget my question about Rick Reynolds, you're wrong. What were you two arguing about?"

"Nothing, really," he said, looking out across the water. "We just didn't get along. I thought he was a boring young twerp. He was trying to talk me into investing with his firm. I told him to get lost. I don't have any money to invest, but even if I did, he'd never see it. Now that he's dead, I feel bad we had words."

He's the second person who has lied to me today, I thought. *Aziza was lying this morning, and Briars is lying now.* He was right about one thing, though. It was nice sitting there, with the sun and the water and the gentle motion of the boat—and the story I had just heard was compelling. I could almost forget for a moment or two the problems that awaited me back at the auberge, and what I had learned from Rob. I could even make the mistake of overlooking the fact that Briars was someone I needed to be very, very careful about.

"It won't happen again, I can assure you," Briars had said to me when I'd first tried to talk to him about his angry conversation with Rick. Maybe he knew only too well at that moment that it could not possibly happen again.

6

*B*AALHANNO STOOD IN THE SHADE OF THE RIGGING *and looked about him, a respite from the backbreaking labor. It was always a good idea to keep a sharp look-out, working or not, always interesting things to observe. And hadn't there been some curious goings-on during this voyage? Infinitely more diverting than most. His fellow crew members might regard this as an ordinary journey. He, Baalhanno, did not.*

There was Abdelmelqart's demise, surely at the hand of someone onboard. The captain, he was reasonably certain, was of the same mind. He'd seen the way Hasdrubal had examined Abdelmelqart's body, the wound, and the angle of the fall. No doubt Hasdrubal had reached the same conclusion he had: that it was not possible for Abdelmelqart to have hit his head and landed faceup, with a wound on the back of his head. That meant the body had been moved, rolled over, after the accident, or Abdelmelqart had been helped on his way.

Then there was the stranger and the special cargo, the cedar box and its mysterious contents. He'd watched the stranger carefully as the ship's cargo had been loaded, and curiosity piqued, had followed him through the dark streets of Qart Hadasht to the luxurious home of one of the city's elite. Now that kind of wealth and power, he, Baalhanno, a metalworker's son, would like to enjoy. The house from the outside was impressive; he could only guess at the riches within. There would be a court-yard, of course, perhaps lined with columns and paved with tiny white marble tesserae, the sign of Tanit in the entranceway to guard the home. There'd be marble ev-erywhere, he was certain, and many rooms, with a bath-room just for the family.

The power, he knew, would never be his. That rested with the great families, ruthless in their protection of their position, though quarrelsome amongst themselves. But wealth, perhaps that was within his grasp, if he played this situation right. Hadn't he always profited from being observant? There were always those pre-pared to pay for his silence.

Mago and the stranger were plotting together. He knew that from the way each one looked about carefully before signaling the other to a meeting place. And wasn't it the stranger who'd brought Mago to the captain to sign on as crew? Mago would not be the first choice for the captain, as he wasn't for others. Mago's reputation as a conniving rascal was well known about the port. So the stranger had a great deal of influence over Has-drubal's decisions, which made this voyage all the more intriguing.

He'd watched Mago go down into the hold, had watched what he'd done, silently from above. It was strange behavior, to be sure. He'd have to think about what it meant. There were conclusions to be drawn from Mago's activities, interesting conclusions at that.

The question was, what to do with what he'd learned, where the most advantage lay. He could go to the captain *and tell him what he'd seen, what he suspected. There'd be a coin or two or three for him in that. But surely there'd be more from the stranger. Someone with connections to the Council of the Hundred and Four would have more resources than the captain.*

He'd wait awhile, see what more there was to see, build his case. And then, when the time was right, he'd make his move. He, Baalhanno, would be enjoying the fruits of his labor soon.

"WE ARE STANDING IN A SACRED AND SOLEMN place," Briars said, and the group became still. "We call this place the tophet, although that is not what it was called back then, and it is here we believe that Carthaginians may well have sacrificed hundreds, if not thousands, of their children, from babies up to about five years of age, to the fires of Baal Hammon in a practice we refer to as molk sacrifice." There was a kind of collective gasp.

"Now before we rush to condemn them," he said, looking right at Jimmy, who had already opened his mouth to say something derogatory, "there are a few things I would like to tell you about them. First, it may well be that the children were already dead—infant mortality was high—and this was a sacred cremation. Two thousand years later, it is impossible for us to say with any conviction, either way. Furthermore, many of the historical references were written centuries after the fact by Romans, enemies of the Carthaginians, who reveled in lurid stories of moonlit ceremonies in which children's throats were slit before they were placed in the arms of a statue of Baal Hammon, then tipped into the flames.

"Second, the Carthaginians were the descendants of the Phoenicians. According to legend, they came from the great Phoenician city of Tyre, which is in present-day Lebanon, and they brought with them many of the customs, traditions, and beliefs of that part of the world. The term tophet appears several times in the Bible, for cxample, and refers to a place where the practice of sacrificing a first-born occurred. Think of the story of Abraham and Isaac.

"Rituals involving fire were also important in this context. If you recall, I told you earlier about the legend surrounding the founding of the city of Carthage, or Qart Hadasht, when Elissa, sister of Pygmalion, the King of Tyre, fled the city after her husband was killed by her brother, and after wandering the Mediterranean, came to the shores of North Africa. Sometime after the city was founded, according to the story in 814 B.C.E., Hiarbas, a Libyan chieftain, demanded that Elissa, by then known as Elissa Dido, Dido meaning the wandering one, marry him or he would kill all her people. Rather than betray her dead husband, she threw herself into a fire. Several centuries later, in 146 B.C.E., the wife of the last leader of Carthage threw herself and her children into the flames rather than submit to Rome. All this is by way of saying that death by fire was an important ritual concept to the Carthaginians.

"Thirdly, molk sacrifice seems to have been practiced, in the later period at least, only in exceedingly difficult times; that is, it was not a regular part of their ritual observances. For example, one of the most dangerous times for Carthage was the period between 310 and 307 B.C.E., when they were locked in a bitter struggle with the Sicilian Agathocles, a ruler who was called the Tyrant of Syracuse, because of his ruthless treatment of the rulers he had deposed, and anyone who opposed him. Carthage had set up a blockade of Syracuse, but the wily Agathocles broke through it, and sailed straight for Carthage, landing on what is referred to as the Beautiful Promontory, what is probably Cap Bon, just across the Bay of Tunis from where we are standing. He arrived with sixty ships and fourteen thousand men. Because he did not have enough men to guard his ships, he burned them, and then started his march overland toward Carthage.

"The Carthaginians were stunned by this. They immediately sent an offering to the Temple of Melqart in their mother city, Tyre. But still Agathocles advanced, pillaging the rich farmlands outside the city, and taking town after town. He also persuaded a lot of Carthage's allies to desert them. A battle was fought not far from Carthage, and Agathocles was the victor.

"The result, however, was not definitive. While Agathocles had won the battle, he was not strong enough to storm the city walls. Inside, the Carthaginians tried to regroup. Being the merchant nation they were, they bought and sold everything, including armies. While they sailed their own ships, including their navy, on land they relied almost entirely on mercenary troops, and they needed time to raise a new army.

"Picture this situation: two implacable enemies staring at each other across the city walls. It is then that the Carthaginians turned again to the molk sacrifice. The leaders, generals, and many of the elite sacrificed their children, probably their firstborn. We're told it was considered a badge of honor that the mothers and fathers would stand there, dry-eyed, as their child was taken from them, and offered to the burning god.

"The Romans regarded the Carthaginians with disgust for a practice they considered barbaric, which it was. But for the Carthaginians this was a sacred ritual. They did not do this for entertainment or sport, nor is there any indication that the elite bought children to substitute for their own. Look at the rows of votive stones here, commemorating their little ones," he said, gesturing toward them. "Some show children with their mothers, others show priests taking the child for the sacred offering, still others depict the goddess Tanit, consort of Baal Hammon, and protectress of many Carthaginian homes. Giving up your firstborn to the fires of Baal Hammon was something you did to save your city from a terrible curse. I think we need to consider it in that context."

"But what happened to the city?" Susie asked.

"The Carthaginians were able to raise an army and send Agathocles packing back to Sicily," Briars said. "But it was only a temporary respite. Just a few decades later, they were locked in a doomed struggle with the mighty power of Rome. Now let's have a look around, and I'll point out more."

The group moved on, all, that is, except Chastity. She stood looking about her, then took a book of matches out of her bag and lit one. It burned as she watched her mother, now hanging on Emile's arm. With a little cry, she dropped the burning match and licked her fingers. The match sputtered and died in the sandy soil.

"That girl is disturbed," Jamila said that evening, taking the lid from a dish and inhaling the heavenly aroma. We were on the outdoor patio of Restaurant Les Oliviers, a lovely place at the edge of town, sharing a specialty called *koucha,* with fish, potatoes, lots of green olives, peppers, and onions in a spicy tomato sauce. I'd ducked my responsibilities of dinner with the gang to meet Jamila. Not that it wasn't legitimate. We were bringing the group to this same restaurant a day or two later, and we had arrangements to discuss. Still, it felt something akin to skipping classes or reading under the blankets with a flashlight long after I was supposed to be asleep. The restaurant was on four or five different levels, a series of outdoor terraces that cascaded down the side of the hill, with a terrific view of the harbor and the yachts and colorful fishing boats that shared the marina.

"She is. No wonder, though. Her mother is absolutely ignoring her."

"Marlene is spending time with Emile, I notice," Jamila said. "Or trying to, anyway."

"I don't know whether she's having much success there, but for sure Chastity is suffering because of it. I don't know what we can do about it."

"I think we both just have to spend as much time as we can with her. I don't like the idea of her lighting those matches. You don't think she had anything to do with that fire at the hotel, do you?"

"No," I said. "I don't. I talked to the policeman overseeing the investigation. The fire started in the mattress—they even found traces of the cigarette that had started it—and the fuel was simply lighter fluid. She may have spilled some. The smoke detector was disconnected. I think Kristi had herself to blame for that one."

We both enjoyed our food and wine for a while without speaking. "Isn't that a new ship in the harbor?" Jamila said, breaking the silence. "That big one, with all the lights. I wonder if it's someone's yacht. If so, I'd like to meet them."

"It does look nice," I said. "Maybe we could stow away on it. Leave the whole group behind."

"Tempting, I agree." She laughed.

"This restaurant is splendid, though," I said. "The food, the view, everything. I'm glad we did this, even if I shouldn't have."

"Me, too," Jamila said. "And we do have a reason for being here. We need to discuss the evening. I'm suggesting we make it a folkloric night. You know, belly dancers, snake charmers, that sort of thing."

"Yuk," I groaned.

"I know," she said. "But people like it. Have some more wine."

We talked for a while about how it would all work, and what it would cost, and finally got the details all nailed down. The owner joined us for a moment or two to close the deal.

"I guess this is not exactly your average tour, Jamila," I said. I'd been wondering how she felt about tourists dying every other day. "You're probably wondering what awful thing you did in a past life to deserve being the successful bidder on the land portion of this tour."

She shrugged. "Accidents happen," she said. "You've just been unlucky on this one. Both of these people were very careless, wouldn't you say? Diving like that, and if Kristi disconnected the smoke detector and then fell asleep, well, I'd have to agree with you that she brought it on herself."

I was tempted to tell her about my dream, and my conversation with Rob, both of which had convinced me that Rick's death was far from accidental. I held my tongue, though. I didn't know her well enough to confide in her, although I wished I did. It was strange being the group leader. I felt very responsible for everyone's welfare, but at the same time, I didn't feel I could be friends with any of them, except perhaps Emile, whom I'd known before.

"It's too bad about the publicity, though, for both of us," Jamila said. "We were hoping, and I'm sure you were, too, to have a good write-up in that American magazine."

"In that regard we may have been lucky, Jamila," I said. "I don't think Kristi was too keen on this tour, or this country."

"But she seemed very positive!" Jamila exclaimed. "I'm surprised."

"I was, too," I said. "But take my word for it. She thought the ruins were boring."

"Carthage? The tophet? How could she?" Jamila looked indignant at the criticism.

"Are you as surprised as I am that Aziza and Curtis haven't packed up and gone home now that's she's out of hospital?" I asked.

"Yes, I am," she said. "If I'd been the one pulled out of Kristi's room barely conscious, I'd have headed straight home as soon as they'd let me."

"Me, too, and I can't help thinking Aziza shares our feelings."

"It must be her husband who wants to stay," Jamila suggested. "What was she doing in that room anyway?"

"She was out for a stroll and noticed that the door was open, and went in to see if there was a problem, I guess. What do you hear from the rest of them?"

"Actually, other than the fact that people are dropping like flies, to use Curtis's expression, I think the tour is going quite well. People seem to be enjoying the sights, and everyone likes the hotel, despite what happened. Everyone has concluded that Rick and Kristi were . . . what's that Jimmy was always calling them?"

"Idiots," I said.

"Idiots," she agreed. "They seem to have almost forgotten all about it. They all seem very nice."

"Nice" wasn't the first word that now came to mind, although I didn't voice my disagreement. Before I could say anything, a loud burst of laughter caught our attention. I looked about for the source of the noise. The place was almost empty: It was just us; a bunch of giggling schoolgirls having soft drinks on the terrace above; a group of four businessmen, smoking the chicha on the terrace below; and, over at the far end of the main terrace where we were, a large group of what appeared to be Americans, about ten of them, enjoying a meal together. It was one of those occasions, apparently, that called for many toasts, and rounds of applause at regular intervals.

"Do you notice those people are all wearing the same blue shirts?" Jamila asked. "Do you think they're a sports team? The fellow sitting at the head of the table could be the coach, or something."

"Could be," I said. "I've got to go to the ladies. I'll have a look on the way by. Back in a minute."

One of the young women from the sports team table was brushing her long blond hair as I came in. We smiled at each other in the mirror.

"Hi," she said.

"Hi," I replied.

"American?" she asked.

"Canadian, actually, although I'm here with a group of Americans. How about you?"

"California," she replied. "I'm sort of here with a group as well. We're working in the area."

"I saw you on the terrace. Do the matching shirts have any significance? And that nice star logo on the pocket?"

"We're with an outfit called Star Salvage," she said. "I'm a diver. We're looking for an old shipwreck. I don't know if you can see the ship in the harbor, the big one, from where you're sitting, but that's ours."

"I did see it," I said. "It's lovely. I think I've heard of your company."

"Have you?" she said, looking pleased. "We've found some great shipwrecks in the Caribbean. There's one, the *Margarita* . . ."

"Oh, yes, of course," I said. "Wasn't there some dispute about who owned the treasure or some such thing?"

"Yes," she replied. "There certainly was. In the end Peter—that's the owner, he's here with us tonight, the older guy at the end of the table—got screwed, but he's trying again. We're going for gold this time."

"That must be very exciting," I said.

"Best job I ever had," she said. "I couldn't believe my good fortune when Peter took me on. Left the desk job, and I've never looked back. My name's Maggie, by the way."

"I'm Lara. Are you the only ones looking for this shipwreck?" I asked in what I hoped was an innocent voice.

"There's another small outfit, a bunch of archaeologists. One of them came down to Sousse a couple of days ago, and accused Peter of sabotaging his operation. Made quite a scene. He was kind of scary, actually. The guy's insane. Why would we bother? We'll find it first. We have all the latest scanning equipment, and if it's down deep, we have an ROV—a remote underwater vehicle, kind of a robot, that can go down for us. All they've got is side scan sonar, and a rather small boat."

"That's sounds just fascinating," I said. "So are you going to be searching in this area?"

"Yes," she replied. "We've been working south of here, out of Sousse, for the last several weeks, and we're gradually working our way north."

"I hope you enjoy the search." Tactful, that. I wasn't about to wish her success, given my association with Briars. "And it's been nice talking to you, Maggie," I said, heading into the cubicle as the young woman packed up her cosmetic bag.

"Same here," she said. "I hope we're not too noisy here, by the way. We usually sleep on the ship out at anchor, so we won't waste any time going out to where we're working during the day. But every now and then we come in to port—we still sleep on the ship, but we get to come ashore for a little R&R—and we can get a little carried away."

"No problem," I assured her.

"Enjoy your stay," she said.

Well, that pretty much confirmed Briars's story, as unlikely as it might all sound. The overwhelming impression I had was that Briars was rather outclassed in terms of technology. "It's a crew from a marine salvage company, Jamila," was all I said back at the table.

"There you are," a familiar voice said. We looked up to see four heads peering down at us from the terrace above: Ben, Ed, Emile, and Chastity. The heads vanished and the foursome descended the stairs to our table.

"Thought you could sneak away, did you?" Ben said.

"You can run, but you can't hide," Ed said, and Chastity giggled.

"We were doing some planning for the next few days," I said, rather primly.

"Nice spot. Do you mind if we join you?" Emile asked as the other men moved a table over to ours. Chastity sat between Emile and me, and Ben and Ed took places next to Jamila.

"Dessert, coffee, ladies?" the waiter asked. "Gentlemen?" The waiter was looking very dashing with a sprig of jasmine blossoms behind one ear.

"Coffee for me," Jamila said.

"Me, too," I said.

"Me, three," Ed joined in. "What's that flower you have behind your ear?" he added.

"Jasmine," the waiter replied. "If a man wears it behind his right ear, then he is married. On the left, he is looking for a wife."

"So you're not married," Chastity said.

He smiled. "Let's just say most men in Tunisia wear the jasmine behind their left ear."

"Don't worry," Jamila said. "The feminist wave will sweep my country yet. But perhaps," she added, "not in our lifetime."

"Do you have baklava?" Ben said, referring to the sweet pastry drenched in honey and nuts.

"Of course," the waiter answered. "Three coffees and one baklava."

"You've already had baklava tonight," Ed scolded.

"I know," Ben replied. "I'm conducting a baklava taste test. At the end of the trip, I'll announce the winner."

"I'll have one, too," Chastity said.

"A brandy for me," Emile said.

"I'd like a brandy, too," Chastity said.

"No, you wouldn't," Ben told her.

"You're just like my mother," Chastity sulked. "Okay, I'll have some of that nice tea with nuts in it."

"Pine nut tea," the waiter said.

"Where *is* your mother?" I asked.

"Headache," she replied. "She's gone to bed. Can I have a cigarette, Emile?"

"No, you can't. I've been put in charge of Chastity," Ben said to me. I thought that might be a tall order. There was something different about Chastity. She'd pulled her hair back into a tight knot, and applied makeup, perhaps more than necessary for someone her age. She was wearing the same little black scoop-neck dress she'd worn the first evening, but she'd pushed the sleeves down past her shoulders to reveal a lot more creamy skin, and I was pretty sure she'd shortened the dress by several inches. She kept crossing and un-crossing her legs rather provocatively.

"We went shopping after dinner," Ed said. "Chastity found a necklace she liked. It was brutal bargaining for it," he added. "Thrust and parry. It took stamina, guts, and determination. For a while I feared defeat, but in the end, the dealer folded, and victory was ours." We all laughed.

"Let's see it," Jamila said, and Chastity carefully unwrapped a tissue package.

"That's lovely," I told her, and it was, a choker of silver beads, some round, some rectangular, interspaced with malachite stones. "Those silver beads are Berber design, Chastity. The one right in the center is supposed to bring you luck, and ward off evil."

"Bravo, Chastity," Ed said. "Excellent choice. Put it on, why don't you?"

"I'll help," I said, but Chastity had already turned to Emile.

"Will you help me, Emile?" she cooed. I looked over at Jamila, who raised her eyebrows. Chastity was growing up very fast, it seemed—something about the way she caressed the choker and her neck. Emile was very careful not to touch her as he put the necklace on, but she maneuvered it so that she brushed his hand. An embarrassed silence followed. CS—Lolita, I thought, just what Kristi wrote. How had I missed all this?

"So, Ben," I said brightly, in an effort to change the subject as quickly as possible. "How are you finding the trip? Is it meeting your expectations? Are you here to study, or just to relax?" My, I sounded perky.

"I'm enjoying myself immensely," he said, digging into the gooey dessert with gusto. "As for your question about study or rest, I guess it's a little of both. I teach classics as you know, and my personal area of study is the Punic Wars and the period leading up to them. You know what I mean by the Punic Wars, Chastity?"

She screwed up her face very prettily for a moment.

"Hannibal, and those elephants in the Alps," she said finally.

"Right." He smiled. "The Punic Wars—there were three of them, from 264 and 146 B.C.E.—were between Rome and Carthage. Hannibal was a Carthaginian general."

"The Carthage we've seen?" Chastity asked.

"One and the same. The term Punic has various derivations, but it applies to the Carthaginians during this period of time. So, yes, the location is part of my area of interest, but I'm really here to have a good time. Of course, I'm always on the lookout for material for my book. It's to be my *magnum opus,* you see. I've been working on it for years."

"What's it about, Ben?" I asked.

"The working title is *Past Imperfect.*"

"*Past Imperfect,*" Jamila repeated. "Is it a history book or a grammar book?"

"I told you," Ed said.

"It's history. Ed is always telling me the title is a problem. But I like it, and until it's finished and a publisher tells me otherwise, *Past Imperfect* it is. One of the things I think people need to know about history is that it's written, by and large, by the victorious, and even more than that, by the dominant group within that victorious culture—usually the elite, and of course, usually men. For example, almost all the reports we have of the Punic Wars come from Rome. As usual, it's the victors who get to give their version of events, while the vanquished do not. There are really no Carthaginian accounts of the wars and the political situation that led up to them. My theory is that the wars were clearly started by Rome for their own internal political reasons, with little if any provocation on the part of the Carthaginians. Others, I might add, are more tolerant of the Romans than I am. But that, you see, is why I called it *Past Imperfect*, because our view of the events of history is skewed in this way."

"It's a great title," I said.

"Thanks. What I tried to do with the book was cast light upon some of the silent voices of history, the people we don't usually hear about or from, either because they lost some war, and the people who won got to write the account of it, or because they were simply regarded as unimportant and were therefore overlooked when the stories of their time were being told."

"Like women," Jamila interjected.

"Exactly," Ben agreed. "Women, the poor, or even whole nations who lost out in battle. The Carthaginians are an excellent example. The Romans by and large absolutely despised the Carthaginians. They'd make an exception for a few they admired, grudgingly, but essentially they described the Carthaginians as dirty, drunken, barbaric louts. There was a Roman expression, *Punica fides,* Punic faith. What do you think it meant? Treachery! Punic faith to the Romans was synonymous with treachery. They were particularly scathing on the subject of the child sacrifices in the tophet. So this is the view of the Carthaginians that has come down to us. The Romans won the war, wrote the history, and it is their side of the story we have. But you heard Briars on the subject of the tophet. It could be it didn't happen, or if it did, it was a sacred ceremony, not a game. The Romans, as we know, had peculiar ideas themselves about what constituted entertainment, and there is no indication the Carthaginians shared that. As for dirty, well, we saw the town of Kerkouane the other day."

"They had bathtubs," Chastity said. "We saw them."

"They did. Right in their homes, in addition to public baths. The archaeological evidence would indicate that they weren't nearly as dirty as the Romans said.

As for barbaric, the Roman alphabet is based on the Phoenician one, and Carthage was a Phoenician city. Also, a Carthaginian by the name of Magon taught the Romans a great deal about the best agricultural practices. There are lots of examples one could give, but we rarely hear them."

"So are you trying to put some of these stories right?" Jamila asked.

"In a way, yes. I've been researching it for years . . ."

"Years and years," Ed interjected. "I keep telling him that at some point he just has to stop researching and writing, and start trying to find a publisher."

"Ed doesn't understand that the research is the best part of it. I'm trying to find old writings or even ancient works of art that depicted common people rather than the kings and queens or gods and goddesses of ancient times. I uncovered a number of examples, just really interesting stories about common people who did something extraordinary, to refute some of the misconceptions we have of the past, and give a voice to the many people who have been silent."

Group intellectual, I thought.

"This is a rather long-winded answer to your question, isn't it?" Ben said. "*Dum loquor, hora fugit.* While I'm talking, time flies." A good thing, too, from my perspective. Chastity had, for the moment, stopped her vamping.

"What language is that?" Chastity asked.

"Latin, of course. I teach classics. Would you prefer Greek? What about you, Emile?" Ben said. "Didn't you say you'd been born here but hadn't been back for years? Has it changed much?"

"It's changed a lot in many ways, but in others, it's very much the same," Emile replied, signaling the waiter for another brandy, and lighting a cigarette. "The countryside is as beautiful as I remember it: the sea, and then the mountains and the desert. Such contrasts in a tiny country! I used to come to Taberda as a boy during the summer to visit friends of the family. All these homes were owned by the French in those days. Now, of course, it is wealthy Arabs who live here. I enjoyed a rather charmed life while I was here, I'm coming to realize. A lovely home in Tunis, private school, a week or two every summer here, and my father had a large estate out in the Sahel, south and west of Tunis. He had vineyards and orchards. Pity, what happened."

"What was that?" Chastity asked.

Emile paused for a moment as another cheer went up from the Star Salvage team. The man I took to be Peter Groves stood up and raised his glass. He was a stocky man, but fit, about five foot ten, and maybe fifty years of age. "Here's not just to finding the treasure first," he said, a little unsteadily, the result of a few too many toasts. "But here's also to crushing the competition! Let's never forget they are the enemy, and we're not just going to beat them to it, we're going to blow them away." The group cheered again, and several banged their beer glasses on the table.

I had a sense of someone above us, and looked up. Standing on the terrace above was Briars, his face flushed with anger, his fists clenched. For a moment he stood there, staring toward the group, and then he stepped back from the wall and disappeared. I looked behind, half expecting to see him come down the steps to start a fight, but he didn't. I had no doubt, though, that this was going to be trouble.

"The Arab population started to agitate for independence from France, and the early 1950's were bloody," Emile continued, oblivious to the little drama that was playing out around him. "The country was formally granted independence in 1956, but the bloodshed did not end there. A lot of our fellow countrymen left for France during those years. But my father stayed on. He firmly believed it would all blow over. Then in 1961 there were riots again, and shortly after, my father's name appeared on a death list. We packed up and left the country overnight with only what we could carry. We lost everything. While some of the French who left earlier had managed to sell their properties, albeit at distressed prices, my father just had to walk away.

"It was very hard after that. The French government did negotiate with the Tunisian president, Habib Bourguiba, for some restitution for the lost farms, but it was too late for my father. He had trouble getting a job back in France. We had to live with some distant relatives who were none too pleased to have us. My mother died a few months after we returned. Ostensibly she died of a stroke. I thought she died of a broken heart. I had to drop out of school—I wanted to be a doctor— to find work to support the family. I have a younger brother and sister.

"I vowed I'd never come back, but I'll admit curiosity got the better of me when I saw your ad, Lara. I left booking the trip right up until the last minute, unable to make up my mind. But I finally called, there was a spot for me, and so here I am," he said. "It's stirred up a lot of memories, but not all of them are bad."

"Oh, Emile!" Chastity exclaimed. "That is so—"

"Tragic?" Ed interjected.

"Sad, very sad," Chastity said. She reached out and placed her hand on Emile's thigh. He looked startled, but not entirely displeased.

"Time to go back to the hotel," Ben said, his baklava not yet gone.

I couldn't have agreed more. I signaled the waiter for our bill.

"I'm heading home," Jamila said. "See you to-morrow."

We walked back together in silence, each of us deep in our own thoughts. I for one, had a lot of thinking to do. The tour was beginning to feel rather surreal to me, a regular little hive of intrigue when I'd thought everybody came for sun, sights, and shopping: Curtis threatening Rick, Briars threatening Rick, Rick dying in the swimming pool, whether by accident or design. Then there was Aziza wandering around in the middle of the night, and just happening to go into a room that's about to go up in smoke taking its occupant with it, a room that belonged to a woman who was keeping a nasty list in which Aziza and her husband were featured prominently. Not to forget Briars, who was locked in a hugely competitive search for a 2000-year-old ship-wreck that, according to someone named Zoubeeir, was to be found offshore lined up with a rock shaped like a camel, and who had just heard some rather inflam-matory talk from his competitor. It was all just too much.

There were so many unanswered questions, it was hard to know where to begin. If Rick had been mur-dered—and both my dream and what Rob had told me convinced me it was murder, then who had done it? Curtis? What were those two men doing on that path late at night? And where had Curtis gone?

He hadn't come back up the path. The fastest way to the hotel, about a fifteen-minute walk, was back the way we all came. I went that way, Rick went that way, and so, presumably, did Kristi. Curtis didn't. Or at least not for some time. I'd waited for him for quite a while. Later the next day, I'd gone and checked where that path went. It ended at the road along the harbor. To get back to the hotel from there would require a very long walk along the harbor in either direction to the main road, and then back up that road to the hotel. It was not possible to climb straight up the cliff to the hotel, of that I was certain, even for an athlete like Curtis. The cliff actually curved back out near the top. You'd have to be a spider, or have rather elaborate climbing equipment, to manage it. The other possibility would be to get a taxi down on the harbor road. I didn't know if taxis regularly cruised along the harbor that late at night, but I doubted it. But there was a telephone, and it would certainly be possible to call for a taxi. If Curtis got one right away, he could have been back at the hotel in about ten minutes. He could have got there before I did, in fact. My ankle hurt and I wasn't moving very fast. But he could also have gone off somewhere else. Where and why, I had no idea. I supposed Aziza would know when Curtis got back, but I very much doubted she'd be saying.

Could it be Briars? He maintained that Rick was trying to get him to invest with his company, and that he found this offensive and told him to get lost. Certainly I would have objected strenuously if Rick had started a sales pitch with me, too, but somehow I didn't believe Briars on this one. There must be more to it than that. Rick told Briars not to threaten him. Why threaten someone just for being a pest?

Then there was the notebook, and the question as to whether or not it played a role in all of this. It was certainly nasty enough. What had happened to it? This really bothered me. What seemed to be such a brilliant idea at six o'clock that morning, tossing the book in the bushes, that is, looked rather more like poor judgment now. The thought of anyone else finding The List with its horrible insinuations was almost more than I could bear. I kept trying to picture Kristi standing by the pool that morning, enjoying the performance. I was certain I would have noticed if she'd been carrying the notebook with her then, even if I was in something of a state at the time. It could have been that the gardeners simply tossed it out, but I didn't think so.

It was also possible that someone just decided they could use a nice leather diary. If that was the case, I'd better hope they tossed all the pages without looking at them, or, at the very least that it was found by a stranger to whom The List would mean nothing.

Could it have been destroyed in the fire? Unlikely. The fire merely smoldered: Kristi died from smoke inhalation, not burning, and the hotel staff quickly extinguished what little fire there was. The diary might have got a little singed, but nothing more than that.

And it hadn't been among her things. I'd volunteered for the unpleasant task of packing up Kristi's belongings in the hope of finding it, without success.

I decided I would have to find two things: the notebook and a murder weapon. If Rick was hit on the head before he was dumped in the pool, as I believed he was, there had to be a weapon. You couldn't inflict that kind of damage on someone's head with your bare hands. It could be anything, a rock, tools used to clean the pool, even a chair. It was possible the murder weapon would have been disposed of in some way, but not if it were something that by its absence would bring attention to it or to the crime.

Perhaps if I could find both these objects, the rest of it would start to make sense.

7

"WE MUST HEAD FOR SHELTER," THE CAPTAIN said. "A cove, if not a harbor. The weather is worsening by the hour." The boy, he knew, was in the corner behind sacks of grain, no doubt listening to every word. He'd told him to hide when he heard the footsteps approaching.

"We must go on," the stranger said. "You know my mission."

"I have been told what your mission is, yes," Hasdrubal replied. "Regardless, we must find shelter."

"You would risk the future of Qart Hadasht!" the stranger exclaimed. "You are a traitor."

"I do not think the future of Qart Hadasht will be secured by the loss of my ship and the death of my men. If your mission is as you have stated it, safe arrival at our destination is paramount."

This man is becoming a nuisance, Hasdrubal thought, what with the advancing storm and a murder to be considered. Well, he'd deal with all of it, with the boy's help. Smart one, that boy. He'd been right about him. Not as *young as he looked, either—a man not a boy. Now that he, Hasdrubal, was a grandfather, he noticed everyone seemed younger. Well, a voyage or two would harden the young man, assuming he survived this one. No matter what his age and experience, he knew who to suspect right away. The short-sword he'd found almost immediately, hidden amongst Mago's belongings.*

The murder weapon, the captain had feared, would never be discovered, thrown overboard at the earliest opportunity. But the boy had found that, too, a silver ingot. Since it was too valuable to discard, and sure to be missed when inventory was taken at the end of the voyage, the killer had instead attempted to wipe it clean before setting it back in its place. The deed was done in haste, however, and there was a trace of what the captain was certain was blood, and a strand or two of matted dark hair. Clever of the boy to figure it out and wait to see who replaced it.

Unfortunate it was not more definitive, though. Too many men had come down to the cargo hold, and the boy, having only a peephole to look through, and worried about being caught, could not see which one of them had replaced the ingot. But he'd narrowed the list of suspects, that was for certain, from the twenty-odd crew members to only three: Mago, Safat, and Malchus. Funny how it was always those three who came to mind: Mago the crafty thief—and what the boy had been able to see of his actions through that tiny opening was strange to be sure—Safat, the unpleasant accomplice, and Malchus, the jealous lover. Still, just being down there didn't make them guilty of murder, any more than the theft of Abdelmelqart's belongings did. With the storm coming, the cargo would be checked and checked again to make sure it was securely fastened so that it wouldn't come loose in the bad weather and destabilize the ship. But one of them had done it, of that the captain was certain. And he had a reason to interrogate one of them. He would confront Mago about the sword and perhaps more when he was ready, but in the meantime he had the storm and the stranger to deal with.

Come to think of it, was there a fourth suspect in all this? This man who stood before him, the one the crew referred to as the stranger, but who he knew to be one Gisco, esteemed member of the Council of the Hundred and Four, and a man now on a diplomatic mission of vital importance to the future of Qart Hadasht? Hadn't the boy seen Mago and Gisco talking together, their heads bent toward each other so no one could hear? What was a man of Gisco's status doing conferring with someone like Mago?

Yes, he knew what his mission was. Hadn't Bomilcar, the great man himself, one of the two generals whose duty it was to defend the city against that scourge, Agathocles, come to his home in the old quarter of Qart Hadasht, to personally ask him to undertake this voyage? He'd recognized him the moment Bomilcar lowered the corner of the robe he'd held in front of his face. The future of the great city hung in the balance, Bomilcar had told him. They must raise an army from amongst the Libyans, persuade them to switch their allegiance back to Qart Hadasht. Well, the cargo was rich enough to help convince them, that much was certain. But to do this, it was necessary to get there, ship and cargo intact.

"I am in command of this ship," Hasdrubal said, rising from his seat. "And we will set a course for shelter now."

The stranger took a bag from his robe and threw it at Hasdrubal's feet. Coins, silver and gold, spilled from its mouth as it hit the floor. "There is no time. Keep going," the stranger said.

Emile St. Laurent ducked his head to clear the awning in front of the little stall.

"Can I help you, monsieur?" the proprietor asked. "Are you looking for something in particular?"

Emile picked up a leather wallet, examined it closely, then set it down.

"Leather, monsieur? Shoes? Perhaps a handbag for your lovely ladies," he said, glancing at Chastity, Marlene, and me. The three of us were browsing.

"I might like to look at those," Emile said, pointing at something through the glass countertop.

"Roman glass? Very good."

"Not the glass," Emile said. "The case, there."

"Ah, the coins. You are interested in coins. I have some very fine ones."

"I'll take a look, please," Emile said. He took a small magnifying glass from his pocket, and for a few moments he studied the coins carefully.

"This one, perhaps," he said, picking the coin up by the edges. "How much for this one?"

"You have a good eye, monsieur," the proprietor said. "This is a Roman coin, very fine condition. It dates to around 200 B.C. I will give you a special price. Are you paying in dollars?"

"I can," Emile said. "How much?"

"Two hundred American dollars," the man said.

Emile laughed. "That is a special price indeed, my good man. The coin is not in very fine condition, only fine, and is reasonably common. While it may be the best coin you have here, it is not worth more than forty dollars, and that is what I am prepared to pay you."

"You may very well be right about the price and condition, monsieur. But price is also set by the market, and tourists are not all as discriminating as you are. I can do rather better than forty dollars, I can assure you. I will sell it to you for one hundred dollars."

"I'm afraid not," Emile said, turning to leave.

"Monsieur," the man called to Emile as he ducked back under the awning. Emile turned. "You obviously know coins," the man said. "Come back tomorrow. I may have something that will interest you."

"I might do that," Emile said. "If you're sure it will be worth my while."

"Tomorrow then," the man said. He rubbed his hands together and smiled.

"I'd say he picked the wrong man to try to deceive," I commented after we left the stall.

Emile smiled. "Yes, he did, and he wouldn't come down, even though he knew I was right. His argument was that people will pay the outrageous prices he asks, and I couldn't disagree with him. People who don't know anything about coins think a Roman coin is something special, and while some of them are, most are essentially worthless, from an economic point of view, anyway. Nice to have, perhaps, and possibly historically interesting, but that's all. Anyway, all the more power to him if he can get the prices he asks, I suppose. Now, who's for some ice cream?"

"I am," Chastity said.

"Me, too," Marlene said.

"Afraid not," I said. "I have to get back to the auberge. Have a good time. Catherine wants to talk to me about something, apparently."

"I REALLY DON'T WANT TO COMPLAIN," CATHERINE whispered. "But you know, this is becoming intolerable." We were talking outside the inn, in the garden.

"What is?" I asked as gently as I could. The woman looked close to tears.

"My belongings," she said. "My cosmetics, my clothes, everything."

"Catherine, I'm sorry, but you are going to have to be a little clearer, here. I don't know what you're talking about."

She blew her nose, and paused for a moment. "Someone is going through my things," she said. "I come back to the room after dinner, and my cosmetics have all been rearranged, and the clothes in the cupboard have been messed up. You'll have to talk to her."

"The housekeeper, you mean?" I said. "You think the staff is moving your belongings about? I'd be happy to speak to the management if that's the case."

"No," she said. "It happens before they've even come in to make up the rooms, or later, after the beds are turned down. We have breakfast at different times, you know. I get up early, and shower first. She's usually still in bed when I leave. And then she goes off jogging for a few minutes. I'm sure she's been in my suitcase. I know she's curious about everything, and she seems good-hearted, but she shouldn't handle my belongings."

"You think Susie is getting into your stuff?"

"Who else could it be? We share a room. Come, I want you to see something while Susie is out."

"Lara! Oh sorry, I didn't realize you were busy," Ed said, coming up to us. "Have either of you seen a croquet mallet? Betty and I are challenging Ben and Marlene to a match, but there are only three mallets."

"It must be around here somewhere," I said, looking about the grounds. "Have you looked in the garden shed?"

"Yes," he replied. "Do you think they might have an extra one at the desk?"

Catherine tugged at my sleeve. "Please," she said. "You must come in now while you-know-who is out."

"All right, Catherine," I said, trying to keep the exasperation out of my voice. "I'll find Mohammed and send him out to help you, Ed. Catherine needs my assistance right now. I'll come back and help you look, too, just as soon as I've taken care of Catherine's problem."

"Okay," he said amiably.

We climbed the stairs to the room Catherine and Susie shared. "Look!" she said, lifting the pillow on one of the beds, uncovering a very pretty blue nightgown. It was all tied in knots. "Now look here," she said, lifting the pillow on the other bed. A rather flamboyant nightshirt featuring a huge green frog, lay there, neatly folded. "It's always my belongings that are tampered with, not hers," Catherine sobbed. "The end of my lipstick got squashed. Then there was my shampoo. It was spilled all over my cosmetic bag. It made such a mess!"

"It's awful when that happens, isn't it," I said. "I've had the same problem. Either the top is substandard, or maybe I didn't quite tighten it."

"But you don't understand!" she said. "It wasn't in my cosmetic bag. It was on the shelf in the shower. She took it from there and emptied it into my cosmetic bag, then put the top on loosely and made it look as if it was an accident, that I'd done what you said, not tightening the top or something. But I know where I left it. Why is she doing this to me? Can you tell me that? I know we're different, but I thought she was a nice person, and we seemed to be getting along fine. I enjoyed her company. Is it because she's jealous I have more money? What is it?"

I stood there wondering if Catherine had an overly vivid imagination, when she exclaimed, walking over to her luggage and unzipping it, "I've tried to ignore it, take it as an attempt at humor, you know, like apple-pie beds at camp, but this is the limit. What is this supposed to mean?" she said, pointing at what lay inside her suitcase. We both stared at it for a moment or two, and then I leaned over and picked up the offending object. Some people might have thought it was just a croquet mallet. Somehow, I knew differently.

"Would you like a room of your own, Catherine?" I asked.

"Yes," she said tearfully. "I know I'll have to pay extra, but I can't take this anymore."

"Let's see what I can do," I told her. "You may not have to pay anything more."

"Thank you," she said. "I will if I have to. I just can't talk to her about it."

"Leave the mallet with me," I said.

A few minutes later I was down at the desk talking to Sylvie. "Oh dear," she said. "We may have a problem here. The room Mme. Ellingham was in is a mess. The contractor has promised to come this week now that the police have cleared the room, but no one could stay in it the way it is, and the room next to it, which was M. Reynolds', is still airing out because of the smell. It's still a little smoky, and I'm not sure Mme. Anderson would like it, particularly because of what happened to M. Reynolds. I just don't have another room," she said.

"Then, I think what we'll have to do is give Catherine my room," I said. "It's lovely. She'll like it."

"So what are you going to do?" Sylvie asked.

"Would there be another hotel nearby that you could contact for me?"

"I'll try," she said. "But it's the November seventh holiday weekend coming up. You know, to celebrate the day our current president, Ben Ali, took office. It's a school holiday, too. I think most places are full. Some of them have been calling here because they've overbooked, and we haven't been able to accommodate them.

"Let me have a look at Rick's room, then," I said.

"If it's not too smoky, I'll stay there. After all, he didn't die in the room."

"True," she agreed. "And it has been airing out. Here, I'll give you the key. See how you feel about it, and if you don't like it, I'll phone around to the other hotels in the area for you."

Rick's room looked just fine, but as Sylvie had said, there was a slightly smoky and damp smell to it. *It will have to do,* I told myself.

"Ah, Emile," I said, as St. Laurent walked through the doorway. "I was hoping I'd see you. I need a favor."

"I hope I can help. What do you need?" he said.

"Could I possibly borrow that magnifying glass of yours?"

"Of course," he replied, pulling it out of his pocket. "Are you checking out an antiquity yourself, perhaps?"

"Not exactly," I said. "I'll bring this right back."

Back in my room, I took the shade off the lamp, and set the croquet mallet on the table. I turned it around very carefully, looking at it from every angle, then put the magnifying glass up to one corner. A tiny dark hair stuck to the surface, held there by what I decided was blood. I carefully placed the mallet in a large plastic bag. The murder weapon had been found.

I called Clive. "Clive," I said. "I think we should send everybody home."

"What are you talking about Lara?"

"I think Rick Reynolds was murdered. I—"

"Whatever would make you think that?" he interrupted.

"I had a dream, a nightmare, really, and then—"

"Lara! Do you realize how that sounds? I've heard of this kind of thing happening to women your age."

"Clive! Let me finish!" Women my age! "I talked to Rob Luczka, and he told me what happens to people's heads when they dive into a pool like that. Rick's injuries were not consistent with a dive. He had a blow to the back of his head."

"Maybe he dove in backwards, did a back flip or something."

"I don't think so. I think he was hit on the head, and I think I've found the murder weapon. Think about it, Clive: If we don't send them home, and something happens to one of the others, it will be on our heads."

"What do the police there say?"

"Well, nothing," I said reluctantly. "They still think Rick's death was an accident."

He was silent for a moment. "Lara, you're going to have to get a grip, here. I know this is hard on you, taking care of all these people, but this is lunacy. Think it through. We'll be bankrupt if we send everybody home. We've prepaid the airfare and the hotel, and there'll be a penalty for changing the flight, which we'll also have to pay. We'll probably be sued for breach of contract. How would we explain why we're calling the whole thing off, when, as far as the police are concerned, these deaths are entirely accidental? Tell them you had a bad dream? Do you know how this sounds?"

"You're right," I said. "We women of a certain age do get all worked up over nothing. I'd better get back to the group."

"BUT WHY IS CATHERINE MOVING TO HER OWN room?" Susie said later. "I thought we were getting along fine. I know we're different, and everything, but she's very nice, and . . . I don't know. I guess she doesn't like me."

"Susie," I said, "you didn't touch Catherine's belongings or anything, did you? Maybe try on her clothes, or use her cosmetics?" There didn't seem any way to be tactful about this.

"Certainly not," she replied indignantly. "I only used her sunblock when I misplaced mine. But I asked her first, and she said I could help myself. We're very careful to keep our belongings separate. Anyway," she said, "her clothes wouldn't fit me, would they?" That was true.

"I don't suppose you brought a croquet mallet to the room?" I asked her.

She looked perplexed. "Why would I want to do that?" she said.

"Did you notice anything about your own stuff, things that had been moved or that looked as if they'd been handled?"

"The housekeeping staff straighten my stuff up a little when they do the room," she said. "I'm kind of untidy. Is that what it is? She can't stand my mess?"

"I don't know what it is, Susie," I said. "Maybe Catherine is just one of those people who need to have their own room."

"Will I have to pay more now that I don't have a roomie?" Susie asked. "I haven't got a lot of money."

"Don't worry," I assured her. "There'll be no extra charge. We'll look after everything. I think you should just forget about this and enjoy the rest of the trip."

"I guess so," Susie said, but she looked very hurt.

STILL NO SIGN OF KRISTI'S NOTEBOOK. I DID FIND Marlene's Swiss Army knife. It was wedged between where the tiles around the swimming pool ended and the garden began. That put Marlene in the pool area, but didn't make her a killer. Rick wasn't stabbed to death, after all.

I thought long and hard about where the notebook might be. It was a long shot, but something just twigged. I walked over to the bookcase in the lounge, and pulled the glass door open. There were dozens of volumes, some lovely old leather books, and double rows of popular paperbacks in several languages, many left behind, I suppose, by various guests.

I scanned the shelves, and then reached for the spine of a book. It was, indeed, Kristi's diary. I quickly flipped through it. The List was gone.

"AND NOW, LADIES AND GENTLEMEN, IT IS MY VERY great pleasure to present to you our folkloric evening at the Restaurant Les Oliviers," the master of ceremonies said. "My name is Tariq. Please sit back and enjoy the show. What we are going to hear first is something called the Malouf. It is a very ancient musical tradition dating back to ninth-century Spain," Tariq explained, "which combines both Middle Eastern music with Andalusian sound. It was brought to North Africa by Muslims and Jews fleeing Christian Spain during the twelfth to fifteenth centuries. Now we consider it our national music, and take great pride in it."

Our group had taken over the main terrace of the restaurant, the establishment having set up a temporary stage at one end. On the terrace above, several diners had moved over to the wall to take in the festivities. The lights went out for a moment, and then came on again to reveal a group of musicians dressed in red and gold who accompanied two singers, a man and a woman. The music began, performed on the Arab lute; the rabab, a two-stringed fiddle played with a bow; and a zither, along with two or three different drums. For many in our little group it was something of an acquired taste. I could tell. Still, it was exotic, and they seemed to be enjoying themselves. Aziza looked pale, but Curtis had convinced her to come along, and the music seemed to cheer her up.

The show took a different turn a few minutes later

as the belly dancers appeared, and the pace picked up. Soon Tariq was calling for volunteers, and Betty, Susie, Chastity, and Ben were up on the stage being taught how to belly dance. Jimmy covered his eyes as Betty, all pink and excited, took her turn at wrapping herself in a veil and gyrating about.

"The things people will do when they're on vacation," Jimmy said. "And when they've had a couple of drinks," he added.

He might well have been talking specifically about Ben. There he was up on the stage trying to get his rather sizable belly to rotate, to everyone's amusement. He was a good sport, there was no question about that, a man of rather Olympian appetite who didn't much care what people thought of him. In many ways I found it rather refreshing.

Susie, too, seemed to have recovered her sunny disposition and got right into the swing of things. The red and blue veils she was given clashed spectacularly with her lime-green pant suit, and she just couldn't get the hang of it, but she was clearly having fun, and the group clapped and cheered her efforts.

The only one up there who was any good at it was Chastity. The girl who just a few days earlier had been knocking people flat with her backpack was becoming quite the little seductress. She was wearing a halter top and low-cut white jeans, and with a little maneuvering on her part, her belly button was much in evidence. At the end, the instructor presented her with the prize, a silk scarf, as Chastity blew kisses to the audience, specifically at Emile.

"For our next act," Tariq said, as Ben, Betty, Susie, and Chastity came back to their places to great cheers from the rest of the group, "we once again need a volunteer, a gentleman please."

"I'd like to try it," Cliff said, rising from his seat. "If Ben can do it, so can I."

"Don't be silly, Cliff," Nora said. "You know exertion is bad for you. Please sit down."

"Yes, Nora," he said meekly, sinking back into his chair.

I leaned over to Jamila. "I wonder what kind of heart condition he has. Don't they usually recommend exercise for people with heart problems? Moderate exercise, anyway? He was certainly active and strong when he and Ben broke down the door into Kristi's room, and you know, he looks good."

"I think so, too," Jamila said. "But I'm no doctor. She sure has him under her thumb, though, doesn't she? It makes you wonder where care-giving stops and intimidation begins."

There it was again. Kristi's list. Wasn't that exactly what Kristi had insinuated? That Nora was manipulating the older man? How I wished I had never seen that list.

"Someone else?" Tariq said.

"Emile," Chastity cooed. "Why don't you try it."

"Not me," he said, with a wave of his hand.

"Jimmy!" a couple of the others called out.

"Not on your life!" he exclaimed.

"Oh, all right, I'll do it," Ed said, mounting the steps to the stage. "What do I have to do?"

"You will assist the snake charmer," Tariq said.

"Whoa!" Ed exclaimed, as several of the women shrieked. "Just a minute here."

"Come, come," the emcee said. "It is perfectly safe, I assure you. You'll enjoy it."

Once again the lights went down, and then came up again to reveal the snake charmer, a round basket in front of him. As he began to play the flute, the fanned head of a cobra swayed up from the basket. Everyone gasped. Ed took a step or two back. "Whoa," he said again. "I hate snakes." The music played, the snake swayed, and Ed looked as if he'd rather be just about anywhere other than where he was.

After a few minutes of cobra swaying, the snake charmer let the snake go back down into the basket, and then brought out another one about five feet long. "Here," he said, draping the snake around Ed's neck. Ed grimaced as the group groaned in sympathy.

"What did I tell you?" Nora said to Cliff. "This would have been too much for you."

"You may touch the snake," Tariq said.

"Oh, thank you," Ed said, patting it gingerly. "Nice snake." The snake charmer then grabbed the waistband of Ed's khakis, and fed the snake down his pant leg. The expression on Ed's face was one of frozen disbelief as the snake wriggled out the bottom of his pants. The women shrieked and the men all looked away.

"A special prize for this gentleman," the emcee said as the snake was carried off stage. Everyone applauded wildly as Ed accepted an engraved brass tray. There was no question in my mind that he deserved it.

"Worst moment of my life," Ed was telling anyone who'd listen as we started to gather ourselves together to leave.

"Oh, look," Betty said, pointing toward the harbor. "That lovely ship. Do you think there's something wrong?"

We all turned to look at the ship I knew to be the *Susannah,* smoke billowing from the stern. There was a loud bang, and flames shot up. We watched helplessly as much of the ship was engulfed in an inferno.

"That should slow them down for a little while," Briars said.

8

*T*HIS WAS DEEPLY DISTURBING NEWS, HASDRUBAL
*thought, to say nothing of being damned inconvenient,
what with the storm coming, and the ship already short
one crew member. But the ship had been searched twice
from bow to stern, and he'd even sent the boy, who was
infinitely more observant than the rest of them, and who
seemed to have found all the nooks and crannies there
were to hide in, to have one last look. The inescapable
conclusion was that Baalhanno was no longer on board.*

*He had been a strange one, that Baalhanno, with aspi-
rations way above his station in life, and always an eye
for the main chance. And the way he was always watching everybody: More than once Hasdrubal had heard
complaints that Baalhanno was a spy; more than once
he'd had to break up fights between Baalhanno and the
object of his scrutiny. Not a terribly popular crew member, it had to be said. Nonetheless, the news was
alarming.*

*He could certainly have fallen overboard. That hap-
pened often enough, regrettable though it might be. On*

the other hand, since Abdelmelqart had been mur-
dered—there was no question in the captain's mind
about that—then perhaps Baalhanno, an innocent if ob-
noxious man, had been helped over the side. But for
now Hasdrubal must put all this aside. There was his
ship to think of, and his men, and these were perilous
times. Anything could happen.

It took a few hours to get the fire on board the *Susannah* under control. Fortunately, all but one crew member was ashore for dinner. For that one, however, Margaret Robinson, the outlook was poor; she was severely burned over much of her body. "I have a horrible feeling that Margaret might be the Maggie I met the night you and I were at the restaurant together," I said to Jamila. "She was lovely, and so excited about her job. What a dreadful thing to happen to her."

It got worse. Later the next day, the police tracked down Briars as we were touring the Roman ruins at Thuburbo Majus, and took him in for questioning. He came to see me at the auberge around ten o'clock that evening.

"Apparently there is evidence that the fire on the *Susannah* was deliberately set," he said, downing what I was afraid was to be the first of several Scotches. "The police know Groves and I are both looking for the same shipwreck. I suppose Groves told them. They certainly seem to be aware of my little tantrum down in Sousse, and are therefore considering the possibility, if not outright assuming, that the fire was my revenge. They haven't thrown me in jail, as you can see, but they've taken my passport."

"You should get in touch with the U.S. embassy in

Tunis first thing tomorrow, Briars," I said. "I think you need to take this very seriously."

"I suppose you're right, and I am taking this seriously. That isn't why I'm here, though. First off, I want you to know that I didn't set that fire. I confess my first thought was that I'd have the field to myself for a little while, but I didn't do it, and I think it's terrible what happened to that young woman. My remark last night was callous, and totally inappropriate."

"You heard that little speech of Peter's at Les Oliviers."

"I did, and there is no question I was furious. Still am, in fact. I wanted to go down there and knock the jerk flat on his ass. But I am not a violent man, Lara, despite my temper. My idea of revenge is finding that ship before he does. I still intend to do that, and I've come to ask you for some help. We're really short-handed, and I'm wondering if you would consider helping us out tomorrow afternoon when we get back from the morning tour. Would you?"

"I'll think about it," I told him. "I'll let you know in the morning. In the meantime," I said, as Briars signaled for another drink, "if I were you, I'd get some sleep. I don't think a hangover is going to help you any."

"You're right," he said, canceling his drink order, and getting up to pay his bill. I, too, got up from my chair. "Lara," he said to me, "it's really important to me that you believe me, about the fire, I mean."

I looked at him for a moment, and then, without a word, turned and went up to my room. I didn't know what to say, because I couldn't decide whether I believed him or not.

"If you're interested," he called after me, "be at the pier at two o'clock."

The next day didn't get any better. That morning

we were exploring an old Byzantine fort north of Taberda. The views of the coastline from the ramparts were magnificent, although one had to dodge chickens and cows to get there, the space having been taken over by an enterprising farmer and his family. Still, it was worth the visit. The place was not as well maintained as it could have been, and we kept cautioning everyone to watch their step. There was one stage that was something of a bottleneck on the way down, and the group was milling about when there was a cry. Catherine tumbled down the broken steps, and lay in a heap at the bottom.

Everyone rushed over to her. She was breathless, and had a rather nasty scrape on one knee. Her wrist, too, was already swelling.

"I'm all right," she said, as she was helped to her feet.

"I'll get the first-aid kit in the bus," Jamila said, rushing away.

"We were told often enough to watch our step," Jimmy said to Betty.

"Oh hush, Jimmy," Betty replied. "Don't be so critical of everybody and everything."

Jimmy looked nonplused. "First time his wife has stood up to him, do you think?" Aziza said quietly.

"Could be," I replied. "I hope Catherine is all right. She hasn't been having much fun lately, has she?"

"I was pushed," she said to me a few minutes later, after the others had moved on and Jamila had taken care of the scrape and taped her wrist. "I did not fall."

"Who do you think pushed you?" I asked. *This is preposterous,* I thought. The woman was paranoid.

"I don't know," she said. "There was a whole bunch of us there, and I didn't see who it was, but I was definitely pushed. Susie was there," she said accusingly. "I think it was her."

"Catherine maintains she was pushed," I said to Jamila, taking her aside.

"What?" she exclaimed. "Do you think that woman is completely sane? Maybe she's embarrassed to admit she's none too steady on her feet."

"I don't know. Did you happen to see her fall?"

"Not really. There were a whole bunch of them milling about on that small landing. I was talking to Cliff and Emile when it happened, so if Catherine's story is true, which I very much doubt, then it wasn't one of them. I think Chastity and Marlene had already gone down. Other than that, it could have been any one of them."

"What about Susie? Where was she?"

"I think she was in the pileup of people, but I couldn't say whether she was right next to Catherine or not."

"Catherine thinks Susie is behind all this, because she's envious of Catherine's money. There's no question Susie worries about money, but I don't think she's the jealous type, somehow."

"I don't think so, either," Jamila said. "Nor do I think she's capable of such a thing. She's a contented little soul. I found her annoying at first. All those personal questions! But now I think she's really sweet."

"Okay, but let's assume for a moment these stories of Catherine's are true. I agree it's a stretch, but let's do it anyway. Who has it in for her? Has she inadvertently offended someone in the group that badly?"

"Not that I know of. I haven't heard any talk to that effect. Very puzzling."

"Keep your eyes and ears open, Jamila," I said. "And let me know what you hear." There was something very wrong with this group of people, but I had no idea what.

For instance, I had to decide whether or not to accept Briars' story. Having had a night to sleep on it, I decided I did. He had a temper, but other than some rather heated language, I'd never seen any indication that he'd be capable of arson.

"I'm going back to that dealer who tried to rip me off yesterday," Emile said when we got back to the auberge. "Do you want to come with me?"

"I'm sure that would be very entertaining, Emile, but Briars asked me to come out and give him a hand on his boat this afternoon, and I think I'm going to do that. It's rather pleasant out on the water. Do you want to come along? I don't expect the work will be very onerous."

"No," he replied. "My curiosity has been piqued. I'm going to have to go and see if he really does have something, although everything I know tells me he doesn't."

"Okay, I'll see you at dinner, then." I changed into my bathing suit, pulled shorts and a T-shirt over it, and headed for the pier.

"I can't tell you how much this means to me that you're here," Briars said, giving me a big hug. "Whether you meant it or not, I'm taking your presence as a vote of confidence in me, a sign that you don't think I had anything to do with the fire on the *Susannah*. It makes me feel as if everything is going to be all right."

"You can safely assume I wouldn't be here if I thought you'd done it," I said, and he beamed. He was an attractive man, with an open face, a lovely smile, and a rather good physique. His beard felt very nice against my cheek. There's nothing like an attractive man who's prepared to admit to some vulnerability to turn me weak at the knees. I thought I was outgrowing this tendency. Apparently not.

"Let's go," he said, untying the outboard. "The others are already out there. This will be our first dive of the day. We had to do some provisioning of both the house and the boat this morning. We'll only get a couple of dives in this afternoon, but it will be better than nothing. Khmais has gone home for the November seventh holiday, and Gus has come down with a whopper of a cold, so we're even more short-handed than usual. It's terrific you've come along. You can keep watch while we're diving, and help Hedi with stuff on the deck." He gave my hand an extra little squeeze as he helped me down into the boat.

"Reinforcements," he called as we pulled up, and Hedi flashed a grin.

"Okay, Ron, are you and I first?"

"Fine with me. I'm ready to go," Ron told him. "Hello again," he said to me, reaching over to shake my hand. In his early twenties, with dark brown hair and eyes, he had a pleasant, easygoing manner, relaxed with people and confident in what he was doing. I liked him.

"I didn't know you were a diver, Briars," I said. "I thought you were just the archaeologist on this job."

"What do you mean *just*?" he said. "I'm a marine archaeologist, that's what I am. I dive, and I do archaeology. Check the pressure in the tanks one more time, will you, Hedi?" he said, stripping to his trunks and starting to pull on his wetsuit. He was in pretty good shape for a guy his age, I'd have to say.

"Three thousand psi, all tanks," Hedi said. "You're ready to go. I've calculated the time you can be down, and Sandy's double-checked it. Are the stage bottles in place?"

"Yup," Ron said.

"What are stage bottles?" I asked.

"Two full tanks with regulators are attached to our anchor line about twenty feet down," Ron said. "It's just in case we need more decompression time than we have air. We can switch to the new tanks at twenty feet and stay there for a while until it's safe to surface."

"Ron thought he saw something yesterday we should check out," Sandy explained to me. "You know our scanning equipment isn't working, so we've been towing the divers behind the boat to have a look. There's a drop-off of several feet here. We've anchored close to the edge. It has a bit of an overhang, so we couldn't see too clearly. Visibility here is good, about seventy to ninety feet, but the overhang blocked the view. So Briars and Ron are going to do some wall diving. They'll go down the face of the drop-off and see what there is to see."

"How far down are they going?" I asked.

"Maybe a hundred fifty feet, max," she said. "We think there might be a ledge at about that depth. Okay, ready to go? Timers set?" she called to the two men. Both nodded and went over the side.

"Okay, now we keep a lookout," Sandy said. I kept my eyes riveted on two tracks of bubbles. Several minutes went by. "They'll be getting down there by now," Sandy said, checking her watch. "Should be at about a hundred ten, a hundred twenty feet by now. They'll only be able to stay down for a few minutes, then they'll start back up, stopping at various depths to decompress."

I found myself feeling nervous for them. I'm a good swimmer, life-guarded summers as a high school student, but there was something about going that far down with a little tank of air strapped to your back that made me feel uncomfortable.

Suddenly I saw first Ron and then Briars surface.

"Trouble," Sandy yelled. "Get them," she said, grabbing at my arm. "I'll get Ron, you get Briars."

I was over the side, shoes, clothes, and all, almost

without thinking, swimming as fast as I could for Briars. "Briars," I cried. "Say something!" But he didn't move. I slung my arm over his shoulder and across his chest and hauled him back to the boat as fast as I could. Hedi was already raising anchor and the engines were revving when Sandy and I reached the ladder. I tried to push Briars up on the deck, but he was too heavy, and it was all I could do to keep his head above water. Hedi rushed to help. It took a tremendous effort on everyone's part, Sandy and I pushing up from the water, and Hedi pulling as hard as he could from the boat, to get first Ron, then Briars, to the deck. "Briars is breathing," I gasped. "What'll I do?"

"Get him lying on his left side with his feet slightly higher than his head if you can," Hedi said. "We'll need to get him to a recompression chamber right away." Sandy helped me roll Briars into position.

"My God, my God," she kept saying, over and over. I turned to see Hedi doing CPR on Ron.

"We've got to get to shore," Hedi yelled. "Sandy, call for help. Lara, can you do CPR?"

"Yes," I said, kneeling beside Ron. "Get going."

One, two, three, four, five, I counted, pressing down on his chest. *Now breathe,* I told myself, pinching his nose and opening his mouth. *Breathe, one, two.* Again. One, two, three, four, five. Keep going, don't quit.

I checked his neck for a pulse. There wasn't one. Don't stop, I told myself again. Don't give up. And I didn't, as long as it took to get to shore, and the waiting medics. But I knew we were too late.

"I filled those tanks personally," Hedi said late that night at the hospital, his fists clenched tight. "I filled them last night so we'd be ready to go whenever Briars could get away."

"We don't know it was the tanks, Hedi," I said, soothingly.

"What else could it be if both of them got in trouble? And now Ron's dead! And Briars . . . What could have been wrong? I checked the pressure again this morning, and then one more time when Briars asked me to. Everything looked fine." He buried his head in his hands.

A doctor came over to us. "You may see Mr. Hatley now, but just for a few minutes."

"I can't talk to him," Hedi said. "This must be my fault. Please, you go."

Briars did not look good. He'd aged ten years in a few hours, and he no longer looked robust, just pale and ill. There didn't seem much point asking him how he felt, so I said nothing, just took his hand and held it.

He tried to smile. "Ron?" he said.

I shook my head, and he turned away from me. I squeezed his hand.

"What happened?" I asked at last.

"I don't know," he said. "Everything seemed to be going just fine. Then with no warning at all, at something over a hundred or a hundred twenty feet, I felt kind of strange: My mouth was tingling and there was a ringing in my ears. Then I could feel my face twitch. I looked over at Ron and realized he was in trouble, too. I signaled him to head for the surface. I nailed the power inflator for my buoyancy compensator to take me up fast, and that's all I remember. I must have blacked out almost immediately."

"Your tanks are being tested now," I said. "Hedi thinks it must have been his fault."

"I don't believe that," Briars said. "He is, if anything, overly cautious. He follows diving protocols to a fault. He checked the pressure in the tanks before we went in, and I know he filled the tanks personally from our own compressor."

"Maybe there was a bad mixture in the tanks? Some chemicals or something?"

"I don't know what that would be. We only use compressed air. We don't use nitrox or other mixtures because by and large we're working too deep for that. I just don't know what could have happened."

"Please, madame," the nurse said. "You should leave now."

Briars looked at me with red-rimmed eyes. "I'm going to have to call his family. I can't bring myself to do it. I can't do this again."

"Rest, Briars," I said. "We'll talk about this tomorrow."

"I'm almost certain it was an embolism that killed that young man," the doctor said. "We'll know for certain tomorrow."

"How could that happen?" I said to Hedi.

"Coming up too fast," Hedi replied.

"Then why didn't Briars have one? He's twenty-five years older than Ron."

"Doesn't matter. Briars probably lost consciousness right away. You're unlikely to have an embolism if you're unconscious. Maybe Ron stayed awake too long."

"Oxygen," the policeman, a man named Ahmed Ben Osman, said the next day. "Apparently that was the problem."

"I thought there was supposed to be oxygen in the tanks," I said, mystified.

"Quite so," Ben Osman said. "But not, apparently, in the quantity that was found. I'm not a diver, but according to an expert we called in, there was way too much oxygen, more than forty-five percent," he added, checking his notes.

"How much is there supposed to be?" I asked.

"About twenty-one percent," Hedi said. "Twenty-one percent oxygen, seventy-nine percent nitrogen."

"Quite so," Ben Osman repeated. "I am told—again, I am not the expert—that at the depths that Mr. Todd and Mr. Hatley were working, this much oxygen is as good as poison. Very little warning of a problem, either."

"So why was there too much oxygen in them?" I said.

"A very good question, Madame McClintoch, and one to which I would like the answer myself," Ben Osman said.

"I don't know how it would have happened. We could check the compressor . . ." Hedi said.

"We are doing that," the policeman said.

"I know that when I tested the mixture after I filled the tanks, everything was okay. That means that the problem occurred after that, overnight. I am really very careful about this, Lara," he said miserably. "I hope you believe me."

"I know you are, Hedi," I said. "Briars does, too. So let's talk about how someone else could have tampered with the tanks overnight. Is it possible to put too much oxygen in the tanks?"

"Sure. I suppose someone could have just let some of the compressed air out of the tanks, take them down to say, a thousand or twelve hundred psi, and then fill them up again with straight oxygen. The pressure would look okay when I tested it."

"Would that be hard to do? Put the oxygen into the tanks? I mean, *I* wouldn't know how to do it."

"I think it is fair to say most people wouldn't know how to do this," Ben Osman said, looking at Hedi.

"Not difficult, no," Hedi said. "You would need the right equipment, and you'd have to get it out to the boat. We leave the boat at anchor, and come in and out on the outboard. It's cheaper than paying the marina fees. But if you had the equipment, it would be easy enough to do."

"So the pressure would look the same, but the contents of the tanks would be different."

"That's right. And there'd be no odor or anything that would warn the divers there was a problem. You wouldn't even notice it until you got down pretty deep. It would have no effect in those proportions until you got down to maybe a hundred twenty feet."

"That's just about where Briars said he was when he realized he was in trouble."

"This is all very interesting," Ben Osman said. "I suppose it could have been an accident, someone making a very bad mistake, or, and personally I think this more likely, it could be the latest strike in a war between two parties looking for treasure. First, the boat belonging to one of these parties is damaged. The head of this particular expedition blames the other. Several people hear his threats. Then, two days ago, the ship belonging to the other party catches fire. Someone who has the misfortune of being on it, is seriously injured. Yesterday, the scuba tanks belonging to the first group in this dispute, are tampered with. One person is injured, another dies. An eye for an eye, perhaps, but rather upping the ante each time, if that is the correct expression, are we not? You may go now," he said. "We are finished here for the moment. Please send in the next person as you leave."

The next person, as it turned out, was a stocky man with graying hair, a paunch, and a ruddy complexion, in a blue shirt with a star logo. He'd been sitting with his head in his hands as we came out, but looked up at us. He had blood-shot eyes, and his hands were shaking. "You're next, Peter Groves," I said, pointing to the door.

9

W<small>HY DID MEN TAKE OTHERS' LIVES IN THIS WAY,</small> *Hasdrubal wondered, not during the heat of battle, nor from a careless act, but in a cold and calculating manner? Greed, perhaps. No doubt many had died to enrich others, and Mago was not, he thought, above such covetousness, nor moreover, incapable of such a deed. And Safat. Never one to come up with an original idea, yet he could almost certainly be talked into such an undertaking. Love? Yes, perhaps as strong a motive, under certain circumstances, as greed. That would point to Malchus, but only, as far as he knew, where Abdelmelqart was concerned. For Baalhanno, he knew of nothing that would have incited such rage. What else? Revenge. Now there was an obsession that ate at the psyche. Was there someone on the ship who burned for retribution? But surely revenge was linked to the other two. When it came right down to it, were there impulses other than greed and love, in all their aspects, that were powerful enough to warp the human soul? How little he knew, really, about the people on his ship. He'd have to think very carefully, listen attentively to what people said, to see if he could find the viper in their midst. He'd talk to the boy again.*

"Does this meet your expectations, monsieur?" the proprietor asked. "Small, I know, but gold. Pure gold."

Emile turned the coin over in his gloved hand and applied the magnifying glass to it once more.

"Not bad," he said. "I will pay you two thousand U.S. dollars for it."

"That is satisfactory. Would you like more than one of them?" the man said, smiling.

"Are there more?" Emile asked.

"Possibly," the man replied.

"And how many more might there possibly be?" Emile said.

"How many more do you want?" the man said, a sly expression crossing his face.

Emile slammed his fist down on the counter. "Answer the question!" he said.

The proprietor started to sweat. "Three, perhaps four."

"Where did you get them?"

The man hesitated for a moment, and licked his lips nervously.

"Where did you get them?" Emile said again. His voice was deadly quiet.

"I have my sources," the man said.

"I will pay you one thousand each for four of them, and only if you sell all that you have to me."

"But, monsieur," the man said. "You offered two thousand dollars. You must pay me two thousand dollars each."

"One thousand each," Emile repeated, and wrote something down on a piece of paper. "You can reach me at L'Auberge du Palmier," he said, handing the man the slip of paper. "I will only be here for a few more days."

"Monsieur," the proprietor said, looking pained. "I am not the expert in numismatics you are, of course. But I have books—" He gestured to a dog-eared row of catalogues behind him. "I know there are very, very few of these coins in existence. This coin is very rare, and worth more than one thousand dollars."

"Not anymore," Emile said. The man looked perplexed. "Think about it," Emile said softly.

"I hate being ripped off," he said to me as we left. "Particularly by amateurs."

"I gather, though, that this fellow is more interesting to you than the last one," I remarked.

"Somewhat," he said. "Now let's try to find those tables you need."

My EXPERIENCE OF GROUP TRAVEL, LIMITED THOUGH it may be, is that there comes a point in every tour where the members of the group begin to feel like old friends. Bonding, I think the psychologists would call it. Perhaps it's just from being so far from home and their real friends, or maybe it's the mutual attraction of like-minded people in a very different—and perhaps threatening, just because it's so different—part of the world. Whatever the reason, they begin to tell each other things about themselves that I am convinced they would never share with such relatively casual acquaintances at home. I could see it happening in my group. But troubled by my suspicions and traumatized by the dreadful happenings of the day before, I did not want to be close to any of them, and felt their confidences something to be endured rather than enjoyed. Indeed, by midafternoon of the day after the diving incident, I was rather uncharitably beginning to feel as if there were a flashing neon sign over my head, visible to everyone but me, that said The Doctor Is In."

First up for a little therapy was Cliff Fielding.

"Lara, I wonder if I might trouble you for a favor," he said, his voice barely rising above a whisper. "I'd appreciate your advice in finding a gift for my daughter. I don't like to ask Nora, you know, and of course, you're so knowledgable about what to buy here."

"I'd be glad to help," I said, setting aside the paperwork I was doing at a poolside table. "Are you thinking of something in particular?"

"No, but something special. Different. Something you couldn't get at home. It doesn't matter how much it costs."

"Okay, tell me about your daughter."

"Gerry's on her own now, divorced. No children. She's a dentist. Takes after her old man," he said proudly.

"Does she have hobbies?" I wasn't sure I could think of gifts with a dentist theme right off the top of my head.

"Oh, yes," Cliff said. "She loves the arts. She's very active in an amateur theater company. They do wonderful productions for kids. She helps paint the scenery, does the makeup, and even ushers in the kids for the performances."

"What does her home look like?"

"What do you mean?"

"Does she have traditional furniture or modern? Does she collect anything special?"

"I don't know what you'd call her furniture," he said. "Kind of a mixture. She has a leather-and-wood dining room set she got on a trip to Mexico. I know she loves that. She has some African carvings, and she likes those done by the Inuit in the Arctic, too. I'm not being very helpful, am I?"

"Sure you are. I have a couple of suggestions. First of all, most women like the silver jewelry here, particularly the kind with the Berber beads. If your daughter likes African and Inuit art, she'd probably like that. Chastity has a necklace. I don't know if you've seen it."

"Oh, yes, I could hardly miss it. She's been showing it off to everybody. She's rather, er, sophisticated, for her age, isn't she?"

I tried not to smile. Then I had the most wonderful idea, the one I'd been waiting for ever since I'd arrived. "My other suggestion, if you're serious about getting something really different, is a puppet. I don't mean the soldier puppets you see hanging in all the gift shops around here. Do you know the ones I mean? They're made of wood, faces painted, often with handlebar mustaches, and they have metal swords and boots, and shields. The ones displayed in the tourist shops are often rather crudely made. But if we could find one of the old puppets, the ones that were used in the French marionette theater here sixty, eighty years ago, that would be quite wonderful. They display beautifully, and they're really unusual. Not inexpensive, though." They would also be absolutely perfect, in my film star client's Rosedale home, exactly the kind of *objet d'art* that would really make the difference. Why hadn't I thought of it before? I could hardly wait to set off looking for them.

"Price doesn't matter," he said. "That sounds just perfect. It fits in with her love of theater perfectly. Do you think you could find one for me?"

"I'll try. I know a couple of dealers around here now, and I'll ask them. I think I might also get at least one or two for my shop. I'll find what I can, and you can have a look. If you see one you like, it's yours. And if not, I've already purchased some very attractive jewelry that can be our fallback."

"Would it be very big?" he said hesitantly.

"Heavy, you mean? Not very."

"No, big. A large parcel."

Good grief, I thought. Not only does he not want Nora to buy this gift for his daughter, he doesn't even want her to know he bought one. "Tell you what," I said, "if I can find a puppet you like, why don't I get it packed up and shipped with the others going to my shop. It should arrive there about a week after I get back. You can go and buy a nice card and write a note to your daughter, give me the note and her address, and when I get back, I'll courier it to her. I'll also gift wrap it if you'd like."

"You wouldn't mind?" he said, looking relieved.

"It would be my pleasure," I told him. He positively beamed, and had his wallet out in a flash, pressing money on me.

"It's okay, Cliff," I said. "Let's see what I can find, and if you like it, we'll settle up then."

"I'll pay for the courier, too, but can this be our little secret?" he asked.

"Certainly," I assured him. "Now you go and get a card. They have lovely ones with either photographs or sketches of Taberda. That might be nice. Give Gerry an idea where the gift came from."

"Thank you," he said. "I don't want you to think I'm sneaking about here, though. Nora is a wonderful woman. I don't know if you've heard this, but she looked after my wife, Annie, when she was dying of cancer. I don't know what we would have done without her. And then, when I had a heart attack after Annie died, she looked after me, too. I don't want to appear ungrateful. This trip, actually, is a little thank-you for everything she's done. She's always wanted to go to Tunisia. I figured that out from things she said, and arranged the trip as a little surprise for her. She's been

wonderful. It's just that Nora and Gerry don't get along
at all. They had words, you know, after Annie died.
I'm not sure what it was all about, but they don't speak.
I haven't seen Gerry in months, and don't get to talk
to her as much as I'd like to. I'd like to send her something really special. I just don't want Nora to know
about it, that's the plain truth. She has very definite
ideas of what's good for me and what's not, and I'm
sure she's right. I think she feels Gerry gets me upset,
which sometimes she does."

"Don't worry, Cliff," I said. "This is between the
two of us. We'll get something really nice for your
daughter."

"It's just that sometimes I feel as if I'd like to be
on my own," he went on. "Oh dear, there I go sounding
ungrateful again. Thank you," he said again. "This is
really wonderful."

"What's wonderful?" Nora Winslow said, unexpect-
edly coming upon us. Cliff stood for a moment, his
mouth opening and closing.

"The view," I said, gesturing across the gardens to
the town and the coast below it. "It seems particularly
clear today, doesn't it? I was telling Cliff I thought I'd
found the best place of all to enjoy it."

"I suppose so," Nora said, looking where I was
pointing.

"Cliff was telling me you've always wanted to come
to Tunisia," I said. "I hope you're seeing everything
you would like to."

Nora looked at Cliff and then at me, with a rather
startled expression, as if dismayed by the idea we'd
been talking about her. "Yes, thank you," she said.
"Now, Cliff, you should be resting. Come along."

"Yes, Nora," he said. "You're right as usual." I
watched the two of them walk slowly away, Nora with
her arm protectively on his. Cliff didn't look back, but

Nora turned back to me, pausing for a moment to let Cliff move on ahead.

"It is very beautiful here, more than I thought," she said. "I wish I could enjoy it." I watched them walk away, wondering what sort of warped sense of duty made her stay by his side every moment, and what perverse sense of loyalty kept him with her. It was one of the saddest comments I'd heard so far.

Next up for a visit with the doctor, was Briars. I went to see him in hospital. He was sitting up, and the nurse assured me he'd be able to leave the next morning. That news, however, did not appear to cheer him up. He sat silently as I chattered away to him on whatever neutral subjects I could come up with, until I decided I should just leave him alone.

"Don't go, Lara, please," he said, when I announced my departure. "I know I'm not a brilliant conversationalist today, but I'm really glad to have your company. I'm just dreading having to call Ron's parents. I know I have to do it, but it makes me ill to think of it."

"Maybe you should leave it for a few days," I said. "I've talked to the embassy, and they've contacted Mr. and Mrs. Todd. His body is being shipped back home tomorrow morning."

"Are they coming over here?" he asked.

"I don't think so. I gather Ron's father has MS, and would have difficulty traveling. The U.S. embassy is helping the family look after the arrangements."

"I've had to do this before," Briars said. "When that young man Mark . . ."

"I know, Briars. You told me about it. You don't have to go over it again."

"I've been thinking about it a lot, today," he said. "I think maybe that was what ended my marriage. It didn't seem like it at the time. I flew home a few weeks later, called Mark's father, then went back to teaching.

But a few months later, right about when I'd be going back to Tunisia for another summer of diving, were it not for the fact that Peter and I had fallen out, I went into a tailspin. I didn't attribute it to the previous summer until today. Stupid, I know, but it just never occurred to me until this moment that it was the terrible accident that caused it. I drank too much, was horrible to my wife and sons, quarreled with my colleagues and even the head of the department, which is a particularly dumb thing to do if you want to get ahead in academia. Finally Emily, that's my wife, told me to get out. My colleagues said I'd better take a break, or I'd probably be out of the university, too. This revelation has come as something of a shock. As you have no doubt already guessed, I'm not a terribly introspective kind of person."

"Sounds like the average man to me," I said, trying to lighten the conversation up a little.

He smiled ever so slightly. "I have a feeling you and Emily would get along."

"You've said that before. Maybe you should call her."

"She threw me out, remember."

"You don't seem to be drinking excessively, at least as far as I have seen, nor do you strike me as a difficult person anymore, if that was the problem."

"I've been trying to straighten myself out," he said. "But I think as far as my marriage is concerned, it's too late." He paused for a moment. "I have a question to ask you, and I'd really appreciate an honest answer. Do you think I'm turning into another Peter Groves? Have I become so obsessed with finding this miserable shipwreck that I'm risking young people's lives, ruining my marriage, destroying any chance I have at my job? Please tell me the truth."

"Briars, I don't know you very well, but I don't

think so. After all, those tanks were deliberately tampered with, weren't they? It's Groves the police are talking to now. It wasn't a case of you sending Ron down under dangerous conditions. You went down with him. Is a shipwreck, no matter how old, worth the loss of a life? No, it isn't. But that's a different question entirely."

"Should I have known, after the fire on the *Susannah,* that something like this was inevitable?"

"I guess that depends on whether you think Peter Groves, in a vengeful mood, is the one who tampered with the tanks, and, if you'll forgive me for saying it, whether or not you set, or arranged to have set, the fire on Peter's ship, and in so doing escalated the conflict."

"I had nothing whatsoever to do with the fire on Peter's ship, although he no doubt thinks I did. As to whether or not he tampered with the tanks, I wouldn't have thought he'd do such a thing. He'd run the risk of killing his own daughter, wouldn't he? They may be estranged, but it's quite a different thing to do something that might get your child killed."

I had a horrible thought. "Did Sandy ask not to dive yesterday?"

"No. We drew lots. Why? Oh, I see what you're getting at. I have great faith in Sandy."

"Okay, just asking."

"To get back to your earlier question: I wouldn't have put Peter down for such a terrible act, but the truth of the matter is, I can't think of anybody else."

My next therapy patient was Marlene. "That daughter of mine!" she exclaimed. "She's just impossible. She won't do anything I tell her. The way she's carrying on! Lighting those matches and everything. It's been so hard since her father left. And she's pestering Emile all the time, follows him everywhere he goes. She's gone into town now to see what he's doing. I can't stop her. The poor man is getting quite embarrassed about it. I'm just trying to get my life straightened out."

Was it that Emile was embarrassed about it, or that Marlene didn't like the competition from her daughter?

"It's her father. Walking out on us like that. Men are all alike, don't you think? Bastards, just like her father. He takes up with a bimbo who is barely older than Chastity and whose IQ is roughly the same as my bra size. And you know what, Chastity blames me for it, can you believe it?"

"I think that happens a lot with mothers and teenage daughters," I said. "I'm sure she'll get over it." Actually I wasn't sure at all. I just didn't know what to say to this woman who was baring her soul to me. "Why don't you try talking to her about all of these things?"

"I can't," she said. "She won't talk to me. Maybe you could say something to her?" she said, brightening. "She thinks you're great."

"That's nice," I said. "But I think you and she need to talk, Marlene."

She sighed. "I'll try. Maybe we can talk about this again."

Who's next? I wondered.

"Lara," Sylvie said. "I have a matter of some delicacy to discuss with you. Do you mind coming into the office for just a minute?"

"I'll be happy to," I said. "Delicate discussions are something I feel I'm gaining more and more experience with by the hour." She looked perplexed for a moment, poured me a cup of tea, and after briefly discussing the weather, sidled into a rant about the hotel business.

"It's not an easy business, Lara," she said. "We aren't like the big hotels that can handle planeloads of German tourists coming in every week. We rely a lot on word of mouth. Also we're small, but we still require plenty of staff to maintain standards. Not having our best suite in use for a few weeks is a real problem for us. Sometimes I wonder why Chantal and I came back. We don't own the hotel anymore, just run it for Khelifa. He's good to us, of course, but at times like this I think of going back to France and starting over again. Paris is so beautiful, and the south of France has a Mediterranean climate. It's not North Africa, but . . ."

Was there something in the air, I wondered, that was making everybody around me so introspective, and worse than that, so talkative? All these people getting in touch with their inner selves and then feeling compelled to share their feelings with me! When times are bad, I confess I take the opposite approach. I throw myself into my work and try not to think or talk about these kinds of things at all. This undoubtedly makes me a shallow person, but sometimes I think that's preferable to all this slobbering about. "Is there something specific that's bothering you that I could help with, Sylvie?" I said finally.

She handed me a piece of paper, a rather long list of phone numbers and charges. "Mme. Ellingham's phone bill," she said. "I am wondering who will pay for it. You know long distance charges here are very high."

"I guess I'll cover it, Sylvie," I replied. "How much is it?"

"Well, if you are paying it, I wouldn't add the hotel surcharge, of course, but even then, at just our cost, it is considerable. A few hundred dollars, in fact."

"My word!" I said. "Did she talk and drink gin at the same time?"

"Not exactly," Sylvie said. "She usually telephoned in the afternoon when she got back from whatever excursion you were on. But as you can see, she made a lot of calls, and some rather long ones at that. Then she drank."

"Okay," I sighed. "Add it to my bill. Can I keep

this list as a receipt? I may try and collect it somehow, from her estate or something. It will be easier for me to do it from home, than for you to try."

"Of course," she said. "Let me make a copy for our records here. And thank you for this, Lara. We really appreciate it."

"What about Rick Reynolds? His phone bill must have been pretty spectacular, too. We might as well settle up on that one, while we're at it."

"He didn't make any calls," Sylvie said.

"You're joking. He was always rushing back to his room to call his office to check on the stock market. At least that's what he told us—*ad nauseum,* I'm sure Ben would say if he were here."

"If he did, it wasn't on our telephone. There wasn't a single long distance call, nor a local one, for that matter."

This was perplexing. "Oh, but there was a call for you while you were out," Sylvie said. "I almost forgot. He said it was urgent. A M. Loo, loo . . ."

"Luczka," I said, pronouncing it Loochka. "Thanks. I'll give him a call." It was Rob's work number, I noticed, as I headed up to my room to phone.

"LARA," ROB SAID. "I'M REALLY GLAD TO HEAR FROM you. Look, after you called the other day, I got to thinking about those questions you asked me. I made a couple of inquiries. This situation may be worse than you thought."

"That would hardly be possible," I muttered.

"I checked to see if an autopsy had been done back here on Rick Reynolds. It was, and the results are disturbing. He didn't dive into that pool, Lara. His injuries are not consistent with that kind of accident. I'd be expecting a broken neck in that case, as I told you when you called. His neck is fine. But there is evidence of bruising and swelling on the back of his head—in other words, he sustained a blow to the head. Now the blow wasn't enough to kill him, maybe, but if he was dumped into the pool unconscious, then he would drown. He did drown, by the way; there was a fair amount of water in his lungs."

"You're saying he was murdered," I said.

"Not necessarily, I suppose," he replied. "He could have fallen—you know how slippery those pool areas can be—and hit his head on something. The top of the ladder, maybe. He then could just have rolled into the pool and drowned. But he'd have to have given himself an awful whack on the head not to come to when he hit the water. I think there's enough here to warrant a second look. I'm trying to see if we can reopen this one."

"Thanks for letting me know," I said.

"Wait, that's not all," he said. "Based on the autopsy on Reynolds, I made a couple of calls to some law enforcement contacts I have in the U.S. Kristi Ellingham died of smoke inhalation, just as you said. However, she was just loaded with alcohol and sedatives, not enough to kill her either, but enough to knock her out cold. She could have ingested them willingly or accidentally, but given the other situation, I think we have to assume there's at least a small possibility that somebody else gave the stuff to her."

"You mean somebody saw to it she was out, and then set the fire?"

"I know it sounds far-fetched. Do you know her drinking habits?"

"I certainly do. Gin, lots of it."

"Well, then, maybe I'm overreacting. Ever see her take pills?"

"No, but that doesn't mean anything."

"I suppose the one thing I can say for certain, then,

is that regardless of how the pills and alcohol got into her, she didn't stand a chance of waking up and getting out of there when the fire started. You be careful, Lara. I think you should just get on a plane and come home right now."

"I can't do that, Rob," I said. "I have responsibilities here. What would they say about McClintoch and Swain, if I just packed up and left? What would these people do?"

"Please be very careful, then," he said. "I'm going to see what I can do from here."

"Thanks, Rob," I said. "I will be careful. Goodbye."

"Lara," he said. "Don't hang up. About this other thing, the other morning when you called. Can we talk about it?"

"No," I said. "Goodbye, Rob." I'd had quite enough handwringing confessions for one day.

Later, now burdened more than ever by suspicion and implied threat, I tried very hard not to find myself alone with any one person during the cocktail and dinner hour. Alas, I was not entirely successful.

"It's started again," Catherine said, cornering me by the staircase. "Someone's been into my belongings, again. I want to go home. You have to help me get out of here."

"Okay, Catherine," I said, as a wave of irritation swept over me. "There's nothing I can do this late tonight. We'll talk about it again tomorrow morning, and if you still want to leave, I'll see what I can do." She sobbed, and then ran upstairs to her room. Following her, I heard the safety chain slide into place, and then a scraping sound as what I assumed was a large piece of furniture was moved against the door.

Realizing rather belatedly that the events of the last couple of days had thrown me into a vile and unkind mood, I, too, headed for my room just as soon as I could.

The trouble was, I couldn't sleep. The truth, when I'd calmed down enough to consider it, was that despite all my efforts that day to persuade myself otherwise, I was growing rather fond of my little band of travelers, foibles and all. The responsibility I felt for them, as the leader of the tour, had begun to weigh heavily on me. I had some serious agonizing to do after the conversation with Rob, on the subject of what to do about the rest of the tour. It had been all very well to carry on when there was nothing more substantial than a bad dream of mine to indicate we might have a problem. It was quite another to continue when Rob thought there was enough evidence to reopen the investigation into Rick's death and possibly even Kristi's as well. Should we just keep going, as if nothing had changed, or should I pack everybody up and send them home before somebody else got murdered, no matter what Clive thought?

I needn't have lost any sleep over any of it. In the end, the matter was out of my hands entirely.

10

"YOU MUST TELL ME ONCE MORE EXACTLY WHAT *you have seen, Carthalon," Hasdrubal said, "that we may reach some conclusions. You observe well, but that in itself is not enough. One must interpret what he sees. You are young, but you will learn. So you hid in the cargo hold, and then . . ."*

"I saw Mago, Safat, and Malchus all come down into the hold."

"Together?"

"No. Malchus came first, but soon he was joined by the others. They talked of checking that the cargo was stable. The storm. All three left together. I was leaving my hiding place to check on the ingot, when I heard someone else coming. It was Mago, again. I don't like Mago."

"He is difficult to like," Hasdrubal said. "So both Malchus and Mago were down there alone. Go on. What did he do?"

"He checked the cargo one more time. He opened an amphora of coins, and a pithos which contained very

beautiful gold jewelry. I thought he was going to steal the coins or the gold, but he didn't, at least I don't think he did. He held a beautiful necklace of gold and lapis lazuli up to the light from above the hold, but then he put it back in the pithos. The coins, too, he returned. I checked the seals on these containers, and they had been resealed. The silver ingot was back in its place, but I regret I did not know which one had left it."

"And how do you interpret what you saw, Carthalon?"

"Perhaps the seal on the amphora and the pithos was broken or defective, and he was repairing them so that they might come to no damage in the storm," Carthalon said doubtfully.

"That is one possible interpretation of what you have seen," Hasdrubal said. "But not, I think, the most likely."

"AH, MADAME MCCLINTOCH," AHMED BEN Osman said, gesturing to a chair. "I thank you for taking the time to come and see me again." My visit to the police station was in no way voluntary, but I decided to regard it as a good sign that Ben Osman was being so polite about it. I set my carry-on bag to one side, and sat down.

"I have been asked by my superiors to have another look at the circumstances surrounding the death of Rick Reynolds. Apparently the Canadian authorities feel that the local police force was not as diligent, perhaps, as they should have been in investigating the death. You may know this already. The matter has now been referred to the National Guard, specifically to me.

"I have asked you here for two reasons. First of all, would you indulge me by recounting again the events leading up to your discovery of the body of Rick Reynolds?"

"Of course. Where should I start? That morning?"

"That will be satisfactory. Tell me all you did, whom you saw, and then exactly the disposition of the body when you found it. I will be taping this if you don't mind," he said. Not waiting for a reply, he pushed the Record button.

I told him about the people I'd seen in the lounge when I went out, about talking briefly to Briars and Hedi, meeting Aziza, then seeing Nora jogging, and talking to Susie. I left nothing out. Except, of course, my ill-considered toss of Kristi's notebook into the bushes. That would have required far too much of an explanation, and I couldn't see that it was relevant. At least that's what I told myself. He made no comment until I came to the part about finding the body.

"There was a kind of haze of blood in the water over his head," I said.

"And the wound? Did you see the wound?"

"I would say it was on the back of his head," I replied.

Ben Osman riffled through some papers on his desk. "That would be consistent with the autopsy findings, yes," he said.

"So I gather you don't get that kind of wound diving into the shallow end of the pool," I said.

"Apparently not. Mr. Reynolds died from drowning, but he also sustained a blow to the back of the head. He was hit with something, then most likely tossed into the pool. Unfortunately the whole pool area has been cleaned several times since, no doubt. Any evidence that might have been there will be long gone."

I reached for my carry-on bag, and started to open it.

"I trust you were searched before you came in," Ben Osman said.

"No," I said.

"No! Then I sincerely hope you don't have a weapon in there."

"Not in the way you're thinking," I said. "You are quite safe with me."

"There is a message here from the Royal Canadian Mounted Police attesting to your good character," Ben Osman said.

Rob did have his good points, even if he was a philandering cad. "So is it okay if I open this bag?"

"I suppose so," he sighed.

"There," I said, laying the croquet mallet out on his desk.

"What is this?" he said.

"A croquet mallet," I said. I felt a surge of relief now that I'd handed it over.

"Ah," he said. "A vestige of European colonialism. Do you want to play croquet?"

"No, I want you to analyze the little bit of blood and hair on it," I replied.

"Ah, I see," he said, peering at the mallet. "You touched this, several times, no doubt," he said severely.

"The handle, yes. Several of us did," I said. "I didn't see any point in worrying about fingerprints anymore."

"Are you going to tell me how you came upon this?" he asked.

"Yes, of course. I have to warn you it sounds improbable, but it is the truth." Then I told him about Catherine, the theft of her necklace and the complaints about someone messing about in her stuff, and how she'd showed me the mallet in her luggage. "She even says someone pushed her down a flight of stairs."

"This woman is quite, uh, well, is she?" Ben Osman said.

"She's very high-strung," I replied. "But have I seen any signs of rampant insanity? No. And her necklace was stolen, we know that. I was able to buy it back from a dealer in the Souk des Orfevres in Tunis."

"Do you have any suspects in mind for this theft?"

"I know who stole it," I replied. "It was Rick Reynolds."

"You blame a dead man? This might be difficult to prove, would it not?"

"Oh, I can prove it," I said. "I couldn't until this morning, but now I can. You see I'm in Rick's former room at the auberge. When Catherine wanted to have her own room, she got mine, and I moved into Rick's. The drawer in the bathroom, the one with the hair dryer in it, has been sticking. It doesn't open and close smoothly. I was in a rush this morning, so I gave it a real yank, and what do you know, out pops this piece of paper." I laid it in front of him. "It's a receipt. Rick signed here for the money in return for the necklace." There'd been something else with it, a note in Kristi's handwriting, suggesting that Rick and she needed to have a little chat. I wasn't going to mention that just yet. After all, Rick didn't kill her, because he was already dead. I couldn't help but wonder, however, how many of the others on her list had received a similar note.

"You can't prove this is for Mme. Anderson's necklace, can you? People do buy and sell lots of jewelry in the Souk des Orfevres."

"Maybe I can't prove it conclusively, but the circumstantial evidence is pretty convincing. First of all, I saw Rick leaving the store. That's why I went in there. The necklace was still sitting on the counter. Secondly," I said, placing another piece of paper in front of Ben Osman, "this is my receipt for buying the necklace. See, same store, same date—I'd say the same handwriting. The proprietor has even described the necklace in the same way."

"The price is quite different," he said, smiling. "Either M. Reynolds did not receive a good price for it, or you paid too much."

"I noticed that," I said. "Irritating, of course. Actually, I got the necklace for a reasonably good price. Rick was either a very poor bargainer, or he was desperate for money."

"So Mme. Anderson realizes Rick stole the necklace and hits him very hard, twice in fact, with a croquet mallet to punish him?"

"Unlikely," I said. "I certainly didn't tell her my suspicions, because that was all they were."

"You told other people?"

"No one," I said. "Except my business partner. But he's back home. Have you heard anything about Kristi Ellingham's autopsy?" While I was having a hard time thinking why anyone would want to murder Rick, I thought Kristi had been practically crying out for it, if anyone else knew about her list.

"No. Am I going to?"

"I don't know. Apparently she had a lot of alcohol and sedatives in her blood."

"You mean she tried to kill herself, or no, you're surmising that someone drugged her and then set fire to the mattress. Rather far-fetched, don't you think?"

"Probably."

"Now I have something else to discuss with you," he said, dismissing my ruminations. "What I require from you is assurance that neither you, nor any member of your party, will leave the country without my permission."

"Yes."

"Yes, what?" he said.

"Yes, I promise that neither I nor any of the members of the tour presently here will leave the country before the tour is over without telling you about it," I said, choosing my words very carefully.

"Why do I feel that your words are—what is the word I am looking for in English?—is it 'elusive'?"

" 'Evasive' might be better," I said. "Or even 'misleading.' "

"Now why would you wish to mislead me, Madame McClintoch?" he said, with a slight smile.

"I'm not trying to do that. I'm attempting to be absolutely accurate. In the first place, the tour ends in six days. I have absolutely no control over these people after that, if I have any control over them now. What would I say? The tour is over, but you can't leave, and by the way, you're on your own for your expenses after this? At the end of the tour, if you don't want them to leave, you're going to have to tell them, not me." We stared across the desk at each other for a few moments.

"You said in the first place. Is there a second place?" he asked, breaking the silence.

"There is a small problem. One of our party is gone. I think she has left for home already."

"And she is?" he said, checking the list again.

"Catherine Anderson."

"Not the one with the croquet mallet!" he exclaimed.

"I'm afraid so."

"Then where is she?" he said. "When did she leave?" He looked annoyed now.

"I don't really know. She checked out of the hotel very early this morning, paid her incidental charges, and asked them to call her a taxi. They tried to reach me, but I guess I was in the shower when they called, because I didn't hear the phone. By the time they got me, she was gone. She was very upset last night. She said that the problem with her clothes, you know, someone moving her belongings around and so on, had started again, even though we'd changed her room, and that she wanted my help to go home immediately. I was in a bad mood yesterday, and although I told her I'd help her today, I know I didn't sound sympathetic enough. She was genuinely frightened, I realized later. She was moving furniture to block her door. In any event, she seems to have taken matters into her own hands, and taken off."

"Did she leave a note for you or anything?"

"No."

"What do you think she would do?"

"Assuming she was serious about wanting to go home, I think she'd go straight to the airport. Either Monastir, to get a flight to Tunis or even somewhere in Europe, or by taxi right to the international airport in Tunis. I think she'd try and get on the first flight out of here that was going anywhere that would get her home. My guess would be, since she has a return ticket on Lufthansa via Frankfurt, that she would exchange that ticket, pay whatever penalty there is, and if there was a seat on the flight out early this afternoon, she'd be on it."

Ben Osman picked up the telephone, spoke rapidly in Arabic, then slammed the receiver down. "We'll see about that," he said.

I looked at my watch. "She may be on her way, by now."

"Then we'll have to get her back."

"I wouldn't worry about it," I said. "I don't think she killed anybody."

"That may or may not be the case, but she's the closest thing to a suspect we have. This is damned inconvenient," he said. "Let me make one thing very clear to you, madame. I will solve this case. The Ministry of Tourism has also expressed an interest in this matter. Needless to say, they do not wish this investigation to harm the tourism industry in this country in any way. Quite frankly, we would all prefer that M. Reynolds' death was an accident, due to his own negligence.

However, I am determined that if he met his death as a result of foul play, then the perpetrator will be brought to justice. If that requires keeping your group here after the tour is over and antagonizing the Ministry of Tourism, then so be it."

"Who's going to pay for their expenses, hotel bills and everything in that case?"

"We are not," he said firmly. "You may go now."

"WHAT ARE YOU TRYING TO TELL ME, LARA?" Clive bellowed.

"You don't have to shout, Clive. The line is quite clear. What I'm saying is that if the police don't find out who killed Rick Reynolds in six days, then our group is going to find itself under house arrest, so to speak. We won't be able to leave the country."

"This is a disaster!" he exclaimed. "Our worst nightmare. We'll be ruined. We'll be on every newscast. Everybody in the whole world will know about the catastrophe called the McClintoch and Swain tour."

"I thought you told me there's no such thing as bad publicity, Clive," I reminded him.

"That is unkind, Lara," he said.

"You're right. I'm sorry."

"Who'll pay their expenses if they have to stay longer?"

"The police have made it pretty clear they won't."

"This is even worse than I thought," he said. "A financial disaster as well."

"Yes," I said. "It may well be."

"Six days!" Clive repeated.

"I'm afraid so."

"Do something, Lara," he said, as he hung up the phone.

Do something, I muttered over and over to myself.

Six days, I told myself: *Think, and think fast.* Irritating though Clive might be—and who could know better than I what self-reproach and regret lay beneath his peremptory tone?—I knew he was right. I had to do something. Nobody else would, or could. *Focus,* I said. That, I decided, meant putting Briars and the shipwreck and the terrible events associated with them, totally out of my mind. There was no reason that I could think of, other than that I rather liked Briars, to get myself involved in what appeared to be, whatever the truth of the matter, a fight to the death, literally, over a two-thousand-year-old shipwreck. Let the police seesaw back and forth between Briars and Groves, questioning each about what had happened to the other one's boat. I had McClintoch & Swain to worry about.

For a minute or two I tried to convince myself that some outside menace was responsible for what had happened to Rick and possibly Kristi, but it didn't work. There were no other guests in the hotel; the staff had not shown any previous inclination to kill off the tourists, and I couldn't think of any reason why they'd start with my troop; and there was no question that at least one or two of our team members had been behaving in a manner that was peculiar at best.

Given that, after a period of reasonably quiet contemplation I reached one conclusion, which was that I perhaps had been a little too much the shopkeeper, of late. It's difficult to make a good living in the antiques business. You really have to work at it. I've moved mountains to deliver purchases where and when I said I would. I try to call as many of my customers as I can by name, and not only remember what they collect, but keep my eyes open on their behalf when I'm on buying trips or at auctions. Now that I find myself, much to my surprise, in my forties, and my memory does not seem to be quite as sharp as it used to be, I keep index cards on my customers' likes and dislikes. And most of all, I keep in mind the cardinal rule of customer service: The customer is always right. When someone returns a purchase that is damaged in some way, do I say something like "any idiot can see you dropped this and then backed your sport utility vehicle over it"? I do not, even when I personally inspected the object, and wrapped it, before it left the store. What I do say is that I want to make it right, either by repairing it, replacing it, or refunding their money.

As much as I wish the various plumbers, appliance salesmen, air-conditioning repair people, and others of that ilk I am forced to deal with, would espouse this philosophy when I am the customer, it seemed to me that this attitude had put me at something of a disadvantage in the situation in which I now found myself.

I was treating all of the people on the tour as customers of McClintoch & Swain, which undoubtedly they were, but such deference was surely more than one of them deserved. All I had felt I needed to know before we left was that they could pay for the trip, and were of sufficiently good character to have a passport. I'd only known one of them, Emile, and him only casually, and with the exception of Aziza and Curtis, had never heard of the rest of the group. Unlike Susie, I'd been too polite to ask a lot of questions. Aziza had told some unconvincing story about wandering around in the middle of the night and just happening into Kristi's bedroom. I knew she was lying, but hadn't pressed her on it. While she was in hospital, that was understandable, but I'd never gone back to it.

With six days to go, I was going to have to be more aggressive, customers or not. I had a very good idea where to start, even though the thought of it made me queasy, as if I were about to throw myself headfirst into a vat of slime. I was desperate. I dug out the copy

I'd made of Kristi's list. If anybody knew what was going on here, it was she, and any one of the items on her list might just have led to murder, Rick's or her own.

"AZIZA," I SAID LATER. "HOW ABOUT A LITTLE walk around the grounds?"

"Certainly," she said, looking surprised.

"I just wanted to warn you that the police are re-opening their investigation into Rick's death," I said, as we paused for a moment to enjoy the view.

"How so?" she asked.

"They think there's a possibility he was murdered," I said. "The autopsy results didn't support the notion of a careless dive into the pool."

"That's dreadful!" she exclaimed.

"Yes," I agreed. "There is also a possibility they'll take another look at Kristi's death."

She stopped abruptly and turned to look at me. "I was wondering if there's anything you'd like to tell me, Aziza," I prompted.

"No," she said. "I mean, what would I have to tell you?"

"What really happened that night you were in Kristi's room?"

"It was exactly as I told you," she said, but her hands were shaking.

"No, it wasn't," I said. "Look, Aziza. This is not going to go away."

"No," she whispered. "Let's sit down somewhere private. Promise me you will not tell the others, the media, anybody, what I'm going to tell you."

"I won't, Aziza, but I can't promise you the police won't ask you or me about it."

"I understand, but no one else." I nodded. "All

right, then. First of all, I want you to know that Kristi Ellingham was a truly evil person. She was blackmailing me. I don't know how she did it, but she found out about some . . . indiscretions . . . when I was young, and just starting in modeling."

"And she sent you a note suggesting you and she needed to talk," I said.

"She did."

"And?"

"I suppose now that I've mentioned them, I'll have to tell you what these indiscretions were," she said, with a catch in her voice. "I signed a contract with a big international agency when I was only fifteen. They sent me to Europe. My parents thought everything was fine. I was supposed to be chaperoned, and I was to stay with other girls my age in a dorm of some sort. The agency supplied a chaperone, all right, or at least what they called a chaperone. Others, more interested in accuracy, would call this person a drug supplier and pimp.

"After six months, I was heavily into drugs, cocaine mostly, and I'd taken up with a string of truly unsuitable men. I think I was almost lost, but one day one of the other girls I was staying with OD'd and died. I cannot tell you how shocked I was by her death, but I owe her a lot. I ran away—they'd never have let me go—got myself home with some help from my parents, and into rehab, and eventually made my way back. I was really lucky not to end up in a body bag, I know.

"I have no idea how Kristi found out about this. I thought that part of my past was long gone and buried. But she did, and she was going to make me pay, big time. Half a million dollars, can you believe it? You know she gave me the impression that she'd been looking into my background for some time, and had actually signed up to cover the trip when she heard Curtis and I were going."

And here Clive thought it was his persuasiveness

that got Kristi to Tunisia. Wouldn't he be disappointed? "Couldn't you just tell her to go ahead and print it? You're really successful, Aziza, and you could probably even turn the story to your advantage. You know, 'model who overcomes a terrible addiction goes on to become huge success,' that sort of thing."

"First of all, I may be a successful model, but I am not wealthy. Curtis has, we have, made some very bad investments, and virtually lost everything in the past year or two. Curtis is a really terrible businessman, I have to admit it. He got into a fight with my manager, and the guy told him to stuff it. Curtis said no problem, he'd be my manager. I love him, but he's a disaster with money. Luckily, I got a very good offer recently, a clothing manufacturer. There's going to be a new line of classy evening wear with my name on it. I even had some say in the design, and I'm happy about the quality. I get well paid for the use of my name, but I also get to model the line everywhere. It'll be worth six figures almost right away."

"That's terrific. Are you going to tell me sex and drugs isn't good for business?"

"Exactly. It's even in my contract that I have to be squeaky clean, and if there is any hint of trouble with drugs or alcohol or anything like that, the deal is off. The company prides itself on being socially responsible. They make much of the fact they don't use child labor, and always pay fair prices to their workers, that kind of thing. If Kristi broke this story, I'd be out on my fanny so fast, you wouldn't even see me go by. We need the money, but Kristi seemed to think we had lots.

"I told her I was broke, but that I'd pay her off over a period of time. The wretched woman said she'd take postdated checks, can you believe it? That's how confident she was I wouldn't go to the police about her. Next thing we know, she's blackmailing Curtis, too. Says she's writing an article for *First Class* about how he's taken all my money and blown it on some really dicey ventures—part of a feature on successful women who take up with the wrong man, it pains me to say. The worst of it was that she was using information we had given her about our financial state.

"I waited until Curtis was asleep that night, and then went to try to reason with her. I was going to tell her that if she wrote this story about Curtis, she wouldn't be getting any money from us, because we'd be ruined.

"I did not kill her, though, if that's what you're thinking. I knocked, and then tried the door. Just as I told you, it was not shut tight, just pulled so it looked closed, but the lock hadn't engaged, if you understand what I'm saying. I just gave it a little push and it opened. The hallway was dark, so I stood there for a minute, to let my eyes adjust. I think that must have been when I pushed the door closed behind me, and this time it latched. I saw what I thought was a light in the bedroom, although it was flickering—that I did notice. And there was a funny smell," she said.

"What kind of funny?" I interrupted.

"Smoke, of course, but something else. It smelled a little the way your house does when it's being painted. Not the paint, though. The other materials they use, to clean the brushes, things like that."

"Lighter fluid," I said. "She had that fancy lighter—no cheap disposables for her, of course. I watched her fill it more than once. She had a little tin of it."

"Could be," Aziza said. "If I could have a sniff, I'd know for sure. Anyway, all of a sudden, there is this sound, a whooshing, sort of, just like I said before, and the smoke gets really bad. I rushed in and tried to wake her, but she didn't move. I tried to pull her off the bed, but the smoke was terrible, and she just fell to the floor. I suddenly realized I had to get out of there. I was feeling dreadful. I couldn't breathe. So I made a run for it, although I didn't get very far, did I? I know you're probably thinking that I was saying good riddance, let her burn. But quite honestly I didn't think about that until later. Did I mourn her passing? Certainly not. In fact it was a great weight off my shoulders. But I wouldn't have left her there to die, if I'd had a choice. I couldn't live with myself if I had, no matter how vile I thought she was.

"I'm quite prepared to tell the police exactly what happened in the room. The story I told you in the hospital was true. I just didn't tell you why I was there. I hope that unless it becomes absolutely necessary, you will keep that part strictly confidential."

"I will," I said. "But tell me, what are you doing in Tunisia?

"We took the trip to celebrate the signing of the contract. We didn't know Kristi was coming, of course, nor did we know she'd be checking up on us. We get a lot of media attention, and I suppose eventually it would have to come out. My past, I mean. Perhaps I was being terribly naive to think it wouldn't. But we didn't know."

"But why Tunisia?"

'It sounded like fun, and we could afford it."

"Who picked it, you or Curtis?"

"Curtis, I think. I voted for Paris, but he thought this would be more interesting and different."

"Why didn't you pack up and go home after the fire?" I asked.

"I wanted to, not because of the trip, you understand. I want you to know that if it weren't for Kristi, I'd really be enjoying this trip. It's a beautiful country, and I've learned a lot, too. It's not your fault this hasn't been exactly the trip I dreamed of. Curtis said we should keep going, not let this get us down, so here we are. And I didn't kill her."

"Hello, BRIARS," I SAID, BEGINNING MY SECOND interview of the day. While I was determined not to get involved in the subject of the shipwreck again, there was still the question of the relationship between Briars and Rick. "I'm glad to see you're out of hospital. Should you be staying all alone in this house, do you think? Where are the others?"

"Hedi's still around. He's a terrific guy. He has a place in town, already, so he stays there. He came by to see me and brought me something to eat, though. Gus and Sandy are taking a break. They've gone to Tunis for a few days. I can hardly blame them. There's nothing doing here, and frankly, I'm not much fun to be around. It's nice of you to come and see me," he said, getting up off the sofa to give me a hug. As we pulled apart, his lips brushed my ear. "Here," he said patting the seat beside him. "Sit down and talk to me awhile."

"I can only stay a few minutes," I said, "I've got lots to do today. I just wanted to make sure you're okay."

"That's nice of you," he said, stretching one arm along the back of the sofa behind me. "Tell me all the things you have to do."

"You don't want to know all the boring stuff I have to do with this trip," I said.

"On the contrary, I'd like to hear about nice, boring, normal stuff," he said. "Anything other than ships and shipwrecks." His hand slid down on to my shoulder and I felt a slight pressure to move me closer to him. Something told me he was feeling a lot better.

"I have to check on arrangements for the excursion out into the desert . . ."

"I don't think you need me for that portion of the trip, do you?"

"No. It would be nice to have you along, but we'll be fine."

"What else are you up to?" he asked.

"Oh, Clive has something he wants me to do in the next day or so," I said. "Have you heard any more from that policemen, Ben Osman?"

"No, and I hope I never have to talk to him again," he said. "Can we talk about something more pleasant?"

"Sure, what?" I said.

"Something like this," he said, leaning over and kissing me. It felt very good, and I realized this was something missing from my life, to put it politely. Pretty soon, the atmosphere was getting quite warm in the room. I was enjoying the feel of the skin on his back, and the touch of his mouth on my neck, when an unbidden thought crossed my mind.

Don't think about it, I told myself, but it was too late.

Leaving aside for a moment the question of why he is doing this, a little voice in the back of my head said, *why are you doing this? Is it because you're feeling sorry for Briars, who is having such a rough time right now? You're not his mother, you know. Or is it because you're ticked off at Rob?*

"Shut up," I said.

"What?" Briars said, pausing for a moment. "Did you say something?"

You're annoyed with Rob, the little voice droned on, *because he has a new pal. Well, won't he be pleased to hear that you're involved with Briars! I mean, do we see a pattern here? This should put any possibility of a relationship back in the freezer for another year or two.*

"Lara," Briars murmured, pulling me down on top of him.

Decision time, the wretched little voice said.

"Briars," I said, sitting up and straightening my blouse. "I think I'm going back to the hotel."

"Oh no," he groaned. "Stay. Please."

"I'm flattered you'd like me to stay," I said, "but I think it would best if I went back."

"I'm not doing this to flatter you," he said, wrapping his arms around me again.

"No," I said. "This won't work. There's someone at home I think I'm attached to, in a way I'm not yet sure I understand. Maybe some other time, for both of us."

"Okay," he said, letting go of me. "I'm sorry, though."

"Me, too," I said, and I meant it. "Oh, Briars," I said, turning back at the door. It's amazing how fast one can forget what one came for. "I saw Ben Osman again this morning. He's thinking about having another look at what happened to Rick. He thinks Rick's death might not have been accidental."

"Do you mean he committed suicide? By diving into a pool? Wouldn't that be difficult to do?"

"Murder, Briars," I said. "About your argument with Rick—Is there anything you'd like to tell me about it?"

"There's nothing to tell," he said, but he looked agitated. "I thought we were done with that topic of conversation."

"Okay," I said. He'd gone really pale, and looked feverish. I didn't think it was his newfound passion for me that was doing it. "Are you feeling all right?"

"I'll be okay," he said. "I'm just tired." I decided I'd have to come back to this one at a later time.

"CLIFF," I SAID, BACK AT THE HOTEL. "I KNOW this is very presumptuous of me, but would you have a look at this tooth of mine?"

"Well, sure," he said. "I have my mirror in my room. I don't have anything else with me, of course, so I couldn't do anything . . ."

"Oh, it's just a second opinion I want. It's the front tooth on the bottom. You probably don't need any equipment to look at it."

"Ah yes, I see it," he said, peering into my mouth. "You've sheared off some of the enamel on the back of that tooth. Does it hurt at all?"

"No. I was just wondering whether to leave it or get it capped."

"If I were you, I'd leave it," he replied. "If it's scratching your tongue, you could have the rough edges filed off. Unfortunately I don't have the tools to do that here."

"Thanks, Cliff. Sorry to bother you with this. I just wanted to make sure I didn't need to find a dentist right away." I'd ascertained with some certainty that Cliff really was a dentist. He'd given me exactly the same advice I'd received from my own dentist before I left. What that did for me, I didn't know.

"People do that all the time." He smiled. "In your case it's the least I can do, what with your help with the gift for my daughter. Have you had any luck finding that puppet?"

"No, I haven't yet," I replied. "But I haven't forgotten. I'll keep looking." But I had forgotten, completely, in the rush to get to the bottom of this mess in six days—forgotten both Cliff and my film star. So much for the self-serving pap about customer service I keep telling myself. I was as bad as the next guy. I rushed into town.

"Madame Lara," Rashid Houari said. "I'm glad you dropped by. I was going to call you at the hotel later. Your brass and copperware went off today. It should arrive shortly after you get back."

"You're too efficient, Rashid," I said. "There's something else I'm looking for. I'm hoping you can help me. I thought perhaps if you did, I'd just add it to the shipment, but you're way ahead of me."

"Don't worry," he said. "I've found something I know you are going to want, anyway. You won't be able to resist."

"Okay, you've got me hooked already. What is it?"

"I will keep you in suspense. First, what are you looking for?"

"One of those lovely old puppets. Not the tourist ones, the real ones."

"I have two or three," he said. "From the old French theater in Sfax. I don't have them here. There isn't much call for them. Most people like these," he said with a shrug, gesturing to new, and not particularly good, copies.

"Can I see them?" I asked him. "And if so, when? I'm a little pressed for time these days."

"The day after tomorrow? I'm closed until then. I must go to Tunis on business."

"That's cutting it a bit fine," I said. "Not any sooner?"

"Perhaps what we could do is go and see them at my warehouse this evening. It's not far from here, down on the harbor road. I close here just before sunset, go to the mosque for prayers, and then go home to see my little girl before she goes to sleep. I could meet you at say, seven-thirty?"

"No, that doesn't work for me," I said. "I have dinner with my group about then, and I have to talk to them about packing smaller bags for the trip to the desert. It's also an opportunity to deal with any problems or questions they have, so I don't like to skip out early. I don't think I could be there until pretty close to nine."

"That would be all right. I have to go there anyway, at some point this evening, to get something for another customer. Here, I'll draw you a map."

"That's right down near the pier the fishing boats use, isn't it?" I said.

"Just a few yards north of it," he said. "There is a small factory there. I use it to warehouse the goods for my shop here, and the one my brother-in-law runs for me in Hammamet. I also have a few people making the new puppets there, and some leatherwork. It has a green door. You can't miss it. Take a taxi, why don't you? and I'll drive you back to town when we're through."

"You're sure you don't mind?"

"For you, this is no problem. Not all my customers are as *gentille* as you. Now, are you ready?" He took me by the hand and led me to a back corner of the store, and pulled a canvas away with a flourish. "It's good, yes? Perfect for your movie star."

"Rashid! It's gorgeous." It was a beautiful little table of inlaid wood, ten-sided, North African style. Old, maybe late 1800's, by the look of it. "You're right. I have to have it. And it's so good, my Rosedale film star may never see it. I may just have to keep it for myself." Falling in love with the merchandise is an occupational hazard for me.

We argued in a friendly fashion about price, but in the end, we had a deal. I told him if the puppets were as good as he said they were, I'd take whatever he had. "See you later, Rashid," I said.

"Nine o'clock," he said. "I have some other merchandise there you might be interested in, very old, very special."

"You never stop, do you, Rashid?" I laughed. "See you at nine."

At about quarter to nine I was in a taxi heading north on the harbor road. I could see the *Elissa Dido* tied up at the pier. As we got closer, I could have sworn I saw a light in the wheelhouse. *It's your imagination, Lara,* I told myself, *or the reflection of car headlights from the road.* But I saw it again. "Pull over," I said to the taxi driver. "I'm getting out here."

"You shouldn't be down here by yourself at night," the driver cautioned.

"It's okay," I told him. "I'm meeting someone over there, at the warehouse with the light over the door."

"Be careful," he said and drove off.

I walked as quietly as I could along the pier, and edged my way toward the wheelhouse. The light came and went, as if someone was moving about with a flashlight. I crouched low and made my way along the length of the boat until I was even with the wheelhouse, then, counting to three to get my nerve up, I straightened and took a look.

It took me about one second to realize I had made a serious miscalculation in thinking I could separate the tour from the shipwreck. Ben Miller was there, sifting through papers. As I watched, he picked up a piece of paper, looked at it carefully, and smiled. A moment later he switched off the flashlight. I ducked down and moved away as fast as I could. At the road, I ran for the warehouse, just a hundred yards away. It was dark inside, but I pushed open the door. The lamp outside shed some light through a tiny window in the door. I found a switch and flipped it on.

"Hello," I called into the interior gloom. No one answered. I suddenly felt vulnerable standing there in a pool of light, with the warehouse dark around me. I could see a passageway leading toward the back, and, when I stepped into the relative darkness, I saw another light farther along. I walked toward it, past rows and rows of puppets, perhaps hundreds of them, soldiers with red faces and white, their armor and boots, swords and shields of metal, occasionally catching a little of the light from farther on, hanging over long work benches from two long rails on each side of the passageway. At the back of the warehouse was another room with the door partially open, and it was from there that the light emanated. I pushed the door open to find myself in an office of sorts. Under the light was a small table, and on it lay three magnificent old puppets, exactly what I was looking for. Rashid was obviously there somewhere. He'd put out the puppets for me to see. I felt myself relax as I held each of them up in turn, admiring the folds of the old textiles, and the artistry of the painting on the faces. They were absolutely perfect. Cliff could have one, and the other two would look fantastic in the film star's living room. I'd get Clive to design display stands for them. Things were looking up.

Thinking Rashid would return at any moment, I took a seat and looked about me. This was obviously where he kept the good stuff. Over in one corner, four large amphorae sat in stands. I wondered if it would be possible to get them home safely. They'd make great decorative items. I speculated on how old they might be. I remembered Briars telling me about Dressel amphora forms, but of course, didn't know enough about them to even guess. They looked vaguely like Zoubeeir's graveyard amphorae, but I'd need an expert opinion.

The room was lined with shelves, some fronted with wooden doors and locked. One cabinet was ajar, the key still in the lock. Curiosity piqued, I went to look. There were a few bronze coins scattered about, along with some broken pieces of terra cotta. But there were some lovely intact pieces as well, one of which particularly caught my eye. I looked at it carefully. Was it possible it was Zoubeeir's wine jug, the one that had gone missing? I'd have to tell Briars that there was a possibility it had turned up. Perhaps the family sold it to Rashid. On closer examination, however, I saw that I was wrong. Lifting it very carefully, I brought it over to the light. Zoubeeir's jug had a piece missing out of the rim, which had been quite distinct in the photograph. I consider that I have a good eye for repairs, no matter how well done, and this piece had been repaired all right, but on the handle, not the rim. Still it was interesting. Two jugs in the same design would no doubt mean something in historical terms, and Briars would be very keen, I was certain, to see this one. I put the jug back in the cupboard, and had a look at the remaining objects.

There was what I believed was a short-sword, bronze probably, given the look of it. It was in very bad condition, and would be in serious need of conservation. Several pieces of gold jewelry, quite lovely, about a dozen gold rings, and an outstanding gold necklace with lapis lazuli had held up rather better. These objects made me just a little bit uncomfortable. They were clearly very old and would certainly qualify as antiquities as opposed to antiques. The antiquities market can be dicey, and it's one in which I try to be cautious. Very often it is illegal to possess, and particularly to take out of the country, objects as old as these. When I do purchase something like this, I insist on the proper export permits and other documentation. I'd rather not spend time in jail, either at home, or, even more so, in many of the countries I visit. I found myself wondering whether Rashid should have these objects at all. Hadn't Briars told me that objects that could conceivably have come from his precious ship were coming on the market? Could Rashid possibly be the source of the antiquities that were causing him so much concern?

Then I heard it: a sound, almost a rustle, or even, perhaps, a shiver. The little puppet soldiers moved, almost imperceptibly at first, then with a louder rattle, swaying on the rails, as if they were all marching to war, sent by some invisible general. "Hello," I said again, but again no one answered. I could feel panic taking over. The shadows became ominous. I was certain someone was down by the front door. In a second the light there went out. Trapped, I moved away from the light of the office, waited until my eyes grew accustomed to the darkness, and then edged my way toward a window to my right.

The little soldiers were still for a moment, and then started swaying again. I ducked under one of the worktables. Were those footsteps I heard, or was it just my imagination? If someone's there it's only Rashid, I kept telling myself. I'll have a great time explaining to him what I was doing crouched under one of his benches. But I was too frightened to stand up and call his name. I wondered if I could crawl along the length of the worktables, thereby making my way back to the door. But it was apparent this wasn't going to work. Just a few feet along, large boxes were piled under the tables, blocking my way.

The pale beam from the office light flickered for a moment, as if someone had passed in front of it. That gave me an idea of where the person, assuming he existed, was situated. I decided to make my move. I slid out from under the bench and started toward the door. The puppets in this row were larger, some as big as three or four feet. In a way, they gave me some cover, and they didn't rattle the way the smaller ones did. I kept close to them and as quietly as I could, eased my way back to the door. Near the end of the row, I came upon a much bigger puppet. About five feet eight inches, I'd say, hanging from the pipe with a noose around its neck. I lunged for the door, almost knocking Ben over as I burst through it.

11

"YOU LACK COURAGE, HASDRUBAL," THE STRANGER said. "What is a little storm to a sailor of Qart Hadasht?"

Hasdrubal chafed at the ropes that bound his arms and feet.

"Mago here will assume command of the ship. Safat will assist him. We are sailing to our destination with all good speed. You have no backbone," the stranger repeated. "And I have taken what measures I must."

Mago leaned so close to Hasdrubal that the captain almost retched from the smell of the man. "You are a fool," Mago said. "And now all the money is mine." Mago grabbed the captain's money bag and emptied it. Abdelmelqart's pendant, he put once more around his neck, laughing as he did so. "I'll have yours soon and Abdelmelqart's, too."

"You'll have to live to spend it, traitor," Hasdrubal said quietly. Mago kicked him, then pulled an empty sack over his head. "Enjoy the voyage," he hissed.

He knew his ship so well, even lying in the dark and

trussed like an animal readied for the slaughter, he could sense what was happening. He heard the groans as his ship hit the troughs, then struggled to rise for the next wave. "We're doomed," he thought. "All of us."

The ship lurched sharply, and he was thrown against something sharp. In pain, he almost missed the touch of a hand on his shoulder. "Hush," Carthalon whispered. "I'm behind you." He felt the boy working away at the ropes at his wrists.

His arms were free. He whipped the sack off his head as the boy tackled the ropes at his ankles. "Quickly," the boy said.

"What is that you are using to cut the cords?" Hasdrubal said.

"Abdelmelqart's short-sword," the boy replied. "It seemed just, somehow, to use it for this purpose."

"Then put it to further good use. Release the slaves, then come up on deck as fast as you can," the captain said.

Mago tried to turn the little ship into the wind as the gale howled, whipping the sea into a frenzy. At the crest of a wave, Hasdrubal looked to the west and, for a brief moment, thought he saw landfall. Perhaps there was some hope. "Drop the sail," Hasdrubal yelled to the men, some of them huddling in terror by the mast. "Now!"

Too late. The mast came down with a terrible crack, the large sail falling like a huge bird onto the deck, trapping many of the men beneath. It smashed through the cedar box as if it were the finest glass. All eyes turned to the cargo revealed, and a collective gasp went up. Mago and Safat moved toward it, hypnotized by what they saw.

The ship lurched again and a wave crashed over the side, carrying a screaming Mago into the sea. Below, the amphorae of oil and wine began to roll. The ship foun-

dered, then righted itself once again. It was the last time.
With a sigh, it rolled precariously to starboard. "Jump,"
Hasdrubal yelled, grabbing the boy.

FIVE DAYS. DO SOMETHING. I JUST WANTED TO
spend the day in bed, sucking my thumb. No, what I
really wanted to do was get on the first plane home, to
my little house, my cat, my friends, and my shop. Catherine had done it. She would have a lot of conversations
with the police there, certainly. But she was home, and
I wasn't.

Rashid had hung himself. As unlikely as it seemed
to me, given our conversation earlier in the day, and
the fact that he'd taken out the puppets—why would
you go to the trouble of laying out puppets before you
killed yourself?—there was no question the signs were
there: the overturned chair, and a note in his pocket in
Arabic that apparently said simply "please forgive me."
I told myself to get a move on. There'd be time for a
nervous breakdown later.

"Give me plenty of coins," I said to the attendant
at the taxiphone, slapping down several bills in front
of him. "I've got a lot of talking to do." Almost as
much as Kristi Ellingham herself. I began making my
way through her phone bill.

Many dinars and some time later, I knew that Kristi
had called Rick Reynold's employer, a Montreal newspaper, a Paris news magazine's offices, and the public prosecutor's office in California. She'd also called the research
department of *First Class* magazine many times.

"*First Class* library, Helen Osborne speaking. How
may I help you?" the lovely voice on the end of the
phone asked.

"Hello, Helen," I said, wondering whether the
phone was answered that way everywhere there: *First*

Class advertising, *First Class* sales, maybe even *First Class* cafeteria. I was beginning to understand how inspired the magazine's name was, despite my initial tendency to sarcasm. "My name is Eliza Dwyer," I said, making it up on the spot. "I'm the lucky individual who's been assigned to finish up some of the work that Kristi Ellingham was doing before she died. I'm feeling at a disadvantage here, because I don't have all the material she asked for. I sure hope you can help me."

"I'll certainly try. Are you working on Prattle or the travel story on that antiques tour to Tunisia?" she asked.

"Both, in a way. I'm in North Africa right now, doing the tour, but I think she was also gathering material for Prattle on some of the people who are on it, if I'm not mistaken." If I was guessing right, Prattle had to be the gossip column. "Aziza and Curtis Clark and so on. I'm having some difficulty piecing all her notes together."

"North Africa. Aren't you lucky. Yes, Kristi was doing some research for Prattle on Aziza. You have the name of the modeling agency Aziza was with when she was young, don't you?"

"Yes," I said. "That I've got."

"I think that's all she needed on her."

"Emile St. Laurent?" I asked. "Anything on him?"

"I gave her the number for a publication in France. I know he's a coin dealer and he went bankrupt a few years ago, but he's back in business: ESL Numismatics. I can get that number for you again. Here it is," she said, giving me one of the numbers on Kristi's bill.

"Great, thanks. Was there anyone else she was looking into that you know of? I should probably follow up on that, too."

"Some fellow by the name of Reynolds. I didn't have anything on him. Are you going to be doing Prattle from now on?"

"No, I don't think so. I just want to make sure I've tied up all of the loose ends, you know."

"That's too bad. You seem much nicer than Kristi, I must say. Although I suppose nice doesn't cut it in a gossip columnist, does it? She also asked me to check on a dentist by the name of Cliff Fielding, and a Nora Winslow. I couldn't find anything interesting there, either. He's a dentist, or he was. I found him on the list of the professional association in Texas. I couldn't even find a phone number for this Winslow person. That's it, I think. No, wait. Just before Kristi died, she asked me to look into someone with a funny name. Hold on a sec, I'll get it. Briars Hatley. Nothing too exciting about him, either."

"Right, got it. By any chance did Kristi ask for anything on a company called Star Salvage?"

"No, I don't think so. I'm sure I'd remember if she did. Do you want me to do some digging on them for you?" That didn't surprise me.

"Thanks, Helen, but that won't be necessary." As tempting as it might be to have *First Class* magazine doing my research for me, I didn't think it was a good idea. "I appreciate your help with all of this, though. Now I'd better get back to the McClintoch and Swain tour."

Helen snickered. "Kristi called them McQuick Talk and Swank," she said.

"Wasn't Kristi hilarious?" I said, sticking my tongue out at the telephone. "We'll certainly miss her sense of humor." It's always edifying when someone does to you what you do to everybody else, in this case making up names for people.

Next call: Montreal. "Rick Reynolds, please," I said.

"I'm sorry, Mr. Reynolds is no longer employed here," the voice said. "Could someone else help you?"

"Sure," I said. The call was transferred, and I was treated to a few moments of elevator music.

"Alex Mathias," the man said.

"I was looking for Rick Reynolds," I said. "I had some dealings with him a while back."

"It must have been a while," Mathias said. His tone was guarded. "He hasn't been with us for over a year. But what can I do for you? Are you looking for some investment advice, or—"

"Yes, I am," I said. "Where did Rick go, do you know?"

"I don't know where he's gone. I don't think you'd want to be dealing with him, though, wherever it is," he said carefully. Either Alex Mathias didn't read obituaries or he had a rather macabre sense of humor.

"Left under a bit of a cloud, did he?" I said brightly.

"I probably shouldn't say," Mathias said. "But I'd be happy to help you with your investment needs."

"Great. Thanks. Oh, dear, there's someone on the other line. Can I call you right back?"

Well, Rick was a total fraud, wasn't he? Feigning employment, pretending to call his office every ten minutes. No doubt Kristi thought so, too. She'd gone and checked with the Montreal newspaper right after the call to Rick's former employer. I planned to do the same, but I had other ways of getting at that one that wouldn't require quite so much lying.

I got nowhere with the public prosecutor's office in California, and nowhere with the Paris publication. Even tossing *First Class* magazine and Kristi's name into the conversation didn't get me anywhere. It was time to try the Internet. That was something of a problem, there being no jacks in the hotel room for my laptop. It was not insurmountable, however. I persuaded Sylvie to let me use their Internet account after promising to pay for the time.

I checked the online archives of the Montreal paper for any mention of Rick Reynolds. He was there, all right, suspended from the company pending an investigation into some of his activities. According to the clips, he had invested personally in stock offerings his firm was responsible for selling—a no-no in that business, or at least in the company he worked for—and he seemed to have misrepresented the firm. It looked to me as if he'd been trying to get people to invest in certain schemes by making it sound as if he were doing it on behalf of the company that employed him, when he was, in fact, doing it on the side. That got him suspended and then sacked. I could find no evidence, however, that there had been any formal charges brought against him. If he'd managed to find employment elsewhere, I could find no indication of that, either. He was a con man and a thief, of that I had absolutely no doubt. He'd made himself out to be a big-time operator, phoning all the time, checking the markets, when clearly he wasn't. What I couldn't figure out was at whom the whole performance had been directed. Was it a general attempt to dupe everybody on the tour, or was it for the benefit of one particular individual? I also found myself wondering how he'd managed to pay for the trip, given that he'd most likely been unemployed for a while. I doubted that under the circumstances there'd have been much of a severance package, if any. I knew what he was doing for pocket money, though: stealing valuable necklaces and selling them in the Souk des Orfevres, and picking Jimmy's wallet.

Next I checked the archives of some French publications, including the one Kristi had called. I found a little more detail about what I knew already. Emile had been a very successful coin dealer, got out of the business about eight years earlier, invested in a big development outside of Paris that had huge cost overruns, and he went bankrupt, along with the project. Nothing illegal in that, or our jails would be even more packed than they already are. He disappeared from view for a while, and then he came back to what he knew, I suppose, and started up a new business, ESL Numismatics. There was no indication of fraud of any sort.

I found a Web site for ESL Numismatics that listed coins for sale through an online auction. Hundreds of coins were listed with descriptions of quality and prices in U.S. dollars. If you wanted to pay the list price for a particular coin, you could buy it on the spot, if your credit card was up to it—mine wouldn't have been for several of the coins listed—or you could put in a lesser bid and wait until the deadline, when you'd find out whether or not you had been the successful bidder. The site was excellent. It appeared to be updated daily, and had a nifty little search feature. You could go back through three years of online catalogues, and there were nice photos of the coins, and a section on the history of money, and so on. Just for fun, I looked up Carthaginian coins, and found three of them under the current listing. The most expensive one was $12,000. I decided not to look further, or envy would definitely get the better of me.

I then checked out Star Salvage. Where ESL had taken the more serious educational approach, Star went for glitz, with links to various underwater organizations and lots of photos of the *Susannah* and of Peter Groves in diving attire: Groves studying charts and looking very serious, he and others looking at some of the loot they'd found. Star claimed to have found numerous wrecks in several places, including the Great Lakes, the Eastern seaboard of the U.S., and the Caribbean, and it was noted that the company was now in the Mediterranean. The company was touted as a great investment opportunity. There were references to the gold on the

Margarita, and so on. People interested in further information on the company could leave an address for a prospectus. It was all pretty convincing, until I remembered that Maggie had told me that Groves had been screwed, to use her term, over the treasure on the *Margarita.* Somehow I rather doubted that Star was quite the sterling investment its Web site trumpeted it to be.

I was running out of time, however, so I did a quick check on Harvard and UCLA. Both Briars and Ben were what they said they were, professors of archaeology and classics, respectively.

I logged off, and thought for a few minutes. I still hadn't firmly established a link between the shipwrecks and the tour. There had to be one. Ben had been on the ship, and had not even tried to deny it. He'd been absolutely unflappable, though. He'd gone with me to the police, and had stayed right at my side until we got back to the hotel. He'd even bought me a drink in the bar, as if this were a perfectly normal evening. Questioned, he said he'd gone over to the warehouse to see if he could find a phone to call a taxi to take him back to the hotel. When I asked him why he was going through papers on the *Elissa Dido,* he'd said he was just curious about what Briars was doing.

"I'll apologize to him when I see him," he said, sphinxlike. "I hope he'll forgive me." And that's all he'd say. Was there another possible connection between the two? I thought back on all I'd found out, not much in and of itself. But there was Rick and his fraudulent claims about investment opportunities, and there was Star Salvage looking for investors. It was a long shot, but the only one I had.

"Aziza! Can I have another minute of your time?" I said shortly thereafter. "Privately."

"Not on the same subject, I hope," she replied, as I took her aside.

"Related. This may sound a bit obscure, but do you think Curtis might have invested in something really speculative recently?"

"He better not have," she said. "He promised me. How speculative?"

"Very. Something like an expedition to find buried treasure on a shipwreck in the Mediterranean."

"Oh please, I hope not," she said. "I'll kill him."

On that less than positive note, I went to check on Briars. "How are you doing today, Briars? Feeling okay. Got enough to eat here?"

"I'm better, thanks," he said. "I suppose I should apologize for my behavior yesterday. I was feeling a little sorry for myself. Not that it wouldn't have been magic, of course, if you'd taken me up on it. But maybe I was a little pushy."

"That's okay," I said. "I didn't find the idea offensive."

"I've been thinking I'd like to come with the group on the desert trip, if you'd let me. It would get me out of here, and I think I could contribute something. I have done some work on Roman Africa."

"Fine with me if you feel up to it."

"Great," he said. "I promise to behave myself. If you agree, it might be a good idea to take Hedi along as well. He grew up in the desert, you know. He hasn't got much to do right now, and he could share a room with me."

"Okay. Sure. I know I've asked you this before, but I'm asking again. What was your conversation with Rick about? I'm sorry, but what you've been telling me just doesn't ring true."

He looked pained. "God, you're persistent. What possible difference could it make now that he's dead?"

"I have no idea what difference it would make, but I'd really appreciate the truth. Quite frankly I feel as if I've been lied to by just about everybody, or at the very least, that people on this tour have other agendas completely unrelated to sightseeing and antiques that they haven't felt the need to mention to the tour leader. As I told you yesterday, the police are reopening the investigation into Rick's death, and I just want to make sure I know what there is to know about the people I'm associating with here."

"Okay, okay. I get your point. It's true, that story about Rick bugging me to invest with him was pure fabrication. The guy was dead by the time you and I got around to discussing it, and I just didn't see the point of bothering you with it, or for that matter, speaking ill of the dead. At that point I just thought he'd done something really dumb by diving into that pool, so there didn't seem any harm in fibbing. I'm trying to convince you I had good intentions in not being too forthcoming on this subject. Am I succeeding?"

"Maybe," I said. I wanted to believe this guy, but he did make it difficult.

"I guess that'll have to do. The truth, then, is that he tried to bribe me not to go on looking for the shipwreck. The little runt offered me ten thousand dollars. At least that's what he worked up to eventually. He started at five, but apparently he took my response as meaning I wanted more."

"And your response was?"

"I'm sorry you feel you had to ask. I told him to fuck off, in those very terms. They say everyone has a price, but mine happens to be just a little more than ten thousand dollars!"

"Just as well. I have a feeling he wouldn't have been able to pay you, anyway. Why do you think he did this?"

"I have no idea. The only reason I could think of is that he invested in Star Salvage, and was worried about losing his money if we found the ship first. I told him to stay away from me, the boat, the shipwreck, and everything else. When the boat got trashed that very night, it did cross my mind that he might have done it, although you know, he was such a little wimp, despite all his posturing, I rejected that idea. Given what's happened lately," Briars said, pausing for a moment, "I'm sure I was right to do so. The weight of evidence definitely points to Groves. Now can we talk about something more pleasant? What time do I have to be ready to leave? Oh, and where are we going to stay? I'll have to tell that fellow Ben Osman where I'll be; otherwise, he'll be sending in the troops for me."

"It might have to be on camels," I said.

He laughed. "Thanks for cheering me up," he said. "And not being too hard on me about Rick. Or for that matter, my rather outrageous behavior yesterday. You wouldn't care to change your mind on that subject, would you?"

"No," I said, heading out the door and back to the hotel.

"TELL HER," AZIZA DEMANDED, HANDS ON HIPS and eyes blazing. "Tell her what you told me."

It was a deflated Curtis who stood between the two of us. Gone was his air of confidence and well-being. Instead he looked uneasy, even defeated. Even his tan looked as if it had faded.

"Please, Roz," he said. It took me a minute to figure out who he was talking to, but of course, Aziza's name was Roslyn Clark.

"Curtis!" she said.

"I met Rick almost a year ago," he said. "I was in Montreal doing some promotion for an upcoming tournament. I can't recall who introduced us. It may

just be we struck up a conversation at one of the cocktail parties the ad agency had arranged. In any event,
he got in touch with me at my hotel, suggested we get
together for drinks. I was on my own, and glad to have
the company. He took me to the old part of Montreal.
We had dinner, some nice wine. Now that I think about
it, I paid for it. That should have told me something.
Somehow the conversation got around to investments.
He told me he was with a big firm in town. I don't
know if Roz told you, but we're a bit strapped financially these days. My fault, I know that. I was looking
for a way out. Rick told me about this great opportunity, a salvage company that had some real success
finding underwater treasure."

"Oh, Curtis," Aziza said. "I can't believe this."

"I'm sorry, Roz," he said. "I really am."

"Continue," I said.

"There's not much else to say. I looked this Star
Salvage company up on the Internet. They have a
pretty impressive Web site, and looked legit. I called
the Montreal firm that Rick said he was employed by,
and he was, in fact, there. He told me I'd be getting in
on the ground floor on this one, that his firm was having a look at the company right then, and I could get
in before the public offering. Not true, I guess," he
said, looking at me.

"Probably not, but if it's any comfort to you, you're
not the only one who was taken in by Rick. His firm
eventually fired him for misrepresentation. And, you
know, all of us on the tour thought he was legit, didn't
we, if a little bit boring about it? We all believed he
was an investment dealer."

Curtis winced. "I found him far from boring. I told
him I'd think about it. A month or so later I got a
call from him, and I gave him five hundred thousand
to invest."

Aziza looked as if she didn't know whether to cry or strangle him. "After a few months, I was beginning to get a little worried about this investment," he went on. "After all, surely the summer would be the right time to do the salvage work, but I had trouble tracking Rick down. I did talk to him once and he said he'd left the company because he wanted to set up on his own. The company was way too conservative, he told me, and there was lots of money to be made for those with vision." Curtis paused. "I know what you're thinking, both of you," he said. "I've been a fool.

"When I saw your tour advertised, Lara, it seemed a great way to check up on Star Salvage. I didn't know Rick would be on the tour, too, and I was none too pleased to see him. I guess he was doing the same thing I was. That's when I found out that not only had Star not yet found the ship—Rick had given me the impression it was just a matter of waiting for the right sea and weather conditions to bring the treasure up—but someone else was looking for it, too.

"Rick told me that everything would be taken care of. When I asked what that meant, he said he was going to discourage the other party. By this time I was in so deep, I actually thought this was a good idea. He didn't succeed, of course. That's all there is."

"No, it isn't," I said. Aziza looked first at me, then at Curtis.

"I don't know what you mean," he said.

"Yes, you do. What were you and Rick doing on the path down to the harbor that night?" He looked wary. "You know, the time you told Rick that he was an incompetent little twit and if he couldn't look after things, you would."

"Curtis!" Aziza exclaimed again. "What night? What path? If you don't tell us everything, absolutely everything, you and I—"

"You were asleep, Roz. It was one of the nights you took a sleeping pill because you were so upset about Kristi. Rick said he was going to take care of the other party looking for the shipwreck. I figured out by then that Rick had money in the scheme, too. He told me Star would find the ship first, but just to make sure, he was going to go down and mess up the other boat a little to slow them down, because he'd made them an offer of some kind which he wanted to reinforce. I think the idea was they'd like his offer a lot more afterwards. I was furious, and I knew if I lost more money, you would maybe never forgive me. I told him to get on with it. He asked me for twenty thousand dollars more to protect my investment!"

"Where did you go after that conversation?" I asked. "It wasn't straight back to the hotel. Down the hill to the harbor? Was it actually you who did the damage to Briars' boat?"

"No, I swear I didn't. I intended to, though. I went down there, to the pier, I mean. I knew the name of the boat: *Elissa Dido*. I didn't know it was Briars at the time, you know. He's a great guy. I mean, I just had no idea. But the boat wasn't at the pier, it was at anchor. I had no way of getting out to it. So I went back to the hotel. Rick was in the bar, even though it was closed already. I told him to pull himself together, figure out some way of getting out to the boat. I told him to swim if he had to. Then I went to bed. Roz says that the police think he might have been murdered. I didn't do it. The last time I saw him he was in the bar."

"Ever gone scuba diving, Curtis?"

"Sure," he said. "I do all kinds of sports, not just golf. I learned years ago. I don't do it much anymore, just out for a day when Roz and I are on holiday in the Caribbean. Why?" I said nothing. "You think I tampered with the tanks on Briars boat? No way! After

Rick died, I just decided to hope for the best, that the right guy would find the treasure, and I'd be home free. After all, Roz had a new contract, so money wasn't going to be a problem if we could just get through this bad patch. I'm sorry, Roz," he said. "I really and truly am. I won't do anything like this again, I promise."

"Do you know how many times you've made that promise, Curtis?" Aziza said.

"I know," he replied miserably. "This time . . ."

"Maybe this is a sickness," she said. "Like compulsive gambling. We could get you help, Curtis. I did when I had a drug problem."

"I don't need help," he said. "I'll stop. I promise."

"You have a choice, Curtis," she said. "You get help, I'll stick with you. You don't, and I'm gone."

"Roz!" he cried. "I got taken in by a crook, that's all. You heard Lara. The guy fooled a lot of people."

"You have a choice, Curtis," she said firmly. She nodded to me and left. In a minute, Curtis went after her.

Later that night, I took out Kristi's list again. So far the woman wasn't batting a thousand, exactly, but she didn't have it all wrong, either. Emile, as far as I'd been able to ascertain, hadn't been charged with fraud. On the other hand, Aziza might not be on drugs now, but she had been. Curtis wasn't blackmailing anyone, but he was being blackmailed by none other than Kristi herself. Rick, too, had been worth checking up on. Kristi most certainly had been right about our little Lolita, Chastity. But there didn't seem much more to be said about that, other than that someone needed to take the young woman in hand, something her mother seemed to be incapable of.

So far Cliff seemed to be pretty much what he said he was, a former dentist with an investment company. I suppose he could have invested in Star Salvage, too, and the best way to find out would be to ask him. That left the trailer-park trash: Nora Winslow. Kristi had hinted that she was manipulating Cliff, which maybe she was. She was certainly overly solicitous about his health. But Kristi had also implied there was something more. Maybe Nora, too, could bear some looking into.

What was interesting about these revelations from Briars and Curtis, is that logically it would seem that damage would be done to only one party, that is the *Elissa Dido* project. But someone had set fire to the *Susannah*. Curtis wouldn't have done it. He wanted Star Salvage to find the shipwreck first. Did Briars do it? Or did he have someone on his side, someone who was just as determined to make sure that Groves didn't find it, as Rick and Curtis were that he did. The only other possibility was that there was someone out there who didn't want either of them to find the shipwreck.

All of this presupposed that Rick had been killed because of the shipwreck. Maybe he'd been killed because he was a con man and a thief. There were a lot of *maybe*s here, a lot of information was coming together, but on the conclusion side, we were a little light. All I had to go on was gut instinct. As inconceivable as it might seem that all of this could have happened because thousands of years ago a ship had gone down at sea, my intuition was now telling me it was the shipwreck.

I didn't think I'd go to sleep, but I did. Soon I was standing in the sanctuary of Baal Hammon in a white dress, a *sifsari* covering my head and face. Everyone on the tour was there with me, although it was hard to tell who was who, because even the men wore robes with hoods.

A great fire was burning there, and its light flickered across the features of a golden god who sat, hands on his thighs, palms facing each other.

We were there for a great and sacred ceremony, although I didn't yet understand what it was. Somehow it became apparent to me that a child was to be sacrificed to the golden god. I wanted to stop it happening, but I couldn't move.

The child, whose face I couldn't see, was wrenched from its mother's arms and carried toward the statue and the fire. A howl so intense it could surely be heard in heaven, went up from the mother.

"Doesn't she know she's not supposed to cry," Jimmy said. "Can't she read?"

As Betty turned her back on her husband and walked away, I noticed an enormous sign that said NO CRYING! DEFENSE DE PLEURER! TRAENEN SIND VERBOTEN!

"Incompetent little twit," Curtis agreed.

"Tragic," said Chastity. She was standing directly behind Emile. If he moved to the right, she did, too. If he turned and walked a few steps, she followed. As she spoke, he turned and looked at her, then flicked his cigarette into the flames. She made the same motion, without the cigarette, and he frowned.

"Mors certa, hora incerta," Ben said. "Although given this is a sacrifice, perhaps it really should be *hora certa,* too, in this particular instance. Will we get dinner after?"

"You and I need to get in shape, Ben," Susie scolded "It's possible, you know. We can jog. Nora's done it."

A snake slithered over the golden god, then turned its eyes, demonic red, toward me. The mouth opened to reveal its fangs. The head swayed closer and closer.

I was back in my room. I looked at my alarm clock. Three in the morning. Four days to go. Who was the snake?

PART III

Tantaene animis caelestibus irae?

Can rage as fierce as this abide in the soul of heaven?

12

ALL NIGHT HASDRUBAL AND THE BOY CLUNG TO A *piece of wood, dashed by the sea, whipped by the winds.*

"I believe this is part of the cedar box," Hasdrubal said. "The gods must have a sense of humor."

"Of a sort," the boy yelled over the roar of the storm.

"You remind me of my son, Carthalon," the captain said. "I trust I do not offend you in saying this."

"Indeed, I am honored," the boy said.

"I do not believe I will survive this night," Hasdrubal went on. "But I think you might. You are young and strong. Therefore I have another task for you, one for which, unfortunately, I am unable to reward you this time, as my money is gone."

"I will do it," the boy replied.

"You are a fine young man. I ask this favor only because I believe that our great city of Qart Hadasht is in grave danger, not just from Agathocles, as you might suspect, but from another."

"Tell me," the boy said.

"My ship was commissioned for a special voyage, a

*secret mission, by a very important person in Qart Ha-
dasht. I was approached by the great man himself. I was
told it was a matter of utmost urgency to the state. This
person was, I believed, beyond reproach. Our task was
to carry a special piece of cargo, which I'm sure you
have guessed was the cedar box, along with money and
goods, on a specified route along the Libyan coast
bound for Tyre. Gisco, the man you call the stranger,
was to accompany it. You caught a glimpse of that
cargo, I believe."*

*"I did," the boy said, "and I have never seen anything
so magnificent. Where did it come from?"*

*"Tartessus, of course, the lands beyond the pillars of
Herakles, where gold and silver and jewels are to be
found. But it is not so much what it is, as what its purpose was to be."*

*Hasdrubal gasped as another large wave hit them.
The boy reached across their tiny makeshift raft to
steady him.*

*"I was told that the statue—it is very old, Carthalon,
older even than Qart Hadasht itself—was a gift to the
city of Tyre to propitiate the god who has seemed to
desert us in our hour of greatest need as the Greek tyrant
tries to destroy us. Many have felt that miseries have
been heaped upon us, because we have been lax in the
worship of our own gods."*

*"I know that," the boy said. "I saw the sacred cere-
monies in the sanctuary of Baal Hammon. But what of
the silver and gold coins and the rest of the cargo? Were
they for the city of Tyre as well?"*

*"No. The cargo was to be used to raise an army
from amongst the Libyans to assist us in the forthcoming
battles with Agathocles. I knew the voyage was dangerous, slipping out alone, without escort, and on such a
bad night. But how could I refuse when I had seen the
sacrifices made by our leaders—their first-born, some-*

times their only children—sacrificed to save us all? And I confess there was profit in it. We citizens of Qart Hadasht are always on the lookout for gain."

"And so you are worried, now that the cargo has not reached its destination, the gods will still be angry with us—and the mercenary troops we hoped to muster, and even you, will not be paid?"

"No, much worse than that. I think the cargo was not really destined for Tyre. I fear that I am a dupe to treachery, an unwitting party to it. I believe the statue was stolen from a sanctuary in the lands near the pillars of Herakles—there is rumor of such a statue, more beautiful than anything we have ever seen, gold, with eyes of diamonds. I think the money was to go to mercenaries all right, but rather than being used to raise an army to support Qart Hadasht, it was to be used against us. The money was to convince the Libyans to support a traitor! And the statue, I believe, was to be used by that same traitor to convince the people to follow him."

The boy gasped. "How can this be? What makes you think this is so?"

"In part, it is just a feeling I have. In part, it is what you told me."

"What do you mean?" the boy said. "I told you nothing of this."

"Ah, but you did. You told me that the stranger conferred with Mago before he went down to the cargo hold, and that while you could not see who had returned the ingot, you did see Mago open an amphora of coins, hold the money for a few moments, but then return it and reseal the container. He did the same with the pithos of gold jewelry."

"So I told you. But . . ."

"Who would have noticed a few missing coins, a gold ring or two, under the circumstances?" Hasdrubal said. "Or for that matter, what could be done about one silver *ingot, given our mission? But Mago didn't take them. That's because they were already promised to him. The cargo was never to arrive at its destination. Some of it was to be used to pay those crew members who were part of the conspiracy; the rest would go into the coffers of the traitor. We were to be overtaken by Mago and his friends, killed, no doubt, and the cargo would simply disappear. Why else would he leave the coins and jewelry there?"*

"But you said the person who sent you on this mission was above reproach."

"I did, but I no longer believe it."

"What do you want me to do?" the boy cried.

"You must survive this night—the sea will take you to shore, I am certain. You must make your way back to Qart Hadasht, taking care not to be captured by Agathocles' men. And then you must get an audience with the Council of the Hundred and Four and tell them this story."

"This is not possible for someone like me," the boy gasped.

"It is," Hasdrubal replied. "Can you reach the pendant around my neck? Yes? Good. Take it to the home of Yadamalek in a place I will tell you. He will recognize the pendant as mine and believe you. He'll see to it that what needs to be done, is carried out quickly. Will you do it?"

"I will," the boy said. "And the name of the traitor?"

Hasdrubal pulled the boy closer and cried the name in his ear.

FOUR DAYS. WE WERE IN THE FORUM OF THE ancient Roman city called Sufetula. Three temples, the largest dedicated to Jupiter, flanked by smaller ones to either side, Juno on the right, Minerva on the left, towered above us. That the Romans built such a magnificent city out here in the Tell, and embellished it with sweeping avenues, soaring arches, and towering columns was a marvel indeed.

But I wasn't studying the temples. Instead I pulled back into the shade of the Antonine Gate that leads into this great space, to study our group. I realized that I had been so wrapped up in the details of the trip— whether the bus would arrive on time, if dinner could be postponed for half an hour to allow a longer visit at a site, if everyone's needs had been accounted for— that I had not really looked at them as individuals at all.

I knew there was an evil presence among them, but I didn't know who. I thought if I looked at them, really looked at them, the answer would be clear. I searched for the jarring note, the misplaced gesture, the momentary slip of the mask. But they all looked like ordinary people to me.

Over in front of Jupiter's temple, Susie and Cliff shared a laugh. Now that Catherine was gone, Susie had apparently set her sights on Cliff as her next husband, and he seemed to be enjoying her company. For a moment or two I wondered if perhaps Susie, desperate for a new mate, had tampered with Catherine's clothes, and even pushed her rival down the stairs to scare her off. Watching Susie, though, as she buzzed about the site, I couldn't believe she was guilty.

Chastity, whose shameless, but somehow innocent, flirtation with Emile had been rebuffed, had gone back to being a distressed, possibly disturbed, teenager. Over in one corner, by herself, she lit a match and watched it burn, dropping it into the sand at her feet only after it had seared the tips of her fingers. She had become very needy for my attention in the last day or two, asking for help buying souvenirs to take back to her friends, or asking me to check her overnight bag to see if she'd brought all the right things. Suddenly I couldn't stand watching her do this anymore. I crossed the forum, grabbed the book of matches, saying "Stop that, Chastity! You'll hurt yourself."

"She doesn't even notice I'm doing it," she said.

"Who?" I asked.

"My mother."

"She notices."

"Then she doesn't care."

"She cares, Chastity, believe me."

"She drove him away," she said.

"Who?" I asked her, wondering for a moment if she meant Emile.

"My dad."

This, then, was what it was all about, wasn't it? The matches, and the pathetic attempts to get Emile to notice her. She was competing with her mother for a man because her mother couldn't get, or keep, one. "Your mother and father don't get along. That's unfortunate. But it doesn't mean that either of them has stopped loving you," I said, trying to put my arm around her. She turned away from me, and looked toward her mother.

Marlene, also spurned by Emile, had now pinned forlorn hopes on Briars. As he spoke, with his expansive gestures, and very comfortable male presence, to which neither she nor I were immune, she stood, eyes riveted on him, with a look of what I can only call longing, crossing her face. "I hate her," Chastity said.

The other person paying grave attention to Briars was Nora, her head turning as he pointed to some feature or other, leaning forward to catch what he said. Behind her, Susie and Cliff laughed, but this time, Nora did not return to his side. It was as if the bonds that linked her to Cliff were loosening in the warmth of the North African sun. She looked over at Chastity for a moment or two, and then walked toward her. I watched her speak to the girl for a moment or two, then take her hand and pull her toward the group. Chastity resisted at first, but then came along. It was such a surprising gesture, so out of character for Nora, a woman who had kept so much to herself, clinging only to Cliff, that I could hardly believe my eyes. I could only admire the way she'd brought Chastity back into the group, something both her mother and I were incapable of doing.

Betty and Ed stood together, Betty giggling at Ed's jokes. They were a strange couple, the sixty-something matron and the young gay man half her age. Clearly, they enjoyed each other's company. Betty and Jimmy no longer sat together on the bus. Nor did Ben and Ed. Ben sat by himself, just as he now stood by himself, hands thrust into his jeans pockets, looking about him. Jimmy had chosen to go to a café across the road from the site, for a drink. "Not another pile of rocks," he said, when the bus pulled up to the ruins. He was becoming more and more isolated from the group and distant from his wife.

Aziza seemed to be enjoying herself, for the first time in many days. As she looked up at the graceful lines of the temple of Minerva, goddess of wisdom, glowing gold in the afternoon sun, she took a very deep breath, then exhaled as if releasing her problems along with her breath. Perhaps feeling my eyes on her, she looked over at me in the archway, and waved.

Curtis followed her about like a lovesick puppy, knowing that in some way, perhaps permanently, he had lost her, or at least, if she had any love left for him, it is tempered by a solid sense of what he was, her hero no more. I wondered briefly whether he would ever regain some stature with her, or if the marriage was doomed.

We were on our way to Tozeur, an oasis town not far from the Algerian border, and a setting-off point for trips to the Chott el-Jerid, a huge salt lake formed when the Mediterranean flooded the land, then retreated, thousands of years ago, and to the Grand Erg Oriental to the south. The Grand Erg is part of the band of desert that separates the North African coast from the subcontinent far to the south. To the west, the Grand Erg Oriental becomes the Grand Erg Occidental. To the east, it is called simply desert, Sahara.

Our route took us through town after town, white houses decorated with garlands of red peppers drying in the sun, and in between, roads lined with acacia and olive trees, through which the outline of distant mountains could be seen. We passed two-wheeled carts pulled by donkeys that looked as if they were three thousand years old, sheep herded by nomads, and dromedaries tethered to posts in the sand.

The group was particularly excited about this part of the trip. At Tozeur, they would transfer to four-wheel-drive vehicles to head out into the desert for two days. Once they'd seen Sufetula, they were impatient to be on their way.

But first there was the market in Tozeur to visit. I like Tozeur. It has something of the air of a frontier town to it, with its dusty streets and a kind of collective thumbing of the nose at authority. At one time it was more powerful in the region than the national government in Tunis, and it has retained the feel of the real North Africa, despite the influx of tourists. One can imagine still the sounds, sights, and smells of the great caravans that passed through here, attracted by both the vibrant marketplace, and the hundreds of springs that water the oasis.

It was harvest time for the dates, the delicate, almost translucent *deglat en nour,* finger of light. They hung in large branches from every stall. The place was a hive of activity. Donkey carts jostled for position with trucks, our group mingled with the locals: women, wrapped in the black *sifsari* common to the town, some with faces covered, shopping for their families, carpet weavers plying their trade right on the street, outside their little stalls packed with the brightly colored carpets whose patterns mimic the dramatic architecture for which Tozeur is famous. Buildings there are constructed of handmade yellow bricks, some pulled out slightly when they are laid to create intricate and three-dimensional geometric designs.

Over to one side, a blind man hawked *roses de sable,* sand roses, beautiful crystalline shapes created by moisture, dew perhaps, sifting through the sand dunes, and over time, hardening to create wonderful sculptural shapes. Farther along, a camel munched on its food. And everywhere there were red and white flags and huge pictures of Zine el-Abidine Ben Ali, President of the Republic of Tunisia, whose ascension to power on November 7, 1987 was being celebrated right across the country.

By now the group had adjusted to Tunisian-style commerce, and, getting into the swing of things, were bargaining for gifts and souvenirs with real aplomb.

Chastity stood off by herself, once again. This time she was staring at a newsstand. The proprietor became annoyed with her, and I went to her rescue. She pointed to a newspaper. "I want one of those," she said.

"You can't read it, Chastity," I said. "It's in Arabic."

"I want it," she said petulantly. "Hedi can tell me what it says. I've got some money."

"Okay," I said, helping her with the coins. An Arabic newspaper would make a souvenir of a different sort for her, but as I handed it over, I saw Rashid

Houari's picture. It was just as well Chastity couldn't read Arabic, and that I couldn't either.

Then, at last, it was time for dinner, which we'd arranged to have served at two large tables beside the hotel pool. The evening was lovely, warm enough, and the moon glowed over the palm trees of the oasis in the distance.

It had been a trying day, in many respects, arranging for the luggage to be stored at the auberge for our return, and getting the smaller bags on and off the bus. Marlene insisted on bringing her large suitcase, and Chastity's. She wasn't for leaving anything behind. The hotel rooms had to be rearranged. We'd canceled Rick's and Kristi's rooms, of course, days earlier, and Catherine's the day before. However, the hotel was overbooked, and I had trouble finding space for Hedi and Briars, although eventually it worked out all right.

After dinner I was eager to get back to my research, reading through a lot of material I'd printed off the Web before we set off, but there were many little details to attend to first. The zipper on Jimmy's bag had broken, which would be a problem in the desert sands, and so I had to find someone to repair it for him overnight.

Susie needed to be soothed about the desert. "Could there be snakes in the tents?" she asked.

"I hope not," Ed declared.

"Of course not," I replied.

Cliff needed reassurance that the gift for his daughter was taken care of. I told him I'd keep looking for the puppet. He didn't know I'd already found three, and I left him none the wiser, because I couldn't bear the thought of calling Rashid's brother and asking if I could still purchase them. Instead I showed Cliff some spectacular bracelets I'd found in the market, telling him we wouldn't give up on the puppet yet, but with the bracelets, we'd be sure of having something for his daughter, no matter what. He appeared satisfied by that, and said he might take them both.

"I should get something for Nora, too," he said. "A memento of the trip. She hasn't bought anything for herself."

I thought the bracelets too restrained for Nora, who that evening was wearing very tight white pants, a cherry-colored low-neck blouse with pink and white ruffles, and very high-heeled slip-on sandals festooned with yellow and green plastic flowers. I suggested some more elaborate filigree earrings for her.

"Oh, the bracelets are for my daughter," he said. "If you find the puppet, I'll give her both. I think Nora would like the earrings, though."

As I watched Nora teeter about on the sandals, I made a mental note to tell her to wear her jogging shoes for the trip into the dunes. She was not looking well at all. When I really looked at her, I could see she was quite pretty, but she didn't know how to make the most of what she had. Colors that were rather charming on Susie did not suit Nora. It was as if she had never really looked at herself in a mirror to see what colors would flatter her. Her bottle-blond hair had not fared well in the North African sun, turning very brassy. I thought of Kristi's mean-spirited comments about her, and wished I could treat Nora to a day at my friend Moira's spa. But it was more than that: There seemed to be some profound sadness at the core of Nora's being, something that had twisted a good nature into something else, a woman who had to dominate Cliff in a way that corrupted her generous impulse to care for him. I didn't think I would ever understand Nora, but I hoped the gesture she had made toward Chastity was a new beginning for her.

"What kind of thing do you invest in, Cliff?" I asked, turning my attention back to him.

He looked startled at the abrupt change of subject, but answered right away. One thing you'd have to say about Cliff is that he was polite to a fault. Perhaps that was why Nora got to boss him around so much. He was too courteous to object. "Right now, Internet stocks, digital media, that kind of thing," he said. "Along with the usual safe blue-chip companies. I try to keep some of my money in secure investments, and have a little fun with the rest."

"Would having a little fun extend to say, a marine salvage company looking for treasure under the sea?"

"Absolutely not," he replied. "I'm not that adventurous. Funny you should mention it, though. That fellow Rick Reynolds suggested I might be interested in putting money into just that kind of thing. I told him he was crazy. If you're suggesting it, I'm afraid I'd have to tell you the same thing."

"I'm not for a minute suggesting it," I assured him. "It's just that I keep hearing that Rick did talk to a few people about it, and I was a bit worried some might take him up on it. I'm not sure Rick was quite what he said he was, as far as being an investment counselor."

"I got rather the same impression," Cliff said. "I hope no one was taken in."

Next, I asked Jimmy the same question. "Not you, too," he said. "Pushing such an stupid idea. What would make you think I was such an idiot?"

"I didn't think you were, Jimmy," I said. "Far from it. I was just concerned that Rick Reynolds was bothering people about it. I gather from your comment that he did bring the subject up."

"He did. I told him he was offensive. People make fun of chicken parts, you know, but they're a damn good business."

"Calm down, Jimmy," Betty said. "Lara just said she was worried about Rick bothering people."

I'd been with these people for about two weeks, and now they were all clicking into place for me. My confidence in my ability to judge people, shattered temporarily by my total failure to recognize the real Kristi, was reasserting itself. Somehow I knew that Jimmy called everyone an idiot because he thought everyone believed he was an idiot for getting into chicken parts. He must have been making excuses for his business, thinking people were making fun of him, all through his adult life. Sad, really.

"I think your chicken parts business idea was inspired," I said. "Not only that, it is ecologically responsible. You found a market for the parts of the bird we didn't want, rather than just throwing them out." He looked absolutely nonplused by my comment, but then he gave me something akin to a smile.

At last, everyone seemed to have settled down. A few were still sitting out by the pool, but nobody seemed to have any problems. I decided to take advantage of the peace and quiet to go to my room.

"Oh, just a minute, Lara," Marlene called to me. "Where's Briars staying? I have something I'd like to show him. His name isn't on the room list you gave us."

Assuming she was off to proposition him, I debated for a moment whether I should plead ignorance or not, but in the end I decided that it was his problem and not mine. "There weren't enough rooms right in the hotel because of all the changes we made," I told her. "He and Hedi are staying in a guest cabin on the edge of the grounds. It doesn't have a number, but you can't miss it. Take the steps on the other side of the pool, and then just follow the path until you see the cabin."

"Hedi's there, too, is he?" she said, with more than a hint of disappointment.

"Did I hear my name?" Hedi said. He was looking very smart, dark pants and white shirt, hair slicked back.

"Going dancing, are you?" I asked.

"Yes." Hedi grinned. "I have friends here. There are many parties to celebrate the holiday. Dancing tonight, and then long speeches from the politicians tomorrow. We'll be on our way by then," he added.

"Too bad we'll have to miss those speeches," I said, smiling back.

"It is, indeed," he said, laughing.

I noticed that Nora was listening to this conversation with some interest, and I wondered if Marlene was once again going to find herself in competition for a man. What do I care? I thought. I had made my decision about Briars and me, hadn't I? I went to my room.

The conclusion I was coming to, as I read through all I'd found, was that by and large the people on the trip were a law-abiding lot, and were indeed what they said they were. Dull, some might say. Star Salvage, however, was a different matter entirely. My conclusion, reached after searching several newspaper-chain online archives, was that Star Salvage was very good at finding shipwrecks, and valuable ones at that. Groves had been all over the place—the Caribbean, the Great Lakes, up the Eastern seaboard of the U.S.—and he managed to find a shipwreck almost every place he went. But while he could find them, he didn't seem to be able to profit from them.

Star Salvage was being challenged every step of the way. For example, Groves found a mid-1880's wreck off Michigan. Michigan was claiming ownership and the court case had been dragging on for a few years. In the Caribbean, there was a diver who claimed he found the wreck off Puerto Rico—it was Spanish, so everyone was expecting lots of gold—before Star did and he had sued to establish his claim. In another case, the U.S. government was asserting its right to the wreck of a warship from the War of 1812, in Lake Erie: the Navy wanted it. Star was challenging them in court. Star Salvage must have been paying a fortune in legal fees to have lawyers working for them all over the place, either suing for them, or defending them.

The only case I could find that had actually been settled was a suit by the parents of Mark Henderson, the young man Briars had told me about who died while working for the company. The parents sued Star, Peter Groves, and Briars Hatley, a fact Briars had failed to mention, claiming negligence on the part of the company and the two individuals. There were all kinds of jurisdictional wrangling, but the case was eventually heard in California. There had been a police investigation of the death in Tunisia, and the U.S. authorities looked into it, too. There were no criminal charges brought, but the couple sued in civil court. The death was ruled accidental, and neither the company nor the two individuals were held responsible. The parents, George and Nora Henderson, had had to pay the court costs. The name Nora had given me a jolt, but I'd been able to find a photo of the parents leaving the courtroom. George Henderson had blocked the view of his wife slightly, but it was possible to see that Nora Henderson was a large woman, overweight, with long dark hair. She was wearing sunglasses, and a very conservative dark suit.

If the Henderson lawsuit hadn't cost Star any money, the others would, however. Furthermore there didn't seem to be much in the way of income while the ownership claims sorted themselves out. On top of that, while I had no idea what it would take to keep a ship like the *Susannah* operating, I had no doubt it was a considerable sum of money. No wonder Star was looking for new investors. Curtis Clark put $500,000 of his wife's money into Star. There could easily be several others just as stupid, but I couldn't shake the feeling that Star Salvage was pretty close to broke.

The last information I had was a lot of material about coins I'd pulled off the ESL Web site. I wasn't sure whether I'd done this as research on the cases in question, or just for my own edification, but I read the data, anyway. There was a bit of history at the start: Carthaginians, it seems, came rather late to the idea of coinage. While coins have been in commercial use since the seventh century B.C., Carthaginian coins only appeared around 400 B.C. Their early coins were minted, if that term can be used back then, in a couple of cities that Carthage controlled in Sicily. Why Carthage got into coins so late, given the Carthaginians were the premier merchants of the Mediterranean, wasn't explained, but maybe they stayed with the barter system longer than others, or they just used other people's coins. In any event, given that Carthage fell to the Romans in 146 B.C., the history of Carthaginian coins was a relatively short one, making them relatively rare.

Most of the Punic/Carthaginian coins that I saw had a lion and/or a palm tree on one side, and the head of a god or goddess—according to the listings, usually Melqart, Herakles, Persephone, or Tanit—on the other. Melqart, I knew, was the city god of ancient Tyre, which was the parent city of Carthage. Melqart was also worshipped in Carthage itself. Tanit was the consort of Baal Hammon, and the couple were jointly the city gods of Carthage. Herakles and Persephone were Greek deities. The coins were made in silver, electrum—silver mixed with some other base metal—bronze, and gold. Nothing unusual there. I found Carthaginian coins listed as low as $750 and as high as $45,000. I could see their appeal from a merchant's point of view: no storage problems, no huge shipping costs. Maybe Clive and I could start with just a few to test the market. Then I found something that made me think I'd made the right career choice after all.

What did strike me, looking through these catalogues, was how volatile the market could be. I followed one type of coin through three years of auctions at ESL. The particular coin I chose for this exercise was said to be special: The head on it was Dido or Elissa, rather than Tanit, and she was wearing a particular head-covering that apparently set this coin apart from others, an Oriental tiara, the data said. There were also some other markings on it that were supposed to be special, too. It caught my eye because it had the highest price I saw, $45,000, due to the fact it was in remarkable condition, but also because it was extremely rare. There were only about ten of them in existence at the start of the three-year period. While my initial instinct had been that I wouldn't mind having one or two of those tucked away somewhere for a rainy day, I wasn't so sure by the time I'd worked my way through all the material. A year after that first listing, there was a similar coin, but it was listed at $25,000. At the end of the three-year period, the coin was down to $12,000. Still a lot of money, but if you'd had a couple of those squirreled away in a drawer somewhere, you might suddenly find they were worth less than you'd paid for them. This might be a temporary situation, as ESL's catalogue argued, or it might not.

I decided there would be only two variables, condition and supply. According to the listings, all these coins got the same very-fine ranking, so that eliminated condition as the reason for the difference in price. That left supply as the explanation; that is to say, a few more of them had been put on the market in the intervening time. So, had I been holding on to a couple of these, I wouldn't want large numbers of them to appear overnight.

I wondered under what circumstances a bunch of these would suddenly turn up. A hoard was one possibility. Historically, people buried objects they valued, including coins, particularly in bad times. From time to time someone found one of these hoards that the owner never got back to, for whatever reason. Maybe he died, or just forgot where he buried them. If they ended up in a museum, fine, but if they got onto the open market, and there were a lot of them, some people might lose.

I sprawled on the bed and tried to sort through in my head all that I'd learned. The material about coins was interesting. Emile was in coins, and given what I'd read, a new supply of coins would certainly have a major impact on his business. If I was looking for a reason someone wouldn't want either expedition to be successful, then this just might be it. But how would he know Star Salvage and Briars were looking for an ancient shipwreck to start with? And even if he did, it didn't necessarily follow there'd be lots of coins to be found. Coins, particularly silver and bronze, wouldn't hold up very well underwater for any significant period of time. Still it did bear some thinking about. Everything did: Star Salvage, which might or might not be in financial hot water. Curtis: Who knew what other mistakes he had made? Somewhere in the group lay the *anguis in herba,* as Ben would no doubt say: the snake in the grass. The *anguis* could even be Ben. Heaven knows he was the only one who'd been in the neighborhood when every single one of the victims had turned up dead.

I found myself getting very sleepy, too sleepy in fact to get myself up to undress and crawl into bed. The pages were blurring before my eyes and I struggled to stay awake. I was afraid if I dozed off I'd be back in the tophet with that horrible snake, with Jimmy making his snide remarks, Ben spouting Latin, and Susie going on and on about jogging, and how much weight you could lose. Forty-five pounds in a year. I'd heard her say it often enough.

I sat up, gasping. I grabbed the telephone, but remembered that there wasn't one in the cabin. I pulled on my shoes and dashed out the door, stumbling on the steps leading down to the path from the pool.

I knocked. There was no response. I tried the door, which was unlocked, and went straight in.

"Come in," Nora said. "You're just in time to witness an execution. Close the door and move away from it." I did as I was told. Briars sat in a chair, his hands on his thighs, a knife held under his chin, a rope wound round and round him, pinning his arms to his sides and his body to the chair. A trickle of blood streamed from a cut on his left cheek. "If you run for help, he's dead."

"What is this about?" Briars gasped.

"You don't even know who I am, do you?" Nora demanded. "You sat in that courtroom day after day, and you didn't even look the mother of the boy you murdered, full in the face. Not once. You and Peter Groves."

"You're Mark's mother," Briars gasped. "You're so thin. Your hair . . ."

"So you admit you killed him," she said.

"No," he whispered. "I just didn't recognize you. You've changed."

"He was my only child," she said.

"I know. I'm sorry."

"Shut up," she said. "Do you have any idea what it is to lose a child? Do you?"

"No," he whispered.

"I lost everything. My son, my husband. You would think losing your only child would bring you closer together. It doesn't. He told me we had to move on, when he left me. Said I was lost in the past. Maybe so. I like the past. My boy is alive in it, handsome, intelligent, and so charming.

"And it was all over in a minute, wasn't it? The life gone from him. And for what? A shipwreck? Some ridiculous story about a graveyard of some kind guarded by the golden god of the sea. There's no such shipwreck, just the obsession of two middle-aged men. Are you surprised I know about this? He wrote me every week, long letters, about everything he was doing. He liked you. He trusted you. Does that bother you at all? Does it?" she said. The knife looked perilously close to slicing into his neck.

"Yes," he whispered. "It has bothered me ever since."

"He got a university scholarship, did you know that?"

"Yes," Briars said. "Mark was a gifted young man."

"Are you going to say that I was lucky to have him for as long as I did? That's what the priest told me. I hated him for it. But you and Peter Groves, that went way beyond hatred. I knew I'd track you down one day. How I laughed when I got the brochure for the tour. Briars Hatley, professor of archaeology and noted expert on the Phoenician period, will show us Carthage as tourists rarely see it: Byrsa Hill, the place of its legendary founding in 814 B.C., Roman Carthage in all its grandeur, and the tophet, where it is said thousands of little children were sacrificed to save the city from its greatest threat. I love ad copy, don't you? Did you write that?" she said to me.

"No. My business partner did."

"Your partner was right. Particularly about the sacrificed children. We know all about that, don't we? A child sacrificed for someone's lust for gold. I couldn't even bury him, you know. I dream of his body being eaten by fish, or washed up on shore and devoured by birds." She stopped for a moment and choked back tears.

I found my voice at last. "You think killing Briars will make up for it," I said, barely recognizing the sound coming out of my mouth. There was no fear in it, just fury. "And I suppose some might say you're right. But what about the other people you killed? Ron was someone's son, too, you know. He was handsome and charming and intelligent. Did you think about *his* mother? And what about that beautiful young woman who was terribly disfigured by the fire on Peter's boat? Her name is Maggie. I met her, and she was cheerful and friendly, and she loved the work she was doing, just the way Mark did. She has a mother, too."

"I don't know what you're talking about," Nora hissed. "I didn't do anything to her. I wanted to kill the other girl, Peter Groves' daughter. Then Groves, too, would know what it was like to lose a child. Just shut up," she barked again. But she hesitated for a moment. I pressed on.

"And Rick Reynolds? Was he just another casualty, too? Boring, I know. But he had a mother. And Kristi. Oh, I know she'd have liked us all to think she'd arrived fully formed as the internationally renowned travel writer, but I'll bet even she had a mother."

"What are you talking about?" Nora shrieked. "Be quiet!" For a moment, she seemed off balance.

"Briars," Ben said, bursting into the room. "I have great—"

I lunged for Nora as Briars ducked away, and he and the chair crashed to the floor. She was so strong, I knew within seconds I couldn't wrestle the knife out of her grasp. She started slashing in all directions, harsh, rasping, wordless sounds coming from her, Ben and I dodging her thrusts, both of us trying to get the knife from her. I heard a thud, a cracking sound, and Ben groaned and fell back. Blood streamed from a wound in his upper chest. I grabbed Nora from behind and just held on. I could feel her dragging me across the floor toward Briars, and I couldn't stop her.

I saw Ben try to get up, but he couldn't. On his hands and knees, he pulled himself over to Briars, and with one hand, the other pressed to the wound in his chest, he loosened the ropes. Free now, Briars scrambled to his feet and grabbed at Nora, too. In the struggle, the knife flew out of her hand, and slid across the floor. The three of us scrambled for it, Nora kicking and punching and howling with rage.

It took all the strength both of us could muster to pin her face down on the ground. "I've got her," Briars said. "Go and get help."

13

"*I* AWOKE THE NEXT MORNING AS MY FEET TOUCHED *a sandy beach,*" Carthalon said. *"The captain had slipped away in the night. I cursed the day I was born, that I should have survived rather than the good captain, but I remembered my pledge to him. I did not know where I was, or how I would reach Qart Hadasht, but I knew I must. I saw far away to the south of me a town, Hadramaut, I believe, but was afraid to go there, for fear it had fallen into Agathocles' hands. For many days I hid, getting scraps of food from the refuse of small towns, seeking directions from the citizens of the countryside, who, rightly enough, regarded me with suspicion, and essentially following the coast northward. If it was not our allies I was dodging, it was Agathocles' troops. In time I made my way to Qart Hadasht and the house of Yadamalek, under whose auspices I am here today.*"

"So now that you are here, what have you come to tell us?" one of the men of the Council said. "That the cargo was lost?"

"We authorized this cargo and mission," another said. *"This lad tells us a lie."*

"The mission itself may have been sanctioned by you," Carthalon said. *"But there were others with plans you knew nothing about. The poisoned air of treachery is all about us, and seeps much closer than you think. The greatest danger to our city, to our political institutions and our way of life, lies not with Agathocles, but well within these walls. Indeed it lies within this chamber. Someone here plots to take advantage of the insecurity of our citizens as we battle the Greek, to play upon our fears of defeat."*

"This is nonsense," several Council members roared. *"If you suspect someone, then name him. But you do so at your peril."*

"This fellow is a traitor," one of the members said, rising to his feet. *"He should be executed."*

"I see I am not the only one to survive the shipwreck," Carthalon continued. *"The honorable member who speaks, one Gisco, was also on that ship."*

"You lie!" the man roared.

"You challenge a member of this Council?" another man called out.

"I do," Carthalon said.

"Then it is your word against his," another said, and many nodded.

"You do not have to take my word for it. As we all know, actions speak louder than words," Carthalon said. *"And I will speak to you of treacherous activities being undertaken right now. The man who commissioned Hasdrubal's ship, and I think you will agree that Hasdrubal is an honorable man, loyal to the city . . ."*

"That's the only reason we're listening to you at all," someone shouted.

"You will see soon enough that what I tell you is true," Carthalon continued, undeterred. *"That person is*

someone whom you have entrusted as one of only two generals who will lead us into battle against Agathocles. Even now he is assembling his troops near the old city, not to take on the Greek, but instead to take Qart Hadasht.

"Even I could hardly fathom it, when Hasdrubal told me his suspicions. The name, the traitor, gentlemen, is Bomilcar. If you have a plan ready to deal with such treachery, may I suggest you put it into action now."

"This is outrageous," some of them called. Several others, however, rushed from the chamber.

"See for yourselves," Carthalon said. "As I have seen with my own eyes. And do it soon."

"WHAT I WAS COMING TO TELL YOU," BEN, propped up by pillows on his hotel bed, said, "when, as you've just pointed out, I so rudely interrupted your execution, was that I have something to show you." He patted a manila envelope beside him. "But first, you've got to tell me everything that's happened. The last thing I remember hearing was Jimmy asking if I was dead. I was certain there would be some cutting comment to follow, something about the world being a better place if there was one less homosexual. You did realize Ed is not my nephew, I assume. We're no longer a couple, though. He's moved out already, and in with a younger, more energetic man. We'd planned this trip for months, though, so we decided to come anyway. A last hurrah, I suppose. Since this is true confessions time, are you two an item, by the way?"

"No," I said.

"I've tried, Ben," Briars said. "She won't have me."

I ignored that. "You may be right about what Jimmy would have said given the chance, Ben, but you'll be delighted, perhaps, to hear that Betty interrupted him in midsentence. She told him she'd been a librarian when she met him, that she'd been what he'd rather condescendingly referred to as his bride for more than thirty years, and that now she thought she'd like to be a librarian again."

"Does this mean I've broken up a heterosexual relationship?"

"I don't believe it was just you, although she's awfully fond of both you and Ed. I remember thinking way back in the Frankfurt airport that I wouldn't be surprised if the marriage didn't last the trip, and for what may be the only time since we left, I was right about somebody."

"And Nora?"

"She's confessed to killing Rick, and tampering with the tanks on Briars' boat. That's all. She's adamant that she had nothing to do with Kristi, didn't set the fire on the *Susannah,* and claims never to have heard of Rashid Houari. Kristi may well have done herself in, and Rashid, too, although I still think that unlikely. But his might be an isolated crime, totally unrelated to the others. I talked to Ben Osman. He's on his way down here. He says to give him a little time with her, and he thinks she might confess to more. Oh, and you know what else she confessed to? Knocking Catherine down the stairs and rearranging her clothes. She was trying to keep Catherine away from Cliff. She seemed surprised that Catherine took so long to get the message to keep away."

"She wanted Cliff all to herself, did she?"

"Probably not in the way you're thinking. She moved in with Cliff and took over his life, but I don't think she ever wanted to marry him, or even have an intimate relationship. What she wanted was security. She got him to sign a legal agreement whereby he agreed to cover all her living expenses as long as she was with him. I think he felt it was the least he could do, given her apparent selflessness in looking after his wife and him. She claimed she'd had to give up her job and her own place, and I'm sure he felt responsible for her. I'm not sure either the job or the apartment was a great loss, however. I'd say it was opportunism rather than self-sacrifice that motivated her, even early on. She was broke and alone, and the loss of her son was like a wound that wouldn't heal. I have a sense of her spending her every waking hour formulating plans to avenge her son's death, but not having the wherewithal to do anything about it. Her husband had left her. They'd lost all their money in legal fees and court costs when they sued Star Salvage and Briars; they'd mortgaged their house to keep the proceedings going. Then she happened to meet the Fieldings.

"According to what she told the police, if Cliff had married again, he would have to pay her a whopping sum of money to break their agreement. I don't know if it would really stand up in court, but she would be almost certain to get something under those circumstances. I just don't think that mattered as much as having the security of everything being paid for and looked after for her."

"This relationship between her and Cliff sounds a little . . . What's the word I'm groping for here?" Briars said.

"Sick?" Ben said. "I'd say so. I'm sorry I can't be more sympathetic, but she really hurt me. Winslow is her maiden name, I take it?"

I nodded. "She went back to it after the divorce."

"I know why she was after me," Briars said. "What did she kill Rick for?"

"Rick stumbled upon her, in a manner of speaking, out on the *Elissa Dido*. He'd gone out to trash the place to try to keep you from finding the shipwreck.

The idiot actually swam out to the boat, by the way. Nora, who is infinitely more resourceful, borrowed, without the owner's permission, a little rowboat. She was probably going to fix the tanks right then and there, but he showed up, so the two of them trashed the boat, she rowed him back to shore, and they made a pact not to tell anybody.

"The trouble was, you know what Rick was like: The man could not stop talking. He droned on all the way back, and by the time they got to the hotel, she decided there was no way he'd be able to keep his trap shut about what they did, nor about the fact she was out there. He even asked her if he could borrow some money. So she hit him with the first thing she could find that would do the job, the croquet mallet, and then tossed him into the pool. She had to get his shirt and shorts off, but he had his bathing suit on already. That's what gave her the idea, apparently. Then she just came in: It was before dawn, and there was no one at the desk. She went upstairs, changed into her jogging outfit, picked up Susie, and off they went for a run. There was no time for her to go back to the boat to finish what she'd started, so she just waited for another opportunity.

"I don't think she realized that Briars was actually a scuba diver. Like me, she thought he was just—I know, I'm not supposed to say *just*—that he was an archaeologist. She would have been very disappointed if he'd died that day, I think. She desperately wanted both Briars and Groves—that's the owner of the *Susannah* and a competitor of Briars', Ben—to know she was the one wreaking vengeance and why. What she hoped would happen is that Sandy Groves would die, so Peter would know what it meant to have a child killed. Then she planned to go after both Peter and Briars.''

"Tantaene animis caelestibus irae?" Ben said. Briars nodded. I expect I looked baffled.

"Latin," Briars explained. "From Virgil's *Aeneid*. Maybe you know the opening line: *Arma virumque cano,* of war and a man I sing. The phrase Ben used means 'Can rage as fierce as this abide in the mind, or soul, of heaven?' or something to that effect. Appropriate, don't you think, given the circumstances, to use a line directed at Juno, mother of the gods, who took such a dislike to Aeneas that she plagued him for many years, among other things changing the winds—*multum ille et terris iactatus,* much buffeted by land and sea— to send him to the North African shores, and the city of Carthage and a love tryst with Queen Dido, rather than where he was fated to go, that is to Italy to found Rome."

"I love it when I get the perfect Latin phrase for a situation," Ben said.

"I feel bad about Nora," Briars said. "Even if she did try to kill me. The last few hours have felt like an emotional roller coaster. I guess she'll be tried here. I don't know anything about the law regarding murderers. I don't even want to think about it. What happened to her son was such a terrible thing. Her only son. I guess her life fell apart. God knows, mine did, after Mark died, and I wasn't his father. What's really bothering me is that I didn't recognize her, just as she said. I didn't look at her, ever, in court, not directly anyway. I couldn't face either of Mark's parents. I only saw the surface, you know—she was just a shape to me. All she had to do was lose a lot of weight, cut and dye her hair, and change the way she dressed, and I didn't know her. I think somewhere, though, I did have some sense of it. I kept dreaming about Mark. I'd start out dreaming about Ron, but then I'd be back in the water looking for Mark again. I suppose it was my subconscious working away. I should have paid more attention to it."

"I dreamed about it, too," I said. "I was in the tophet, and a child was sacrificed. Unlike in ancient times, if we believe the stories, the mother cried. I guess my subconscious was trying to tell me it was the mother. I just had to figure out who that was."

"We still don't know who set the fire on the *Susannah,* do we? Any theories on that one?" Ben asked.

"I swear it wasn't me," Briars said.

"I do have a theory," I said. "At first, I thought that it must be someone who didn't want the shipwreck found at all: in other words, one individual who had something to gain by having the wreck stay down there was trying to stop both Briars and Peter. But Nora has confessed to one of these things, and unless Briars here has a secret admirer who is doing his dirty work for him, I can say goodbye to that theory.

"But I have another. I checked out a number of individuals on this tour . . ."

"Including us?" Ben asked.

"Including both of you," I said. "And Star Salvage. I noticed that Star is really good at finding wrecks, and not so good at making any money at it."

"That's true," Briars agreed. "More and more jurisdictions are claiming offshore wrecks as their own, and there are a number of competing interests that are often in conflict."

"Exactly. At some point, and my theory is that it has already begun to happen, investors are going to stay away, in droves, unless they're compulsive gamblers like Curtis Clark."

"Did he invest in Star?" Briars asked indignantly.

I nodded. "A half million dollars of Aziza's money. If it makes you feel any better, Briars, he didn't know the other guy was you. He's not all that bright. He should have stuck to golf."

"Was that a sexist comment?" Ben said. "I think it was."

"Do you two want to hear my theory or not? I've suggested to Ben Osman that he take Groves in for questioning again, not for the tanks but for arson. I think Groves took advantage of a golden opportunity, Briars, one that you and your temper provided. You went down to Sousse, created a big scene that several people witnessed, threatened Groves with who knows what, and then stomped off. Groves needed the insurance money, and I'll bet he set the fire himself. He did it at a time that he thought no one would be on board, but Maggie went back for some reason, and got badly hurt. I think that really rocked him. He'd been drinking heavily when I saw him later at the police station. I thought he was shattered at the loss of his boat and the girl's injuries and because he was a suspect in Ron's murder. I now think it went much further than that: He was feeling guilty about *causing* Maggie's injuries."

"Interesting idea," Briars said. "I guess we'll have to wait and see about that one."

"But didn't you just say that Curtis gave him a half a million bucks? Why would you think he'd be hurting for money?" Ben asked.

"You saw that boat, Ben? They don't come cheap."

"Lara's right," Briars said. "It could cost as much as twenty-five thousand or more per day to run an operation like that. Aziza's money wouldn't last very long."

"I see. And Kristi?" Ben said. "Do you have a theory on her, too?"

"No," I said. "It's possible she could actually have done herself in. I suppose I can tell you now that Kristi was a blackmailer. She used her reporting skills and the entrée they bought her to find out things about people they wouldn't want anyone else to know, and then tried to extort money from them. I figured she was a sure candidate for murder. I guess I was wrong."

We all sat digesting that for a minute. "So what have you got to show us, Ben?" Briars said. "I hope it's a little more upbeat than what we've been talking about so far."

"Prepare to be cheered up. You have to promise, though, we'll work together. We could co-publish. I've already completed most of what I need. It was to be one of the stories in *Past Imperfect*. But that doesn't change the fact that with what we know now, and what you can do, it'll be an even bigger story."

"Do you think it's the drugs they've given him, or am I still in shock?" Briars said, turning to me. "I can't understand a word he's saying."

"Me neither," I said.

"Sorry. I'm quite excited about this. It's given me a whole new lease on life, really. As you can probably tell, I'm a little manic at the moment. Even getting stabbed can't spoil my mood. I was depressed about Ed and me. If you knew me, you'd have realized that. I eat when I'm down; the worse the situation, the more I eat. You must have had quite a time keeping enough food within my grasp, Lara." I smiled. "But then, I realized something. And it was so wonderful, it pulled me right out of the funk I've been in."

"I still don't get this," Briars said. "But whatever the doctors have given you, I want some."

"Okay, okay. Without further ado," Ben said, opening the envelope. "Have a look." He pulled out a black-and-white photograph.

"What is it?" I asked.

"It's a tablet. Black limestone. Beautiful stuff, although it's difficult, I'll grant you, to see that in this picture."

"And these lines? It looks like writing of some kind."

"It is," Ben said. "It's a Punic text, as I'm sure Briars knows. Now you need to understand, Lara, that examples of Punic script are rare. The Phoenicians are credited by some with devising a predecessor alphabet to the Roman alphabet and therefore ours. The Carthaginians would have brought that with them. But there are relatively few examples of their writing still in existence, even in the later Punic period, other than rather stilted ceremonial inscriptions, for example, on the votive stones from the tophet. I found this when I was doing some research in the Louvre many years ago, took a picture of it and then took the photo home. I spent a lot of time trying to translate the tablet, and it didn't make much sense."

"I see Qart Hadasht here," Briars said, pointing to one corner of the picture.

"Yes, you do. But don't try translating it, because, as I finally figured out, it's only half the tablet. It doesn't make sense in and of itself. But then, fast forward twenty years, and in one of those serendipitous occurrences, while I was researching my book, I found the other half in Greece. So, here it is," he said, producing a second photograph. "See, if you put the two photos together—you have to overlap them a little—presto, they fit."

"This is fantastic," Briars said. "Shall I have a go at translating it?"

"Spare yourself the effort," Ben said, handing Briars a sheet of paper. "Here's my translation. You can see it in a minute, Lara."

Briars took the piece of paper and studied it for a moment. "I can do this!" he exclaimed. "Ben, I can find it from this. I can calculate wind speeds about that time of year. We have a fairly good idea how fast those ships could travel. Maybe I could even calculate drift time, and work back from Sousse, and forward from Carthage. Oh, yes, I can find it. And we will co-publish."

"I knew you'd get it right away," Ben said. "I went and looked on your boat, Briars, one evening, without asking your permission. I told Lara I'd apologize to you, and I do. I just wasn't sure, until I saw some of your records, and that lovely sketch you have, that we were running in parallel tracks here."

"Briars may have gotten it right away, but I haven't," I said. "You're going to tell me this is a map to sunken treasure? X marks the spot?"

"It's not a map," Briars said. "It's a plaque, isn't it, Ben? This is a plaque put up by the citizens of Qart Hadasht and the Council of the Hundred and Four, which was probably the magistrature or court in Carthage, to commemorate a good deed done by someone by the name of Carthalon at a time when Qart Hadasht was threatened by Agathocles, the Greek tyrant from Syracuse.

"This Carthalon fellow left Qart Hadasht on a ship which was on some special mission. But the ship was taken over by the forces of evil. The cargo which was to be used to raise an army to support Qart Hadasht, was actually destined for a traitor. I'd guess Bomilcar, wouldn't you, Ben?"

Ben nodded. "That was my assumption, too."

"Something tells me you're going to announce that this is Zoubeeir's ship," I said.

There was a soft knock at the door, and Hedi poked his head in. "Sorry to interrupt. How are you feeling, Ben?"

"Not bad," he said. "The doctors tell me Nora didn't

hit anything important, just a surface wound. I guess there are certain advantages to being somewhat rotound. I'm going to miss the desert trip, though."

"I know and I'm sorry. Speaking of that, though, we're almost ready to go, Lara. Everybody is back from the museum and the tour of the old town, the bags are outside, and the four-wheel-drive Land Cruisers are also here. We'll need to get going to make sure we get to the desert in time for the sunset."

"Okay, give us just a few more minutes. I have to hear the end of this story. Okay, you two, is it Zoubeeir's ship?"

"It could be," Briars exulted. "It absolutely could be. Look," he said pointing to the translation. "The ship was carrying a cargo of wine, oil, coins—these might all be in amphorae, or possible pitoi, another kind of terra-cotta container—and, believe it or not, a gold statue of Baal Hammon. Not only that, but this ship went down somewhere north of a place called Hadramaut, probably present-day Sousse. We know Sousse was called Hadrumetum during Roman times, and that's what the Romans regularly did. They took the old place name and Latinized it. So Hadramaut, Hadrumetum, and eventually, Sousse. You know, Ben, if I can find this ship, and the cargo matches the description of the cargo on Carthalon's ship, and if we can date some of the cargo and they come close, we will have dated an ancient shipwreck to within a year or two, probably 308 B.C.E. It's almost impossible to do, but we might just do it. Sorry, Lara, we should explain. Agathocles was threatening Carthage between 310 and 307 B.C.E., and Bomilcar, one of the generals who was supposed to be mounting Carthage's defense, launched a coup d'etat, trying to take over Carthage while it was in this rather delicate position. He was unsuccessful. Got himself executed. But the fact that both Agathocles and a traitor are mentioned in the plaque, really narrows the time frame. And if we find the ship mentioned, or something that closely matches the cargo, then we've essentially done the impossible."

"You know your assignment," Ben said. "I'm the desk guy. You find the ship."

"I'm going to do that," Briars said.

"I'd give you a high five, but I hurt too much," Ben said. "Let's just shake hands very carefully."

I was really happy for the two of them, but I couldn't get as excited about it as I probably should have. There were too many loose ends. And there was something bothering me about this discussion, a not quite fully formed thought hovering around the edges of my consciousness.

"So of this cargo, the stuff that's listed here on the plaque, what would you expect to still find, given that over two thousand years have passed, Briars?" Ben asked.

"The silver and copper ingots would probably not be in good shape, unless they got completely buried in a great deal of silt. Anything gold would be fine. Gold is essentially inert. The statue should be okay, although it probably isn't solid gold, so it depends what's under it and how well protected that might be. If the coins were gold, they'd be fine, although if they're small, they might easily have been washed away by currents. Silver and bronze coins would survive only if they were well sealed in the terra cotta. In fact, anything in the terra cotta might do just fine, if well sealed. You never know, we might even be able to drink the dregs of the wine."

The terra-cotta wine jug in Rashid's warehouse! "I hope this doesn't throw a damper on this conversation," I said. "But you remember, Briars, you told me that you thought someone else might have found the ship; that there were artifacts coming on the market that made you suspicious?"

"I do. I'm not going to like this, am I?"

"I saw four large amphorae, and a wine jug that matched the one in the photo you showed me, Briars—the jug Zoubeeir took from the wreck—in Rashid Houari's warehouse the night he died. I'd completely forgotten to tell you about it. I don't know what happened to me."

"Seeing Rashid hanging up there with his puppets might have something to do with it," Ben said.

"Now I'm wondering if Rashid was very carefully placing these things for sale one at a time, so that no one would get really suspicious, or if they did, there wasn't enough of it, to raise a hue and cry."

"What kinds of objects did you see? Just the wine jug and amphorae?"

"No. Gold jewelry, quite a bit of it, an old bronze sword, and a handful of coins."

"This isn't good, Ben," Briars said. "I had a feeling this stuff was leaking onto the market. If a lot of it's gone, then we'll have trouble reconciling the plaque and the wreck." He looked at his watch, and stood up. "We've got to go, Lara. Take care of yourself, Ben. We'll be back in a couple of days to get you and we'll talk about this some more. I'm going to go pick up my bag, and I'll meet you out front, Lara."

"I've got to get going, too, Ben," I said, a few minutes later.

"Is something bothering you?" he asked.

"Sort of," I replied. "You know that feeling when a thought is lurking at the back of your mind, and you keep trying to pull it up and you can't and . . . Coins," I said, rising from my chair. "It's coins. It's Emile. He's been looking for the source of some Carthaginian coins that are destroying his business. Chastity's been following him everywhere. She's in danger."

I raced toward the lobby. Out on the street I could see four Toyota Land Cruisers lined up, engines running, luggage already loaded, the members of our group milling about, and the drivers having a last-minute smoke nearby. I couldn't see either Chastity or Emile. "Hedi," I said, grabbing his arm. "Where's Chastity?"

"She's just on the other side of the driveway, talking to Emile," he said, looking surprised at my tone.

They didn't see me at first. Chastity was crying. "But I love you, Emile," she sobbed. "I won't tell anybody you were there."

Seeing me, Emile grabbed her arm and started pulling her toward the first Land Cruiser. "Don't, Emile," I shouted. "Leave her alone."

He had a gun. He opened the back door and pushed her inside. "Get in," he said to me, gesturing toward the front seat, and climbing in the back beside Chastity. "Drive!"

I drove. I gunned it up the hill to the street, looking in the rearview mirror for any sign of Briars. At the main road, I expected Emile to tell me to turn right and head for the airport or possibly the Algerian border, but he ordered me to go left.

We passed a policeman on the outskirts of town, but I was going the speed limit, and he just waved us through. We looped down an old road, and then hit a causeway that stretched straight as an arrow ahead of us.

"Keep going," Emile said. "Drive as fast as you can, but watch out for police. If you get stopped, she's dead." Chastity whimpered.

We were on the Chott el-Jerid, I was reasonably certain, a landlocked and dry salt lake. To either side of us was an arid landscape with shimmering sands but very little water. Small pyramids of salt were piled on either side of the raised roadway which, if memory served me correctly, stretched almost sixty miles across the Chott. In places the salty crust had broken through to reveal a little water beneath the surface, sometimes green, sometimes pink, a mirage of sorts. The landscape was painfully bright as the sun caught the salt crystals in the soil. I reached across the front seat for my bag.

"What are you doing?" Emile barked from the back seat.

"I need my sunglasses," I said.

"Get them from her bag," Emile said to Chastity, who fumbled nervously with the clasp before finding them for me.

I checked the rearview mirror. Way back, there was a plume of dust. Other than that, there was nothing. From time to time, a tent or two would break the otherwise uniform vistas, and to the north and east the thin brown line of the Jebel El Asker, the El Asker mountains, could be seen through the haze.

We stopped at a Berber tent at the roadside to get water. "Don't even think about calling for help," Emile said. We didn't get out of the car. In a minute or two we were on our way again. The plume of dust stayed with us, a little closer, I thought, or perhaps I was only willing it to be so. Let it be Briars, the police, help, I prayed. I tried letting up on the gas pedal just slightly, hoping Emile wouldn't notice.

"Step on it," he snarled.

At the far end of the causeway, we swept through Kebili, stopping just once to get gas. Emile kept the gun out of sight, but there was no way for me to signal the attendant at the gas station. I just hoped, by some miracle, that someone was following us, would find this gas station, and the man would remember the woman driver with the nattily attired European and the girl in the back. A long shot, I knew, but hope was all there was.

I had no idea where we were going. Logically, if I remembered the map I'd studied the day before, we would head northeast from here, up to Gafsa, and then on to much better roads, which would take us to international airports in Monastir or even Tunis. But it looked to me as if we were angling south to Douz. Why he would do this, I didn't know. It seemed to me that south of Douz there was nothing but sand.

The road out of Douz got progressively worse, broken pavement, really, with dunes to either side. From time to time I had to weave my way through sand that had blown across the road. I could taste sand in my mouth, and my skin had a grittiness to it, that seemed to mirror the grating of my nerves. The road, with its curves and rises, made it impossible to see if anyone was behind us. Occasionally I thought I saw an oasis, but I wasn't certain. The light was playing tricks on me.

Soon even scattered houses and reed huts were few and far between. It was like being at the edge of the world. The dying sun touched the dunes, turning them first golden, then pink, then the most extraordinary shade of red, shot through with yellow. It was almost as if the desert were in flames, or had been changed to molten lava that undulated like the sea. It seemed a cruel quirk of fate that such a dangerous, no desperate, situation could play out against a landscape so impossibly beautiful.

How do people survive out here, how do they find their way, I wondered, in a place that looks the same everywhere, yet is always changing, the dunes shaping and reshaping themselves with the wind and the shadows, and where the eyes play tricks on the brain? Were there markers that those with eyes like mine, formed by a different climate, couldn't see? I knew in this desolate place we could not survive on our own. Even if I wanted to leave the Toyota, there was no way I could. Chastity and I were as good as dead on our own.

"Where are we going, Emile?" I said.

"Just drive," he said.

Night was falling, and I switched on the headlights. "Turn those off," he ordered.

"I can't drive in the dark," I said. "The road is terrible. Where are we going?"

"Libya," he said. Chastity started to cry. "Quiet!" he ordered. She gave one last snuffle and was silent.

"Isn't there a highway to the Libyan border?" I asked.

"There is, but they'll be looking for me there by now," he said. "Just drive."

At the top of a hill, I thought I caught a glimpse of headlights behind me in the dusk. Emile looked back over his shoulder, and I think he saw them, too. The fading light was playing tricks, but I hoped the headlights were real, because it would have to be help. Nobody would be out driving in this just for fun.

We crested another small hill, and the road just vanished. I hit the sand so hard that if we hadn't been wearing seat belts, we'd all have been hurt. I wrestled with the wheel, but I had no experience with this kind of terrain, and the truck slid into the sand and came to a halt. Ahead was a mountain of sand.

"I hate this godforsaken country," Emile shouted. The man was coming unhinged. "Get out," he said. "Start digging."

Two men materialized over the sandy slopes, and came to our aid. "Careful," Emile warned as they approached. In a few minutes, the Toyota was back on the road, and one of the men pointed out the best way around the sand.

"Storm coming," he said to us. "Take shelter."

I looked around. Storm? The sky was clear, and the first stars were coming out. But these men were nomads, Mrazig, and they should know. Did it rain in the desert?

We drove on a little farther, but it became evident that we would have to stop for a few hours at least. There was no more sign of the headlights. We hunkered down in the car to wait out the night. Despite her fear, Chastity dozed off reasonably quickly. I couldn't sleep. I looked through the windshield at the stars. There were millions of them, more than I'd ever seen, and they were close: You could delude yourself that with a very tall ladder you would be able to touch them. They stretched to the horizon in every direction. I watched them for a long time, trying to think how to get Chastity and me away from Emile, but the stars didn't say.

At some point in the night, I realized that to one side of us the stars were gone. Clouds, maybe, I didn't know. Just before dawn, I drifted into troubled sleep.

It started with just a hissing sound, millions of tiny needles blasting the outside of the car. In a minute, sand began seeping in through every crack. "What's happening?" Chastity said, wrenched awake by the sound. "Where am I?"

"Sandstorm," Emile replied. "Shut the vents and windows!" The hissing became more insistent, and the Toyota rocked gently. I had never heard sounds like this before, and I felt almost lost, a tiny molecule cut off from any contact with the outside world.

"God, I hate this place," Emile said.

"Then why did you come here?" I snapped. Heaven knows, we could have done with one less murderer on the tour.

"This place ruined my life!" he said. "My father was a good man. He didn't deserve what happened to him.

Tunisia could have been independent without destroying him and my family."

"I expect essentially good people do get caught up
in these waves of history, Emile. But your family,
whether you like it or not, was part of an imperialist
force. Your country took the land from its owners in
the first place, part of the spoils of war and empire. I
understand how you feel about what happened to your
family. I'm not sure I can say the same about what
you're doing now."

"No," he said very quietly. "Once you start, you just
keep getting in deeper and deeper."

"I don't think I want to know this, Emile," I said.
The less he thought Chastity and I knew, the better,
although Chastity obviously had seen something he
wouldn't want her talking about.

"Gold coins. Roman, Greek, even Carthaginian.
You name it. Hundreds of them, maybe thousands. I
don't know where they found them. I tried to make
him tell me.

"Rashid Houari," he said. "He was an imbecile.
Anybody who knows anything about the market would
know what to do with a hoard of coins. All I needed
was a little time, you know. If I could have found the
source, I could have done something about it, controlled their release, just hung on to them for a little
while until I'd sold the business."

He paused for a moment. "That bitch figured it out
though, didn't she? She tried to blackmail me. Told me
what I was planning was fraud. She knew I was about
to go bankrupt again, and she'd keep quiet for a price
to give me time to try to recover. I don't know how
she knew."

"She probably did the same thing I did. Traced the
plummeting prices of coins on your own Web site. So
you went to see her, slipped some barbituates into her

gin, waited until she dozed off, doused the bed with lighter fluid, and then lit a match. Did I get that about right?"

"Pretty much," he said.

"So what are you going to do when we get to the border?" I said.

"I don't know," he replied. "Maybe I'll shoot you both. Maybe I'll just leave you there to fend for yourselves. I'll think about it."

Either way we'd be dead.

I realized there was now no sound, save our breathing. "Is the storm over?" I said.

"I guess so," he said. "Let's get out and see." I tried the door. It wouldn't budge. We were buried, entombed, in sand.

Chastity started to scream. "Let me out, let me out!" She tried sliding the back door open.

"Stop!" Emile said. "We'll suffocate in sand if you open that."

Chastity sobbed uncontrollably. "For God's sake, Emile, let her climb into the front seat with me." He signaled her to move. I put my arm around her, and put my mouth to her ear. "Help's coming," I whispered to her.

"I know," she said. Oh, the self-delusion of which we are capable.

The air got worse and worse. Chastity's head fell on my shoulder.

"I should kill both of you," Emile said. "There'd be more air for me."

"To prolong the agony?" I gasped. He said nothing, but he didn't pull the trigger.

I came to at the sound of smashing glass and the rush of fresh air.

Hedi stood outside the car, a jack in his hand, Marlene and Briars behind him. About fifty yards back was another Land Cruiser. "Get out," he said. "Fast." The three of us tumbled from the car.

"He has a gun," I said, quite unnecessarily. Emile had recovered quickly and was pointing it at Chastity.

"Don't come near me," Emile said. "I'll shoot. I mean it."

"Mummy!" Chastity sobbed.

"Take me instead," Marlene cried. "Don't hurt my baby. I'll go with you, Emile. Please let her go."

"What are you going to do, Emile?" Briars said. "Kill all five of us? It's over."

"The Libyan border is just a few miles over there," Hedi said pointing. "We take Chastity and Lara back with us, and you go wherever you like. We won't be in Douz for several hours. By then you can be across the border."

Myriad emotions played themselves out across Emile's face. "You have a cell phone," he said.

Hedi took it out of his pocket and threw it on the ground. "Take it," he said.

Emile stared at it for a moment, then back at us. "Look at this," he said, waving his free arm about him. "Nothing. Sand. Scrub. A thin line of green along the coast. Yet, it has betrayed me, time and time again, wiped out years of hard work just like that," he said, snapping his fingers. "I'm taking your car," he said at last. "All of you, stay back."

He walked backward, watching us, until he reached the Land Cruiser, put it in gear, and pulled away. We never took our eyes off the car, hardly even breathed, until it disappeared.

"I knew you'd come," Chastity said, hugging her mother.

"Me, too," I said. "What do we do now? Start digging?"

It took us about an hour to get the stranded Toyota

completely uncovered. Hedi got in and turned the key. We all cheered when it started.

"Hedi," I said as he drove, somehow finding traces of a road I couldn't see. "I must have gotten turned around out here in all this sand. I thought the Libyan border would be over there." I pointed at right angles to where Hedi had directed Emile.

"It is," he said in a voice so low I could barely hear him. "The desert has a way of taking care of matters like this."

14

"WE ARE GATHERED HERE TODAY TO HONOR CAR-
thalon, citizen of Qart Hadasht," the old statesman said.
*"For his services to our great city. Were it not for his
warning, our city might have fallen into the hands of
Bomilcar, a man who held our trust, and who abused it
for personal gain. He will pay with his life for what he
did, death by crucifixion in the public square.*

*"But that is not why we are here today. Today, the
Council of the Hundred and Four dedicates our magnificent new sea gate to our wise young friend, Carthalon. A plaque which is being prepared by our best
artisans will be placed here, to remind us daily of what
we owe him. Carthalon has asked that the tablet also
contain the name of Hasdrubal, a most honorable man,
who gave his life in the service of Qart Hadasht."*

"Here, here," several people cried.

"We honor your request, Carthalon," the statesman
said. *"Hasdrubal's name, too, shall be on this plaque,
along with the story of what you both accomplished.*

"There still remains one question, does there not?"

the statesman said to Carthalon after the crowd had dispersed.

"There are many," Carthalon said. "But I assume you are wondering who killed Abdelmelqart and Baalhanno."

"I am. Did they met their deaths as pawns or participants in this tawdry plot to take over the city?"

"Ah," Carthalon replied. "That we may never know for certain, although I can tell you what I believe to have happened. Hasdrubal taught me that on balance there are really only two motives for the taking of another life: greed and love. I've thought a lot about that, and have tried to understand the meaning behind what I saw take place on that ship. As tempting as it is to attribute all that happened to the work of one man, or at least that both deaths were as a result of the plot against Qart Hadasht, I believe that the victims lost their lives at the hands of different people, and for different reasons. Baalhanno died because of greed, both his own, and that of the others. He was the man who watched everything, and then tried to gain advantage from it. He accosted Gisco and told him all that he had seen, and asked to be a part of it, threatening to expose him if he did not agree. Gisco saw to it that Baalhanno would never reveal the plot, nor share in the wealth. Mago, I would guess, was the one who shoved Baalhanno over the side, at Gisco's behest. Gisco will meet his fate along with Bomilcar."

"And Abdelmelqart?"

"Hasdrubal found evidence that the cedar box containing the statue of the ancient baal had been tampered with; that is, an attempt had been made to pry it open, either by Abdelmelqart himself, who was on watch that night, or by someone else whom Abdelmelqart caught in the act. Both Hasdrubal and I thought this meant his death was linked to the plot. However, now I am not *certain of this. It was early in the voyage, the crew was well aware the cargo was a rich one, and they were being exceedingly well paid to undertake the trip. Did it matter if Abdelmelqart saw the statue? Probably not. He was generally respected by the rest of the crew, and while I am uncertain of the intentions of Gisco and the others for the end of the voyage, with bad weather coming, all hands were needed on the ship. I concluded that in that matter, at least, Mago was a thief, but not the killer.*

"This way of thinking made me look for another motive: love, or perhaps the death of love. Hasdrubal knew Malchus to be Abdelmelqart's rival for the hand of Bodastart. I believe Malchus was the kind of person in whom this rejection and loss would fester. Hasdrubal told me that Abdelmelqart had objected to Malchus's presence on the journey, that he felt the man had never reconciled himself to what had happened. Malchus, in my estimation, rather than getting on with his life, instead preferred to plot his revenge. He simply saw an opportunity, finally, signed up for the same voyage as his rival, and took advantage of a moment when Abdelmelqart was alone."

"And that is the end of it?"

"Mago and Malchus were both swept overboard. That much I know. Neither has been seen in Qart Hadasht since. Perhaps it is safe to assume that the sea has prevailed in this matter."

I NEVER SAW EMILE AGAIN. I HAVE NO IDEA whether he got his bearings and made his way into Libya or not. He had bank accounts in several places. All were seized. There wasn't much money in them. Either he was broke, or he had already made plans to get away and is living the good life, somewhere far from home. Sometimes in my dreams I see his bleached bones, stark against the desert landscape. At other times he's in a tropical paradise surrounded by women who dote on him.

Nora languishes in what I am sure is a dreadful prison, awaiting her sentence. Peter Groves, convicted of arson, is luckier. He is serving out his sentence in a U.S. jail.

On a more positive note, Susie and Cliff, I'm told, are conducting their romance via long distance, and Cliff is giving Aziza advice on her money. She and Curtis are still together, which I can only assume means he got help.

More important, perhaps, Aziza has told all about her problems as a young model. She's started a program for young people in that profession to help them avoid what happened to her. The company she thought would throw her out on her fanny so fast we wouldn't see her go by—to use her expression—is a sponsor. I admire her courage greatly.

I got the puppets, eventually, and Clive and I were the hit of the housewarming party in Rosedale.

And while the trip to the desert for the McClintoch & Swain tour was inevitably cut short by unforeseen events, they all did see the sun go down over the dunes, something I believe everyone should have the opportunity to do at least once in their lives. Some of them even said they'd sign on for the next M&S trip wherever it was going, which just goes to prove something. I have no idea what.

It was a great relief to put my charges onto their various flights back home, and to have a couple of days and the flight over the Atlantic to sort out my thoughts. One of the things I was going to have to decide, unless it had already been decided for me, was what I was going to do about any future relationship with Rob. Briars, stunned by all that had happened, called his wife, Emily, when we got back to Taberda. She told him she'd be on the next plane. She's a very nice woman, and I think they'll be okay. What struck me was that the relationship wasn't perfect, but they were better together than apart.

Rob and I bicker a lot, and we disagree about many things, which I suppose makes us pretty much like every other couple on the planet. I think he sees the world in black and white, he thinks I worry too much about all the shades of gray. On the fundamentals, though, I think we concur right down the line. Maybe that's as good as it gets. I decided that when I got home, I was going to send his new woman, whoever she was, packing.

Rob, Clive, and Moira met me at the airport. Rob was holding the biggest bunch of flowers I'd ever seen. I took that as a sign he'd reached the same conclusion about our relationship as I had.

"I guess you're kind of annoyed with me," Clive said.

"Maybe a little," I conceded.

"We put everything in the store back just the way it was when you left," he said. Moira nodded.

"That's good," I said.

"Still mad?" he asked. I said nothing. "I guess that was a yes," he said. "Okay, go ahead. Get if off your chest. Say it. If I ever have another one of these brilliant ideas, I can do it myself. I know. But I'd like to say something in my defense. It's not as bad as you think. *First Class* has asked Aziza to write up the tour. She called the minute she got home and found their message. She said you're to let her know if it's okay with you, and if it is, she says you can rest assured her article will be very positive. We're going to be okay here, Lara."

Some days, despite all efforts to tell myself I shouldn't feel this way, I'm convinced I'm dancing on Kristi Ellingham's grave.

Epilogue

"THAT'S IT FOR MY PART OF THE PRESENTATION. I'D now like to call on my colleague, Professor Briars Hatley."

"Thanks, Ben. Professor Miller has told you of his discovery and subsequent study of the Carthalon Tablet.

"I would now like to share with you the findings from our archaeological survey of what we are calling the Taberda shipwreck. It was lying at a depth of approximately one hundred and eighty feet, less than a mile offshore of the town of Taberda, Tunisia.

"The ship and the objects found with it have been mapped, photographed, and studied extensively using the latest techniques, and I have distributed a list of the finds from the wreck. You will appreciate the fact that there are thousands of items, from olives to some very small wood pieces from the original hull, protected under the cargo, that have been useful for us in dating the wreck. Although the ship had been systematically looted over a period of approximately a year by a local diver named Habib Ouled, and sold through his brother-in-law, the late Rashid Houari, Ouled has co-operated with both us and the Tunisian authorities to assist in the recovery of a number of objects taken from the wreck. While this may not be ideal from a provenence perspective, it does permit us to cross-reference the ship's cargo, as outlined on the tablet, with the archaeological survey of the ship.

"Professor Miller and I believe, and we will attempt to prove to you here today, that the Taberda wreck is none other than the ship that set sail from Carthage in the year 308 B.C.E. with Carthalon aboard. The most significant factor in support of our argument, is, of course, the remains of a gold statue of a god we have identified as a smiting god, a divinity of Syrio-Phoenician tradition. While it would, under normal circumstances, be risky, if not downright foolhardy, to suppose the Taberda ship carried a statue some centuries older than the ship itself, in this particular case, with the aid of the Carthalon tablet, we believe we can say with some assurance that it did. As you will see from this first photograph . . ."